SWEET SALVATION

LILY MILES

Published by Written Warrior Press, New York
writtenwarriorpress@gmail.com

ISBN-13: 978-1-951346-07-2 (paperback)

ISBN-10: 978-1-951346-12-6 (ebook)

Cover design: Najla Qamber

Connect with us at: lilymilesromance.com

Facebook: Facebook.com/LilyMilesRomanceAuthor

Instagram: https://www.instagram.com/lilymilesromance/

Twitter: https://twitter.com/LilyRomance

CONTENTS

1

MARGARET

Through dank, dark halls and over cobbled floors, we walk together in a long line. The heels of our black shoes tap in synchronous time, our hands folded gracefully at the center of our chests, our chins tipped down, piously.

As we march down the hall, rays of sunlight spill through the stained glass windows that cut through the stone walls; the battered base of the ancient convent seems to glow red and blue and green. Through my cracked eyelashes I watch the rainbow of light swirl and spot the feet of Mother Superior Antonia Humilitas ahead of us.

I swallow hard, my nerves fluttering.

The reverend mother doesn't call us to her personal office chamber for pleasant talks. Then again, no conversation with the mother superior is *ever* pleasant. With a shake of my head, I chastise myself for being critical of the reverend mother. It wouldn't do for a nun to think ill of her superior—I'd have to pray on this later. Being a sister of the Benedictine order, I should hold myself to higher standards than criticizing my mother superior.

Heaps of black fabric flutter as we fall to our knees on the floor of the mother superior's office; the room smells vaguely of sage and dust. We keep our hands primly folded, our eyes now carefully squeezed shut. I can feel the mother superior examining us closely to make sure our holy Catholic garb is perfectly in place. I'm glad now that my best friend Sister Catherine and I looked each other over before we were called down for the meeting, otherwise Mother Antonia would've punished me for the wisps of black hair curling across my forehead, now safely concealed—it wouldn't do for a wife of God to be immodest and show her hair. I'd had to push Catherine's own strawberry blonde locks into her black veil because she hadn't cared enough to do so herself. Unlike me, she enjoys pressing the reverend mother's buttons, like a child testing a parent's limits.

Not every nun is perfectly saintly, it would seem, but I do my best. After all, at our core, we are all flawed. We can only hope to become beautiful and immaculate by the light of the Holy Spirit. And though Sister Catherine may be more flawed than the rest of us, she is kind and my only true confidante in the halls of this Gothic castle of a convent. I may be surrounded by sisters here, but Cat is one who truly feels like family.

Even our breathing is in perfect time, as the reverend mother's black shoes click against the cold stone digging into our knees.

Mother Antonia's office is a small one, with stark gray stone walls and a lone crucifix hung on the wall. Jesus writhes across the wooden cross, crimson blood beading on his palms and feet, his half-open eyes seemingly able to follow you, no matter which corner of the office you're in.

The Convent of the Blessed Virgin has been my home for almost a year and a half now, but I'm still barely able to keep track of myself among the spiraling stone chambers and corridors. I much prefer the outside walkways, where I can feel the sun warming the ebony cotton of my habit. When possible, I escape out there to study my Bible.

Though the huge convent is home to over a hundred nuns, the ones gathered around me now are the youngest, freshest bunch. Because we're so new to the holy order, we don't often get to mingle with the older sisters. According to our reverend mother, it is because we still have so much to repent for and so much to learn.

"Sister Margaret," Mother Antonia suddenly barks, her voice as cold as the stone walls surrounding us. "Are you listening?"

The hair on the back of my neck stands up and my back straightens stiff as a board. I open my eyes to find the rest of the sisters, still hunched beside me, looking on silently. Most are just grateful not to be the ones called out, no matter where their minds might have been wandering. Sister Grace's lips are pursed and Sister Eva looks rather content that I'm getting scolded, but Cat looks concerned, her glass blue eyes flashing. The only one who isn't paying attention is Sister Monica, whose eyes are playful slits and narrowed right on Sister Eva. As usual, she probably has something up her sleeve. Quite literally, if I know the mischievous young woman enough.

Meanwhile, plump Sister Isabelle clasps her hands and pretends to be deep in her prayers, while at her side biological twin sisters Lucy and Genevieve hastily follow her lead. Sister Lucy and Sister Genevieve are perfectly identical, from their almond-shaped, hazel eyes and dark blonde hair, down to the cinnamon mole on their right cheekbone.

"Oh, you know Maggie, Mother," Catherine offers with a

convincing sincerity to her tone, "I'm sure she was just deep in her afternoon prayers."

"Maggie?" gasps the reverend mother, dramatically, one hand clutching at the silver cross on her aged breast as though Cat had stripped off her habit to show off her nude body. "Sister Catherine, you've forgotten your place. To call this holy child by such an unceremonious name, you are dismissing the vow that Sister Margaret made to the convent."

"I apologize, Mother," Catherine blurts out hastily, realizing she'd made quite the opposite impression she'd intended to make.

Unfortunately, the reverend mother's expression has gone stormy, threatening clouds of gray fury floating over her countenance.

Sometimes I like to imagine what stocky Mother Superior Antonia, now in her early fifties, must have been like as a young woman of my own tender age. I've caught occasional glimpses of tendrils of faded, gray hair under her veil, but I imagine she had dark hair like I do. And her gray eyes —now hooded with age—seem like they could have once been attractive. But even though her mouth is a harsh, cold line now, surely there was a time she once knew mirth and laughter? Well, perhaps not.

Occasionally, I worry that I may turn into someone like her. Is this what being in the convent does to a woman? Having the joy sucked right out of your bones until everything has crumbled away from your spirit, everything except devotion?

"Your Reverence," another voice says from the corner of the office, her tone much more gentle and kind. Sister Ruth Ellen emerges from beside the crucifix, her hands clasped in front of her to mirror our own stiff stances. "I think that our young sisters are just a little worn out from the fast you ordered last week. It's been over six days since they've had anything but water and occasional sips of vegetable broth."

As assistant mother superior, Sister Ruth is only the mother superior's inferior by a hair, but it's not a hair that Mother Antonia would let any of us—including Ruth—forget. Though she has been at this convent longer than anyone else, unfortunately for all of us, compassionate Sister Ruth had never felt the calling to climb the nun hierarchy as high as Mother Antonia Humilitas had.

Mother Antonia trains her cold, gray eyes on us once more. We all flinch except for Sister Eva, who beams any time the reverend mother even coughs in her direction.

"Clearly a week-long fast was not enough to show you all how important it is to remain pious and devoted to your vows," the mother superior snarls in a low voice, her wrinkled jowls quivering.

At my side, Grace shrinks slightly as though trying to hide behind me. A small girl with an even smaller personality, pretty Sister Grace Sabina rarely speaks. Instead, she chooses to adhere to a staunch vow of silence only periodically broken. Never without her Bible, she is often found kneeling on the stone floor in front of the church's altar, sometimes until her knees bruise. Grace is the epitome of piety, and even she fears the mother superior's often cruel retribution. Though she tries to hide behind her Bible, her saintly cloak can barely conceal the ample swell of her breast or the supple curve of her hips—neither her devotion nor her habit can hide her beauty.

At the mention of the fast that had left all of us with growling stomachs and dizzy heads, a few of the other nuns glance towards rascally Sister Monica, who is slowly nudging some kind of small pouch under Sister Eva's habit with her toe.

The redheaded young woman had not only dared to sneak into Mother Antonia's office. She'd stolen a box of fine chocolates from a gift basket the mother superior had received from the principal of the nearby town's elementary school, where some of us occasionally volunteered. Though Mother Antonia hadn't set foot in that school for years, it was she who'd claimed the entire basket of treats for herself. Until now, no one had confessed to being the culprit, and even our snitch of a sister, Eva, hadn't managed to sniff it out. When the fast was swiftly implemented to punish us and smoke out the wrongdoer, Sister Monica covertly returned the half-eaten box in the hopes of getting our punitive starvation sentence reduced. But Mother Antonia had extended it instead, just to rub our noses in the punishment. Just because she *could*.

For the past six and a half days we'd had nothing but water, our communion and the occasional bowl of broth, and my stomach ached and my body felt feeble. Sister Catherine had snuck me fragments of a chocolate bar from God only knows where, which I'd hungrily devoured after offering Sister Grace some, who'd declined with a simple shake of her head and a disapproving grimace. Judging by the rosy glow of Sister Eva's face, I have a sneaking suspicion she'd managed to pilfer food from the kitchen.

Mother Antonia strides nonchalantly back to her desk. "Your Reverence ..." Sister Ruth whispers grimly, sensing something bad is going to happen before the rest of us do. Mother Antonia frowns at Sister Ruth, who immediately goes silent and lowers her gaze. Again the hair on the back of my neck begins to rise.

This isn't good. We'd all known this meeting the mother

superior called wasn't going to be a cheerful one, but now I get the feeling that it's going to be worse than expected. I join the rest of the nuns in secretively scowling at Monica, though she doesn't appear to notice. She's still busy forcing some kind of small paper bag under the hem of Eva's habit; a sniff tells me whatever is in that tiny bag is disgusting.

Reverend Mother picks up a large, wooden cross that is always perched on the corner of her desk and holds it in her hands, turning it over a few times and inspecting it as though she expected to find the thief's name printed on it in black ink. When no such proof emerges, her eyes lift to scan all of our faces.

"Corinthians 6:10," she states firmly, eyes widening with irritation.

My heart beats faster, drowning out the whirl of my thoughts. What was the verse? I know this game, and the consequences of losing are severe.

"Nor thieves nor the greedy nor drunkards nor slanderers nor swindlers will inherit the kingdom of God," recites Sister Eva smugly, before any of us get a chance to suck in a sharp breath.

Mother Antonia doesn't even glance at the young brunette, her eyes continuing to wander over the rest of us, looking for shreds of guilt. She'll find none on Sister Monica, who might be to blame but has the ability to arrange her delicate features into an expression of perfectly pious innocence, one that would make even righteous Sister Grace look crude.

Mother Antonia taps the cross again on her palm, holding it firmly in her other closed fist. I shut my eyes, dropping my chin as though I'm in prayer, which I am.

Please let her leave me alone. Please let me be invisible.

But I can feel the heat of her stare concentrating directly

upon *me*. A red flush blooms over my cheeks, a blush that I know she'll take for guilt. Even if she doesn't actually think I'd committed the crime, she would punish me all the same as a message to the true perpetrator.

"Ephesians 4:28," the Reverend Mother continues, her tone growing more and more harsh.

I know this one, I realize, and I scramble to put together the words, but it's Sister Grace's light voice that pierces the silence.

"Anyone who has been stealing must steal no longer, but must work, doing something useful with their own hands," says Grace.

"I believe that's enough," Sister Ruth interrupts. My eyes fly open, relief surging through me. Hopefully, the game is over without a victim. "I think our sisters understand what they did was wrong. Whoever is guilty won't do this again, I'm sure."

Sister Ruth looks directly at Sister Monica as she says this, who simply smiles pleasantly in response.

"Oh, I do agree," Mother Superior answers with a smile of her own. Though, then again, calling the twisted scowl on her face right now a smile would be generous. "Those who cause trouble must do something useful with their hands, just as Sister Grace detailed. It's the Lord's will, and who are we but sheep to His wishes? Sister Margaret, will you join me?"

It's not a question, but a demand—Mother Antonia's tone makes that clear enough.

I climb as slowly as possible to my feet, as though hoping that my lazy tempo will make the reverend mother grow disinterested in me, but she waits with uncharacteristic patience until I come stand at her side.

"Hold out your hands," she commands, shrilly.

My fingers curl into fists, unwilling to extend. In front of me, the bowed maidens dressed in black are watching with looks of equal grim severity. Even Sister Eva frowns, and Monica shows just the faintest hint of regret for getting me in trouble for her actions.

"*Now*, Sister Margaret," Mother Antonia barks.

This time, I do as I'm told. I stare down at my white palms splayed out in front of me, watching the light from the single candle flickering on Reverend Mother's desk. There are no windows breaking through the stone dungeon of this room, and Mother Antonia has opted for candlelight over electrical light, making this all the more creepy. Outside, a strong wind blows and the Gothic convent groans.

I close my eyes again as the mother superior begins to talk, trying to convince myself that I'm outside under the sun, the warm wind whipping at my ankles, and this isn't happening right now.

"You girls have had too much free time on your hands; that much has become apparent to me lately," Mother Antonia informs us, coldly. This, despite the fact that we travel frequently to town to sell our hand-stitched quilts at the farmer's market to raise donations for the poor—that is, when we're not helping out at the local soup kitchen or school, or our own convent clinic. "Each of you will have to come up with a personal mission for the next few weeks that will connect you not only with our Heavenly Father above, but with our treasured convent as well."

Fabric swishes as a hand is raised. I don't open my eyes to look, but I recognize the smug tone of the woman speaking. "What sort of mission should we seek, Mother?" Eva asks.

"The kind that keeps your devil hands free of idle time,"

she answers sternly, inviting no further questions. As usual, the details of the mother's requests are intentionally vague, so that at least a few of us will fail to please her.

From beyond my closed eyelids, there's a faint whistle and then a shock of pain jolts through me. My eyes snap open, bulging, as a thick red line appears on my extended palms. The pain has come so quickly and so intensely that it literally took my breath away. The rest of the sisters look on with various shades of shock on their own faces.

Mother Antonia grips the hard wooden cross tighter, lifting it up again over my now throbbing hands.

"Idle hands are the devil's workshop, my sisters," Mother Antonia hisses as she lashes my palms once again, "and you must keep in mind that wickedness loves company and leads others into sin."

I fight tears as blood trickles over my stinging flesh. But only after the cross cracks across my palms two more times does the reverend mother place it back on the corner of her desk. The dark oak of the wood is now tinted the faintest sheen of red. I hold my breath, biting back a whimper that would only satisfy the brutal woman—I refuse to give her that.

"Go now and pray for forgiveness, all of you who may have abetted the criminal who stole from my office. We'll meet again to discuss what mission you will each take up around the convent. Have a *blessed* day," she adds with a faint smirk.

Catherine loops an arm around my back, guiding me hastily out of the office among the group, but neither of us says anything. I keep my head lifted, eyes locked ahead, even as hot tears sting the corners of my eyes. No one asks if I'm alright, unwilling to appear too sympathetic to my pain in case the reverend mother's vindictive eyes turn in *their* direction.

Is this truly what God would want? Are we meant to suffer like this? I squash the doubt immediately, biting my lip hard. Mother would know best ... wouldn't she?

"You should go see the doctor, Maggie," Catherine whispers in my ear under her hushed breath as she drags me out a side door, while the rest of our sisters make their way towards the church.

I sniffle and shake my head. If I were to present these wounds to the doctor, he would ask questions, and I would have to tell him it was the mother superior who'd done it. He'd then question her and I would only end up in deeper trouble, and probably in deeper pain.

"I'll be fine, Sister Catherine," I reply in an attempt to be firm, though my voice quavers.

She rolls her eyes and squeezes me into a hug. "It's so weird when you call me that, Mags. No one can hear us out here."

"You never know who's listening," I murmur back, knowing all too well that Sister Eva has ears like a bat.

Eva takes great pride in hoarding secrets like a dragon does over heaps of treasure, though she's happy to share that treasure with Mother Antonia when the time is right. She can't be trusted, that's for sure, though I don't know how many of our sisters can be.

Catherine smiles and shrugs, taking my hands gently in hers and inspecting the crisscross of wounds running over the flesh.

"At least they're not too deep," she finally sighs with a bite of her lip. "If you're not going to tell the doctor, wash them and wrap them in clean socks. I'll see if I can smuggle you some gauze later tonight. Hopefully they won't take long to heal."

"Damn. What happened?" a deep voice asks from behind us.

Both Cat and I whirl around, shocked to come eye to eye with a pair of deep green eyes set in a tan, handsome face. A tall, young man stares at us, his head slightly cocked, a potted green plant nestled lightly on his hip. The arm wrapped around the pot is muscled and long, his fingernails dark with fresh earth. With his free hand he nonchalantly rakes the sun-kissed, dirty blond hair off his forehead.

Without waiting for one of us to answer, he sets down the pot and breaks off the tip of a prickled leaf, ambling towards us. He grabs my hand with his large, calloused one, forcing the palm up so he can dab the plant gently over the wounded flesh.

I give a cry and try to yank back, not because of pain— the plant is actually soothing— but because it's the first time that a man has touched me. I haven't even let the handsome, young convent doctor give me a full exam, because I'm so horribly shy when it comes to the opposite sex.

He frowns at me and holds my hand tighter. "If you're not going to see Doctor Cliff, then just let me do this. It's aloe, it'll help heal you faster plus keep you from getting infected. I don't think even prayer will keep that away."

"You *heard* us?" Catherine asks idly, much less perturbed by the young man's presence than I am. She leans back against the castle wall, her eyes drifting over him, taking in the sweat-dampened white tee shirt that clings to his body, and the denim jeans that strain over his sturdy thighs—and crotch.

"I could hear you two chatting up and down the whole hall," he answers. "I'm Trevor, by the way. A gardener here."

He grins amiably but doesn't look at Cat. Instead, he stares intently at me with those haunting green eyes that could be carved from emeralds. I've never coveted gems before, but I suddenly understand the desire to possess such things. My breath hitches, my hand limp in his. His big palm is so rough against my soft one, it feels like he could crush me if he wanted.

Why am I noticing this? Why can't I look away from him?

As soon as he's finished applying the cooling aloe, I rip my hand away, jerking my head down to look at my feet as I mutter a strained thanks.

My heart throbs a distinctive, single beat in my chest—I tell myself it's only because of the lingering discomfort in my hand.

"Sister Catherine, we need to get back to our devotions," I croak as soon as I can remember how to suck in a shallow breath.

I turn around, racing down the hall and leaving Cat to chase after me, but I can feel the gardener's eyes following me the entire way.

I refuse to look back, keeping my mind solidly on my prayers for the day and how I'm going to have to pray extra hard, since I allowed that strange man to touch my virginal flesh. Where he touched my hands there's heat and tingling, which is strange considering the aloe plant he'd smothered my palms with had cooled them and eased the pain.

What is this strange sensation that seems to flow from pore to pore? Why can't I push his lingering green eyes out of my thoughts, no matter how hard I try to recite the Lord's Prayer?

2

TREVOR

All around me, gray spires shoot upwards on a mission to pierce through a blue sky and cotton-white clouds. I tip my head back to admire them, welcoming sunbeams that warm my slightly burnt cheeks.

It's another beautiful day at the convent.

I still can hardly believe this is the place I ended up. I guess it shouldn't surprise me all that much, considering what my life was like before arriving here. True, I also didn't have that much of a choice. It was either I come to this place and behave myself and learn to live a decent life, or I get a one-way ticket straight to jail. The decision was obvious.

Anyway, the path my life was taking me on before I wound up working as a convent groundskeeper wasn't exactly getting it done for me. I'd always wanted to change, I just never knew how. It always seemed like I would take one step forward and two steps back, because I could never seem to put enough distance between trouble and myself—I'd just get pulled right back into it.

Maybe it was because I never knew my parents and I got passed around between countless foster homes, or maybe it was because I never had any real ties to anyone who could set me straight and help me gain a solid footing in life. Either way, I fell in with the "bad crowd"—that's how everyone always put it when they were discussing my past. But my friends weren't bad people, no matter how much anyone wanted to label them that. They were just desperate, like me. You need money to survive and when you're at the bottom of the food chain, you do whatever you can to get by. We were people who made bad decisions, but we weren't bad people. Not at our core. I mean, I've never hurt anyone in my life, except myself.

In court, after one of my buddies got busted trafficking some crystal meth out of the house I shared with him, I sat behind the table, mutely watching lawyers argue in front of the judge over my past and what kind of future I'd ever be able to scrounge. Thing is, I hadn't even been *participating* in the drug deals. In fact, I'd finally managed to get a job at a local convenience store making just over minimum wage and wanted nothing to do with that kind of trouble anymore. I hadn't even known about him dealing, because my buddy thought if I was ignorant, I'd be safe, but he was wrong. My lawyer drew a flimsy picture of me as a weak-willed boy who was more or less dragged into trouble while resisting all the way. I kept my mouth shut and tried not to roll my eyes too frequently, and for whatever reason, the judge took pity on me.

That's when I was given my choice: convent or jail.

I thought it was just misbehaving girls who were shipped off to a nunnery, but it turns out they need men around, too. Someone has to look after the grounds and gardens. I'd seen a male doctor only a few years older than myself as well, along with a few carpenters and contractors who keep the building up and running. There's also a kitchen staff and a chef, but he keeps mostly to himself. I'm not the only gardener here, but I am the youngest and the one with the least amount of skill.

Still, I like being elbow-deep in earth. And I like the fragrance of the flowers and plants that I'm tending. There's something powerful about holding seedlings and being the one to protect them and keep them safe. They're so fragile, but they grow so strong. I like to think with a little hard work and a little sunlight, I'll be strong like these green stems, too.

It's only been about three weeks since I arrived here, and I'm starting to adjust to life out in the middle of nowhere. I'm living with some of the other male staff in a dorm-like building on the outskirts of the convent—that way we don't risk seeing any of the sisters when it's late and inappropriate.

The convent itself is like something out of a storybook, a Gothic castle where a fairytale could happen. When the taxi rolled up over green hills speckled with a rainbow of wild-flowers, I'd pressed my face up against the window in awe. The building is old and looks like it could come tumbling down at any minute, but it's also huge. It's surrounded by various orchards that scent the air sweetly with spring blooms; the fields go far until they reach the thick line of a forest.

I'd only taken this job because it was either this or life behind bars, but I'd come to enjoy the quiet and solitude that such a remote, peaceful location offered. Everyone likes to keep to themselves for the most part, and though we eat our meals together, there's not a lot of awkward small talk or idle chatter. That suits me just fine.

Plus, I'm mostly invisible here. No one seems to see me, and I like that. I like the feeling of disappearing—it means

I'm not in trouble. When I was stuck with my various foster parents who had no actual interest in me, I was always content as long as they were ignoring me. With them, you knew you were in trouble when you'd hear your name called out.

"Trevor!" a silky but sprightly voice shouts from behind me. The abrupt call makes me jump.

"Yes?" I gulp, climbing clumsily to my feet. I swipe my palms on my pants, hoping to clear off some of the smeared dirt, but my fingers are still sticky with aloe from when I'd helped the injured nun. How had she managed to get those odd cuts on her palms, anyway? I couldn't stop thinking about her, worrying that she may still be in pain. But it wasn't just my concern. In fact, I just couldn't stop thinking about her. Period.

An old woman stands before me now, her face plump and pleasant like the pink petals of a peony, but her blue eyes are slightly sad.

I recognize this particular woe-eyed nun. Ruby? No. It was something biblical.

"Sister Ruth," she says as if reading my mind. It makes me gulp again.

She doesn't extend a hand to shake my own, though I don't know if that's because it would be inappropriate, or because my fingernails are filthy with dirt. Either way, I end up doing an awkward half bow in greeting. I still haven't gotten the knack of how to address the sisters of the convent, nor have I quite understood how the hierarchy falls. It seems obvious enough, however, with the scary, cruel-looking mother superior at the top of the pyramid and the pretty, fresh-faced nuns—only a bit younger than I am—at the bottom. I guess that would put me at the bottom, too.

Sister Ruth was the first one to greet me when I arrived

here a few weeks back, and I'd made the mistake of assuming she was the mother superior of the place; in fact, she was the assistant mother superior. I shudder, thinking of the actual reverend mother, and then push her frightening, cold eyes out of my mind. I'd been doing my best to completely avoid running into Mother Antonia, and had for the most part, succeeded.

"How can I help you, ma'am?" I ask, peering down at her and then looking away, as though I wasn't allowed to have eye contact with her.

She gives a faint laugh and then a sigh. "You can look at me, child. And call me Sister Ruth. I don't bite. I've only come to see you because I think you may know what this is …"

From a pocket inside her black habit, she draws a small brown paper bag, and with it comes a strong and putrid scent. Sister Ruth arches an eyebrow, and a faintly suppressed smile twitches at the corners of her mouth, but it does not reach her eyes.

"I … uh, yes, that is mine. I mean, it isn't mine but I know what it is," I stammer, shifting from foot to foot and then dragging a hand through my earth-scented hair. I managed to get soil everywhere: when I showered at the end of my shift, the water would fall off me in brown waves.

"Did one of the young sisters here request this of you?" Sister Ruth presses. "I found it in Mother Antonia's office this afternoon after a meeting we had together."

"One of the young ladies did ask me to clip the leaves off one of the plants. She said it was her favorite plant and she wanted to make a tea out of it that would help her with her prayers. I know that they smell bad, but I thought … I don't know …"

To me it seemed being a nun would be a life of suffering.

Why not have terrible tea if you're going to deprive yourself of all earthly pleasures, to begin with? Still, that didn't seem like something I should say to a nun as old and wise as Sister Ruth, so I just shrug my shoulders instead.

"I can assure you that none of the nuns here use putrid-smelling plants such as this in their prayers. This particular sister is known to be a bit of a mischief-maker. Next time Sister Monica asks you for anything, you would do well to contemplate the task thoroughly before entertaining her ideas."

"Yes, Sister," I whisper, chin falling slightly.

I'd come here to make a positive difference in my life, not to cause trouble for more people. How was I supposed to know that nuns could be troublemakers? Weren't they too holy for shenanigans?

Sister Ruth bows her head slightly and then turns and retreats back towards the convent. I step after her, calling her name once.

"Yes, Trevor?" she asks with another pleasant smile.

"I saw one of the younger sisters earlier. She was injured. Do you know if she's okay?" I ask hesitantly, uncertain if I'm breaking some rule by even mentioning what I saw.

Sister Ruth's face freezes into a smiling mask, but her eyes have gone even more bleak than normal. "I can assure you that all of our nuns are in peak health."

Digging my toe into the soft earth, I nod after realizing that I was not going to be getting any more information than this. Again Ruth turns and trundles back towards the convent, her steps labored as she sways back and forth. It must be difficult to be her age and have to live in such modest and grim surroundings. I'd been told that our dorm basically mirrored the female sleeping chambers in the Gothic convent. Our beds were little more than wooden cots with old, hard mattresses that left all of our bodies aching the next day; the sheets were so stiff they seemed to be starched; and the blankets were scratchy, woolen things that somehow managed to be both too heavy and too thin at the same time.

I watch her leave before opening the small bag and dumping out the clipped leaves of the butterfly flower I'd trimmed them from earlier in the morning. Though the pretty purple buds are delicate and sweet, the clipped leaves are a terror on the nose. I try to remember exactly what Sister Monica may have looked like when she approached me earlier, but the only one of the nun's whose faces I can clearly recall is that of the lovely dark-eyed one with the injured hands.

I know nothing about her, but I've seen her from time to time outside of the shadowy halls of the cloistered convent. She's always with the blue-eyed, strawberry blonde sister, the one who seems even more prone to trouble than Sister Monica. I know that the dark-eyed girl has a lovely voice as well: I can often hear her singing quietly to herself from down in the halls, or out in the courtyard.

Religion is a mystery to me, as are women in general, but even with that nun's habit enveloping her, I could still see the curves of her body. It's hard not to stare at something as beautiful as she is. It makes no sense to me why she would dedicate her entire self to a higher power in the way that she has. Wouldn't she have more fun out in the world exploring and going on adventures? Sure, I brought myself to this convent to cloister myself as well, but for me it's temporary: I can leave and return to the modern world when my sentence is up. Here, the women stay for their entire lives, living in a bubble—the advancement of the world means nothing to them.

Being here is like being on another planet. Everything feels mysterious and secretive, not less so considering the vast property is enclosed in stone walls. Even though we're only forty-five minutes from the town, the convent sits alone on lush green acres so far from any well-traveled roads that you never hear the rumble of cars. Once you pass through the stone gate with the sign "Convent of the Blessed Virgin," the old, rutted road that leads to the convent is made of gravel. It's easy to forget that outside these walls, people are living in high-rises filled with smart devices. The phone network is so random out here, I probably won't even try to use my cellphone.

Life feels simple here, but I haven't decided if I like that yet or not. Is living here an homage to the past, or is it a way to escape the future?

From a little bit away, the sound of a breathy giggle drifts over the warm wind.

I glance towards the noise, silently peering up and down the convent walls. I stay out of the convent unless it's absolutely necessary. Once, I'd only gone one step inside when I accidentally shattered a ceramic pot near an open door, and needed to sweep up the shards before someone stepped on it. I'm terrified of accidentally breaching some sacred oath the nuns have taken, despite being told it would be perfectly fine for me to step in the main doors of the church, but I also fear getting lost in there.

Once you step inside the convent, the air is dusty and slightly damp, the scent that comes from generations of use. This building is probably older than some countries, and that's intimidating. I don't want to be the one who bumps into some ancient artwork and ruins it forever—that would certainly be my luck.

Again, a feminine giggle drifts towards me; I curiously

peer around the other side of the wall to catch a flurry of black and white fabric and the flash of a pair of ebony eyes.

It's her. The beautiful nun. I can't help but watch her, transfixed by the way she moves.

"Hush, Cat!" the dark-eyed nun cries, though she has a grin on her face as well.

"Oh, Sister Margaret," Catherine answers with a dramatic intonation and a roll of her eyes. "Are you to tell me this mirth won't amuse the Lord? Psalms whatever, whatever clearly states that every laugh grants an angel its wings."

Margaret. It suits the black-eyed beauty.

I watch them, creeping along the outer wall just to keep my eyes on her a little longer. I know I shouldn't follow them like this, but there's something so captivating about the woman there. I want to know more about her. I want to hear her speak.

"Don't make fun of the Bible like that, Cat," Margaret sighs, her laughter ebbing slightly.

The girls flop unceremoniously onto a patch of green grass near freshly-planted daisies; Margaret reaches out a pale hand to stroke the flowers. She's wrapped what looks like thick black socks around the wounds on her palms.

Had someone hurt her? Or had it been an accident? I'd wanted to ask her, but the conversation had been too brief and I doubt, judging by her tone, she would've even answered me. She'd looked more like she wanted to escape from me than speak to me.

"Maggie, do you want to work together on this mission thing that Mother Antonia's demanding?" Catherine continues, laying back in the grass so that her black cloak and cape sprawls out around her.

"I don't know if Mother would allow that, Catherine,"

Margaret answers. "And besides, I know that would mean me doing the entire thing for you!" she laughs.

They chat a little longer about whatever mysterious project they've been given, but I don't care about any of that. All I want to do is watch the way Margaret's perfectly rosy lips form each word as she speaks and the way that occasionally, not knowing she's being watched, a brazen smile brightens her entire face. I've never seen any fruit as lush and sweet-looking as the red lips on that beauty there. I lean my cheek against the stone wall; it's cool against the heat rising within me.

It's wrong to desire a nun—you don't have to be religious to know that—but I can't help myself.

After a few minutes of watching them from where I'm crouched behind the building, Margaret's black eyes suddenly lock on mine.

She'd been in the middle of telling some story, but she freezes abruptly, her eyes widening, her lips going still. One of her hands is still lifted in an animated gesture, but is suddenly immobilized by my gaze. My heart races in my chest when our stares collide, but I'm unable to even remind myself how to move, until the one named Catherine pushes herself up onto her palms to see what her friend is looking at. Only when both of them are staring at me do I turn and rush back to my waiting flowers. I fall to my knees in the dirt, trying to pretend like I was only scoping out the grounds for my next task, but my ears burn red and my heart thrums in my chest.

She'd caught me staring at her, trying to imagine how her hair would tumble over her shoulders if I pushed back the white and black veil from her pretty face.

There's a slight fluttering and the two women get back to their feet and pad back into the hall, their quiet voices drifting after them. I glance over my shoulder to catch just the last glimpse of their habits before they disappear. Then I groan while turning back to the rose bushes I'd been hurriedly pretending to prune. In my haste, I'd messed up and now the bush is lopsided and the flowers sag on their stems. I pluck a few of them, running my fingers over the smooth, velvet red that reminds me so much of Margaret's lips. I drop the flower with a faint sigh.

Margaret is truly a rose among daisies.

I know I can't have her. I know I should stop even looking at her ... but what's the problem with admiring a flower in a vase from a distance?

3
———

"I think those are enough tears, Sister Eva," Mother Antonia Humilitas sighs as the young woman perched in the chair before the mother superior's desk dabs at her eyes and gives a choked wail. "No harm came to you."

"My habit is going to smell like cat urine for a week!" whimpers the young woman, jerking forward to grasp another tissue and bury her face in it. She acts as though she'd been severely tortured, instead of just having a few foul-scented leaves buried in her habit at some point this morning. "I'm telling you it was Sister Monica. Or perhaps even Sister Catherine, that girl is the devil's spawn herself. She doesn't even like being here."

"You aren't one to judge why the other women around you have chosen to join the convent. Only the Father above is able to do that," Mother Antonia answers.

"And you," whispers Eva, beseechingly. She raises her long, gaunt face to the mother superior, her dark eyes—beautiful in a more conventional face—fawning in an attempt to gain favor. Her high cheekbones, always too prominent, are now particularly jutting from the fast;

Mother Antonia stares at her, considering how Eva looks more like a skeleton than usual.

But enough of this drama. The reverend mother rolls her eyes, glancing up gratefully when the door opens and Sister Ruth Ellen steps in to interrupt the scene. Mother Antonia had no time for tears. It soured her mood even more than usual, and Eva was one of the most tear-prone nuns within the convent walls.

"Oh, Sister Eva!" gushes Ruth, who liked to think of herself as somewhat of a mother hen to all the clucking little chicks of her congregation. "Why are you crying?"

The elderly woman hobbles quickly forward and gives the young woman a comforting pat on the shoulder. But even though Ruth did love to tend to her fledgling nuns, she wasn't going to coddle Eva, because it would only make her cry harder and wail louder to get her way.

"Because of this nasty prank that has been played on me!" Eva cries, after loudly blowing her large, slightly hooked nose. "I'm being targeted by someone jealous of my bond with God. This heinous act has clearly been done by someone struggling with their own sacred vows."

Sister Ruth again pats the young nun's shoulder, only to be shaken off—Sister Eva had no use for anyone who wasn't the mother superior. Mother Antonia was the only one in the convent who struck fear in nearly everyone's hearts, and Eva wanted to get as close to that power as possible. Before joining the convent at eighteen a couple years prior, in her life Eva had felt a powerlessness that still haunted her dreams. She'd vowed while taking her sacred covenant that she would never feel that way again. What she found she enjoyed, however, was making those around her feel that lack of control she formerly felt. She wanted docile Sister Margaret and annoying Sister

Catherine and even virtuous Sister Grace to suffer like she had.

"Now, now," Ruth chides gently, silently noting the wicked wrath in the young woman's eyes. Nuns, Ruth knew, were not impervious to human emotion; just because they took the veil did not make them less prone to earthly temptations than any other person. "I've cleared up the whole mess. It was all just a silly misunderstanding. A mistake, even."

Ruth had struggled with how to share what she'd learned from the young gardener regarding Monica's involvement in the stinky leaves prank. She'd ended up deciding that there was no way to prove Sister Monica had done it on purpose, and so it was safe to assume that Monica had only wanted the leaves for tea and nothing more. There didn't seem to be any reason to drag Monica under the mother superior's vengeful eye. Or Eva's, for that matter.

"It was Sister Monica, wasn't it?" demands Eva ferociously. "I could feel her doing something under my skirt while we were all bowed in prayer. Before Sister Margaret was punished."

Sister Ruth winces. Punished, indeed. And for something young Margaret had no part in. But the reverend mother has strict rules and if they are not abided by, no one can prevent her from doling out punishments she feels are just. Ruth just hoped that Margaret's hands weren't badly injured. She'd wanted to look them over, but Sister Catherine had whisked Margaret away before any further harm could come to the girl. Though Catherine likes to claim she is disinterested in her own religious vows, she cares for Margaret like a younger sister and Ruth saw that; but, then again, Ruth sees most things. Margaret and

Catherine had all but become inseparable since Margaret arrived a few months after Sister Catherine. While most of the girls were here because of their own personal beliefs and choices, Catherine was an exception to that rule.

What Catherine was not an exception to was that she ended up here because she was searching for something. Eva sought dominance. Grace sought purity. Even Sister Monica was here for a reason of her own, as was Catherine. But Margaret was a different story to Ruth. Just what did that young nun seek?

"We have no proof it was Sister Monica," Ruth answers with a firm look at Mother Antonia, who was disinterested in the trite tiff and was only seeking an opportunity to serve swift justice on a sinner. "Especially because the new gardener told me he believed one of the nuns was going to make tea with the leaves. I have a feeling that the bag was simply dropped and there was no ill will involved."

Eva sniffles, looking both unconvinced and disappointed that she wasn't going to get someone in trouble. Ruth again pats her shoulder and turns back to the reverend mother.

"Is this meeting over with then, Mother Antonia?" Ruth asks, eager to leave the room.

The Mother Superior's office was not a place that anyone, even Sister Eva, enjoyed remaining in for long. Plus, Ruth always got nervous when standing in front of the giant crucifix on the Mother's wall. While most depictions of Christ filled the old nun with bittersweet feelings of love and sorrow, this one just made her skin crawl: it was just too morbid.

"Sister Eva ..." Mother Antonia begins, ignoring Sister Ruth's question. That meant none of them could leave.

Ruth rests her hand on the back of Eva's chair, trying to mentally warn her against saying anything at all. When you dealt with the reverend mother, everything was a double-edged sword. No matter how you thought you were speaking of someone else, you were undoubtedly getting yourself embroiled in the trouble as well.

Mother Antonia locks her eyes on Eva's, all but mesmerizing her. Eva straightens, swelling under the attention of the older woman. "Do you agree that your sisters have been more ... lax lately with their cloistered duties, Sister Eva? Have they been sticking to their fast, for instance? Skipping bedtime prayers? Anything else I should be aware of? The Lord may be omnipotent but I, unfortunately, am not." The mother superior speaks slowly, leaning forward on her elbows and narrowing her faded, gray eyes on the young woman before her.

Sister Eva swallows and hesitates for only a fraction of a second before nodding. Ruth's hands twitch, almost curling. Eva never hesitated to throw one of her sisters under the bus, especially if it meant saving her own skin. She wanted to slap a hand over the young woman's mouth and quiet her, but instead Sister Ruth tucked her chin against her chest and prayed that Eva would have no useful information, though she knew that would be a stretch.

Eva had the ability to soak up information like a sponge: anywhere she went, she was listening. Some were skilled in carpentry, or calligraphy, or singing. But Eva's talent was snooping. And she was a dangerous snoop, at that.

The mother superior smiles one of her ghastly smiles that made chills go up the elderly nun's spine. "Do tell, child."

Eva blinks her round eyes. "Well, for starters, I am almost certain I saw Sister Margaret eating chocolate the other day, Your Reverence. I caught her trying to wash it off her lips afterward in the bathroom. I asked what it was and she just turned the brightest shade of scarlet I've ever seen."

Mother Antonia leans back in her chair and folds her arms over her chest with a slow and condemning shake of her head.

"Sister Margaret is one of the ones that I am most concerned about," she sighs. "There's something in her countenance that worries me regarding her oath to the church. I think if we're not careful with her she may shed her vows and live a life of damnation instead. We wouldn't want that, would we?"

Ruth straightens, her mouth opening to say something, but one sharp look from the mother superior and she quiets down once more, shaking her head. This pleases Mother Antonia, who ruffles slightly like a preening bird.

"We certainly wouldn't," Sister Eva agrees eagerly, chomping at the bit to be of use to her mother superior.

She observes the tension between Mother Antonia and Sister Ruth and then bats innocent eyes up at the elderly woman behind her chair. While Monica and Catherine could charm snakes with their feigned virtue, Ruth found Eva much more transparent.

"Don't you think it would be prudent to help Sister Margaret before she falls out of touch with the Lord?" Eva asks, prodding Ruth into disagreeing with the mother.

"It's always good to support our fellow sisters," Ruth responds, her tone strangely dry. "But perhaps more of a gentle touch rather than a punitive one will work better with Sister Margaret. If her state is as fragile as you believe, then it wouldn't do to frighten her off with harsh severity."

Sister Ruth inhales a shallow breath and risks a furtive glance towards the mother superior. She'd seen a lot of things in the last decade since Mother Antonia came to power at the convent, and each one frightened her more than the last. Even this simple clashing statement may be enough to sic Mother Antonia on Ruth.

The mother superior leans back in her chair, her arms still folded over her chest. She rocks, the chair creaking under her body. Each second that scrapes by makes Ruth's throat go dry.

"Are you implying something, *Sister*?" Mother Antonia asks, emphasizing the title to make her point.

Though assistant mother superior, Sister Ruth Ellen is still just a simple nun under Mother Antonia; despite her long tenure at the convent, it is Mother Antonia who makes the rules. Now she's reminding Ruth of her place.

"I would never be vague with you, Your Reverence," Ruth answers softly, ducking her chin.

Meanwhile, Sister Eva looks on silently as the two women speak, her eyes flashing delight at the tension between the two older nuns. Only when the reverend mother looks back at the far younger nun does Eva blanch slightly—she'd forgotten just how terrifying Mother Antonia's cold, gray eyes could be.

"I believe a strict hand is always best," Sister Eva offers hopefully, longing to earn a bit more favor with the reverend mother. Despite Eva's best attempts, though, Mother Antonia always remained unfeeling towards the young sister.

Mother Antonia nods, her eyes drifting back to the cross perched on the corner of her desk. In the light of the candle, flecks of dried and peeling red stains are still visible. She smiles to herself, reliving that moment again—the crack of wood on the tender palms, the slow bubbling of red on white flesh. That type of domination pleased Mother Antonia Humilitas. Her nuns would be perfect, Christ-like creatures who lived and breathed their sacred vows. The little lesson from earlier had been merely a taste of what she could do and would surely keep Sister Margaret on her best behavior, at least until she could figure out a way to control her better. That's what this entire convent was about —control.

These young women, Mother Antonia believed, have no self-control whatsoever.

They're flighty and wicked at heart and prone to disastrous temptation. Mother Antonia has no problem disciplining them in any way that will keep them firmly on the most righteous path. There's nothing the mother superior wouldn't do to keep control of her flock of disobedient sheep in black robes. If they stepped out of line, she would crush them back into place.

It made no difference to Mother Antonia whether or not Sister Margaret had been the one to actually steal the chocolates off her desk. In fact, the mother superior knew full well that it was Sister Monica who'd not only stolen the chocolates, but had played this prank on Sister Eva as well, and she also knew Monica's punishment would come. But Mother Antonia was also not concerned about Sister Monica losing her path; she could play her artless tricks. Margaret's soul was the one that worried her.

"I don't trust our fresh round of sisters, Sister Ruth," Mother Antonia continues after a long moment of silent contemplation. "We need to be sure that they each remember their places in the church and that they remember that it's an eternity spent in heaven or hell at risk here. Sister Eva, perhaps you could keep a closer eye on Sister Margaret? Make sure she's sticking to the holy word. Keep an eye on her for transgressions that need to be punished. Can you do that?"

Sister Eva practically squirms in her chair with delight. It's the first time she was actually given a direct order by her superior, and she is eager to prove her value.

"Of course, Mother Superior!" gushes the young nun, "I would be honored to do such a task for you. I'll find Sister Margaret and do an extra devotional with her tonight before we break our fast at dinner."

"Break our fast?" chuckles the reverend mother as Sister Ruth's grimace turns even more grim. "Oh, Sister Eva, surely you wouldn't suggest such a thing during these trying times? You young nuns need discipline, and I feel that fasting for at least another twenty-four hours will bring you closer to the Lord."

"But, Mother ..." Eve starts to whisper, her jaw falling slightly. One of her hands creeps towards her empty, starving stomach.

"You question me?" Mother Antonia snarls, and Eve quickly shakes her head and scrambles to her feet.

"Of course not. You're right. We need the extra trial of further fasting to strengthen our faith," she croaks. "I will still find Sister Margaret to aid her in strengthening hers."

"Go, child. May the Lord walk with you," Mother Antonia answers, smirking as the young woman dashes out of the room. "And don't forget the promise that you have made to Him in this office. You must look after Sister Margaret for her own good."

"It's for her own good," Eva answers with a nod, smiling brightly.

The door swings heavily behind her, smacking against the doorframe as Sister Ruth and Mother Antonia gaze at one another in contemptful silence. The pair have never seen eye to eye.

"Sister Ruth," Mother Antonia begins after allowing the

silence between the two to stew for a while longer. "As I reminded Sister Eva, I am the one in charge of this place. I am the one tasked with keeping everyone walking the line of piety and reverence. Don't make me doubt your place here, or I will send you to another convent."

"I wouldn't dream of it, Reverend Mother," Ruth hisses back, her cheeks flaring red with restraint.

4

———

MARGARET

Catherine grabs me, whirling me around so that my back smacks firmly against the convent's stone wall. My cheeks flame red, my eyes darting towards the now closed doors hiding Trevor from view.

That face when he was looking at me ... what had that expression meant? It was the kind of look I'd never once seen in my life. It was a look that made my veins suddenly feel as though my blood had been replaced with fire; I don't understand what that could possibly mean. These feelings, that expression, it's all too confusing. I may not be able to grasp what all of it signifies, but one thing's for sure: it feels like trouble.

I fear I've gone against my oath of purity to the Catholic church.

"Was he watching us?" Cat whispers, her voice strangely hungry. She bites her lower lip, eyes wide and dilated.

Why does she look like that? My head spins and I press my body roughly against the stone wall in an attempt to make everything go still once more. This time yesterday, I had none of these conflicting emotions surging through me.

How was it that a man could lock eyes with me and flip everything on its axis?

There was only one thing to do now and that was pray—I had to pray these strange urges away. I had to forget Trevor and the dirt under his fingernails and the way his eyes had been burning right through my cloak when I noticed him.

"Of course not," I answer swiftly, though my entire body is tingling, and I know better.

I suck in a deep breath and the shifting of my robe over my nipples ignites the fire in my veins even further. I give a grunt as though in pain and double over, hands on my knees, squeezing my eyes shut.

This is surely just like any other illness. With time and rest it will pass.

The gardener had been looking right at me—through me, in fact—his eyes like emerald lasers. It was like he could see all of me, even though I'm wrapped in my habit from head to toe. When I blink, I can still see his strained expression etched onto the backs of my eyelids.

"Are you alright?" Catherine asks, taking my hands in hers and pulling me away from the cool stone.

I nod and lean against her. "I want to go to the library. The private one. I need some quiet meditation. Maybe we can work on our mission idea as well."

Though Catherine wasn't normally one to go to the library without argument, she nods. Her arm wraps around my own as we hurtle through the halls of the convent. Our shoes slap loudly against the floor as we rush on, but I don't care about how much noise we make: it's still early in the evening and no one will be trying to rest. We'll probably have interrupted one of Grace's constant rituals, but at least she doesn't speak enough to complain to the mother superior.

We slip past one of the barricades that marks a secluded portion of the convent and make our way towards the private library. This is a library solely for members of the Holy Church, though no one except the convent nuns have made use of it for generations.

Sometimes I like to go to the library all by myself and lose myself among the aisles of books, inhaling the scent of furled, yellowed paper. I like brushing delicate fingers across the faded titles, and imagining the hundreds of women who have taken the same steps I have around the library, or who have carefully handled the same books I do. There's something almost magical about that connection, a connection I'd always been looking for while growing up.

The Catholic Church has always played a pivotal role in my life. My parents, both former missionaries, are still intensely involved in the Catholic world, and it only made sense that in my own way, I would join them. At times, it was clear to me that they loved the Church much more than they did me, and even perhaps each other, but I thought that was just the way it worked. Your connection with the Holy Spirit was the only one that mattered: no other human bond could compare. Perhaps there was a part of me that thought my parents would finally love and value me if I followed this path, but I haven't even spoken to them since arriving here. They'd dropped me off, my father shaking my hand and my mother patting my cheek, briefly greeted Mother Antonia, and then left without looking back. I stared after them, feeling the very first twinge of uncertainty.

But when I conveyed those concerns to Sister Ruth, she'd laughed and told me that every nun had a doubt here and there. The most important thing was to let the Lord take care of it. Push it from your mind and pretend it isn't there, and eventually, it will fade. This has proved true—for the most part.

I'd first heard of a nunnery when I was eight years old and my mother mentioned that there was a special castle where the purest of girls went to devote themselves to their faith and their God. That appealed to me, of course, because I always fancied myself a princess in one way or another, and she worded it in such a fantastical, mythical way. After learning of this magic castle where I could go if I stayed pure, I threw myself into the biblical teachings of the church. I told everyone I met that I wanted to be a nun. I had meeting after meeting with my priest and my parents, grilling me on whether or not I could actually follow through on this desire. I committed myself to learning everything I could about the church at my all-girls Catholic school. Of course, I rebuffed any man that ever even glanced my way. And through it all, I memorized the Bible frontwards and backwards.

Eventually, I got my wish.

But I didn't understand until I set foot in the convent, just what it meant to give up everything in order to become a nun.

This isn't an enchanted castle. I don't get to spend my days with my nose in the Bible, studying the teachings there. Instead, I'm hounded by Mother Superior and lashed on my hands every time I speak out of turn. I enjoy the evenings when we all come together after dinner to sing hymns and pray together, but the rest of the time I live in fear. I'm glad that I have Cat who makes this entire lifestyle bearable, but what will I do if she leaves the convent? I can't imagine her staying her forever.

Though when they come up, I am able to will my doubts

away, the questions persist and I feel that I can no longer bring them to Ruth; I feel like I can't bring them to anyone.

Will I make a misstep in my pursuit of salvation? Will I make my parents proud? Am I making the right choice? But, even if I did decide I was making the wrong choice, it's too late now: I've already made my vow, I'm already a part of this convent. Renouncing the cloth is not an option. This is the rest of my life, forever.

"I've been thinking," Catherine muses as we walk in through the great doors of the library.

I take in a breath, inhaling the comforting scent of the dusty books. A stained glass rosette window is carved high up on the wall looking down upon the library; I can see wisps of white clouds floating by through the shimmering glass.

"About what?" I murmur, one hand finding my heart over the black cloth. Its beat is stilling—I'm returning to normal.

I give a relieved sigh and shake my head. I'll just have to avoid the gardener. I don't know what it is about him that sets my heart racing, but it can't be healthy for my faith. Only the Lord should make me feel that way.

"That you're right," Cat continues breezily as she parts from me.

We walk down two aisles separated by one huge bookcase, though she drags a loose book free to stare at me from between the pages. "He wasn't looking at us. He was looking at *you,* Maggie. He was looking all over you. Like he wanted you. Like he was imagining what it would be like to peel the layers of your habit away until you were bare in front of him." Her blue eyes gleam as she speaks, widening with that same hungry expression she had earlier. She rambles fast, trying to get in the words before I plug my ears and sing a devotional hymn to drown out her scandalous claim.

She thrusts the book back into place and giggles, letting her laughter bounce over the walls as though no one else could possibly be in here. I gather up my black skirt in my hand and rush around the side of the bookcase to confront her, glaring.

"Don't say such blasphemous things, Sister Catherine!" I whisper, my nervous eyes flitting over the large room.

My ears strain, listening for any hint of feet swishing over the creaking floorboards, but there isn't so much as a breath of noise to be heard. There's only the groan of the ancient building as it weathers the same warm, early spring winds it has for decades.

Catherine brushes aside my anger with a cavalier chuckle. She never takes anything seriously, but doesn't she remember how I was abused this morning? Words such as hers could garner me an even worse punishment. Or perhaps it would be her with her palms extended next.

"Stop it, Mags, there's no one else in here, I promise," says Catherine as she continues to smirk. "If anyone is in here then it's Gracie, and that girl doesn't talk enough to tell anyone what we're saying, anyway."

"Sister Grace has taken an oath of silence. Just because she dedicates herself to something doesn't mean you have to be negative about it," I shoot back, keeping my voice quiet and careful so that anyone who may be listening may not take negative things back to the mother superior.

It's not Sister Grace that I'm worried about. It's Sister Eva. She longs to be the nun equivalent of a teacher's pet and she's always eager to inch closer and closer to the reverend mother. She would absolutely love to take snippets of this conversation back to Mother Antonia to get my hands lashed again. I wince at the thought, hazarding a look down at my palms. The aloe from the gardener had helped quite a bit, but I'd still wrapped clean socks around my hands to keep from getting dust in the cuts. My palms hurt every time I stretched my fingers, however, and reading my Bible had proved difficult. It was going to be hard to come up with a suitable mission, while I was struggling to turn the pages of the most holy book.

Catherine slowly wets her pink lips, her head tipping to the side. Strawberry blonde silk escapes her cap, gliding in silky strands towards her shoulder. It's like her hair has a will of its own to break free. No matter how tightly I braid her hair beneath her veil, it always manages to spring free. She'd gotten rebuked for it so many times by Mother Antonia that I've lost count now.

"Have I ever told you about my life before I came to the convent, Maggie?" Catherine asks after a few minutes, dragging a finger over the dusty shelf and inspecting the long smear.

Of course she had, at least a dozen times. Laying in our cots at night, she would gaze at me from across the shadowed room, her eyes glowing blue, and she would tell me all about where she came from.

"You didn't come here because you wanted to devote yourself to your faith. You came because your parents forced you," I recite quietly, biting my lip.

She nods and inspects her perfectly trimmed fingernails. "I got sent here because I was a naughty girl, Maggie. A very naughty girl indeed."

As she speaks, her eyes slowly turn to slits that gleam a pale, perilous blue.

I've seen this expression on her face before, usually before she makes some off-color joke that makes me blush.

But this time she stares directly at me the same way that Trevor had. Again that same, strange simmering begins to lazily churn through my core. She takes my hand in hers, lacing her fingers with my own. Her thumb trails sluggishly over the back of my hand. I almost try to pull away, but there's something paralyzing about the way Catherine is looking at me.

She licks her lips slowly, pink-tipped tongue dragging over her upper lip. I look away and clear my throat.

"If you're struggling with your virtue, then this place is definitely for the best," I answer haltingly, my throat dry. "Here you can be free of plight and temptation and you can focus on establishing a love of the Holy Spirit."

This time it's me blurting out my words as quickly as possible. My heart keeps fluttering in my chest and I can't seem to control it.

"I'm definitely struggling," she giggles, voice dropping to a breathy hiss as she leans in close. "Because I know what it feels like to have a man touch me. I know what it's like to have my clothes ripped piece by piece from my body, his mouth on mine, our arms around each other ... have you ever imagined that? Have you ever wanted to taste the salt of a man's skin?"

"No!" I cry out, jerking away from Catherine and putting ample space between us. "Of course not! My vows are made to the Church and I have no intention of ever breaking them!"

"Sweet Maggie, that's because you haven't experienced anything else. But when his body rubs against yours and you can run your fingers down his chest, and press your cheek over his heartbeat while his fingertips slip slowly past your navel, then you'll have a different point of view."

"Catherine, you can't talk like that in this place!" I cry out.

I don't know why she's torturing me like this. I don't know what sort of game she's playing. All I know is that the room is spinning again, so fast that I feel like it's going to hurl me right out through the stained glass rosette. My face feels flushed and hot, the same way it did when I came down with the flu last winter.

"Why?" she asks innocently, batting her long lashes. "Because it's turning you on? That's what that feeling is. That twisting inside of you like a stretching rubber band begging to be snapped. Think of Trevor's face buried between your thighs, his breath hot on your—"

"Stop!" I shriek, refusing to acknowledge the twisting tendrils of heat that have slowly begun to coil below my belly, making something between my inner thighs ache. I press my legs hard together and will the warmth to stop.

I don't want to hear anymore. It's too confusing. And it can't be holy, that's for sure.

There's a faint shuffling of noise behind us, and we both whip around to see Sister Grace Sabina emerge from among the books. She gazes at us, plump, pink lips set in a line, narrowed brown eyes cloudy with irritation and hunger. Though our habits are designed to conceal, the cloak hides little of Grace's curvy, hourglass figure. Though she's petite and slender, she has a tiny waist and an ample bust and hips. With every movement she makes, her hips languidly roll side to side with a sensuality that she'd never be able to see in herself. So when she catches men staring at her as she passes in town, she always assumes they're gazing at her cross necklace, and not at the swell of her breasts that the chain nestles between.

"You're supposed to be quiet in a library, sisters." She

swallows hard, trying to pretend she hadn't heard a single disgraceful word of what Sister Catherine had been spouting.

"What?" gasps Cat with mock astonishment. "You don't say?"

Grace frowns at Catherine's tone. "I hope you two know it's your fault our fasting got extended," she says with a sigh. Her voice is fragile, delicate, virtuous.

"You're talking now?" Cat prods with a roll of her eyes. "I thought you were never going to talk again or whatever. Isn't that what a vow of silence is?"

"I choose to dedicate my energy more to my studies than my speech, but I never said I wasn't talking anymore. Maybe if you paid as much attention to your surroundings or your Bible as you did to torturing everyone else around you, you'd know that," Grace continues.

"Sister Grace!" I gasp out. "That isn't kind."

"I guess good little Gracie isn't as good as she pretends to be," mocks Catherine.

I throw up my hands, separating them. Everyone is on edge, but I'm almost grateful for their disagreement, because it's distracted me from the gardener and the heat welling between my thighs.

"We're all irritable because we're hungry," I say gently. "That's all. Once we're able to break this fast, everyone will go back to being much more even-tempered."

Sister Grace bites her lip and nods. "I do apologize for my curt tongue, Sisters," she says softly, returning to her demure nature. "I haven't had anything but water in a week and it's getting hard to stay focused and to remember compassion."

"Mags and I tried giving you chocolate," Catherine notes, earning another harsh look from Grace.

"We're supposed to be fasting," Grace responds. "And I don't partake in sweets to begin with. It's just another form of temptation."

"And what did you say about the fast getting extended?" I ask, interrupting their bickering and pressing my hands on my belly. I've never been this hungry before.

I'd done plenty of occasional, much briefer fasts growing up, and then there was Lent when I always deprived myself of good food and lived off little more than breadcrumbs, but I'd never gone this long while only sneaking bits here and there. I'd made it four whole days before caving after watching Catherine take down a whole Hershey bar that she'd somehow snuck into the convent. Catherine was always managing to get prohibited things inside the fortress walls. Chocolate, magazines, even wine once.

"I ran into Sister Eva on my way to the library. She mentioned that we would not be having dinner tonight ... again," Grace murmurs with a grimace. "Mother Superior ordered it because she feels we haven't been diligent enough in our worshiping lately. Apparently, the reverend mother also believes there are some among us who have broken their fasts early."

Grace eyes us both, but I'm grateful she hasn't turned anyone in. That's probably because it's only she who's stuck perfectly to the fast the entire week.

"Have you decided what your mission is going to be, Gracie?" Catherine asks, trying to change the subject. Talking about food just reminded her that even she hadn't been able to conjure a decent meal all week.

The young woman gets a contemplative look on her face, her head tilting one way and then the other. "I think I'll do something with stained glass in the main church. Maybe I'll help clean it. Or perhaps there are some other studies I can do with it on its history and its meaning pertaining to the Lord."

"That sounds just like you," Catherine murmurs before turning to look at me with questioning, lifted eyebrows. "And you, Mags?"

I nod my head towards the books on the library shelves. "I'm probably going to transcribe some old manuscripts. I like looking at all the pictures that have been drawn in the margins, so it'll be something to keep me occupied until we're allowed to eat again."

Catherine's nose wrinkles and she gives her head a small shake. "Really? You're going to lock yourself up in a dusty room to stare at books all day? You do that already too much."

When I just shrug, Catherine wraps an arm around my shoulder, that sly gleam lighting her face once more. She gives me a squeeze, one hand on the small of my back. Grace looks away, cheeks pink.

"I think we can come up with something more interesting than that, Maggie," Catherine promises me before slipping away towards the library doors.

5

TREVOR

With a faint grunt, I lift my arms and sharply twist my body back and forth. I'm resting on a simple wooden chair under the shade of the convent, hoping my muscles will ease. I still have a few more hours of work to do, but my back is stiff and my thighs are sore. I'd always worked out, but garden work around the convent had pushed my body to the limit.

On the one hand, I loved how toned and tan I was getting. On the other, who am I going to impress *here?*

The middle-aged man sitting next to me, Henry, the head gardener, leans back in his chair, his legs propped up on the overturned barrel in front of us. Handsome and weathered, and almost never without his dusty, beat up cowboy hat, he looks like the cowboy in the Marlboro cigarette ads I've seen in old *Life* magazines. I nibble at my ham sandwich, keeping one eye on him. He reminds me of somebody but for the life of me, I can't remember whom. He'd more or less ignored me since I arrived, only occasionally giving me even the simplest of instructions, and so it was odd that he'd plopped himself right down beside me today when I stopped to have a late lunch.

After he'd offered a cool greeting, we were quiet now. While I eat the sandwich, he digs a steel fork into a bowl of microwaved beans.

The convent kitchen serves both the nuns residing within the nunnery as well as the staff from the dorm, but it had been shut down today for spring cleaning. All I could get for lunch was a ham sandwich, but that was fine with me —I'm a simple guy when it comes to food. Plus, I no longer trust the kitchen like I had when I first arrived. It was there that I'd run into Sister Monica, who I now recalled had auburn bangs falling into pretty green eyes. It was she who asked me to cut the leaves of the butterfly flower for her prayer tea. I felt foolish now for taking her word, but who would've expected a nun of all people to lie? It'd seemed innocent enough at the time, especially since I have no idea what weirdo rituals go on inside the mysterious building. For all I know, it's cult sacrifice. Hell, that may be why I was even brought here to begin with. Lol.

Henry takes a drag from his cigarette, seeming to blow the smoke purposefully towards the convent in giant, practiced circles. He looks pleased when they drift in the right direction, watching the smoke rings float on, with a smirk. I take another bite of my ham sandwich and wonder what the hell is up with this guy.

Everyone here is strange, I decide. You have to be if you're willing to hole yourself up in a place like this.

"I saw you talking to one of the sisters," Henry says abruptly, swinging forward so that his feet plant firmly on the soft earth. For a gardener, he has no qualms about crushing the sprightly green blades. He even digs his heel down a bit as if to prove to the lawn who's in charge.

"Is that not allowed?" I ask honestly, frowning. "Sister Ruth approached me."

"I'm not talking about the old lady," Henry chuckles. He runs his fingers over the brim of his cowboy hat, letting dust fall free. He gazes at me, taking another slow drag of his cigarette. He speaks so slowly, I find myself tapping my foot in an attempt to hurry him on. "I'm talking about one of the young ones."

"Is that not allowed?" I repeat, still frowning.

He blinks eyes the same shade as faded copper pennies. There's something unsettling about the way he looks at me, like he can see right through me, like every thought I have flying through my head is bared for him to read like the pages of an open book.

"It's not ... not allowed," he settles on saying eventually, almost smiling.

I can't tell if he's trying to make a joke or if he's messing with me. It's probably a little of both. Either way, it's irritating. I'd been hoping that I could have a moment of peace and quiet with my sandwich and think about Margaret. I want to hear her voice again. I want to hear her say my name. I want to let my mind wonder about what she's got going on under all that black fabric.

My eyes narrow, scrutinizing his expression. "Okay."

"You just have to be careful with those young ones," he continues, after flinging his still- burning cigarette onto the grass. He doesn't bother to put it out, watching the way one of the blades slowly begins to burn, embers floating up off the green blade. I reach over with my own foot to stomp the small flame out before it can get too high. We worked way too hard maintaining the grounds here to ruin them ourselves.

"How so?" I ask, wishing the conversation was over and

regretting urging the man on. I should've just agreed and stuffed my face with the rest of my ham sandwich.

I don't know much about Henry, but I know he's been part of the convent's staff since he was young himself. I'd seen an old black and white photo of him in the dorm's kitchen. He's the only one of us that has a nice, large room, tucked away on the bottom floor of the dorm building, with its own private bath and shower. When he's not working on the grounds, he's always locked away in his quarters—he's a loner. Henry doesn't even eat with the rest of us during the usual dining hours when everyone is in the kitchen. But he sure can be annoying: among other rude habits, he always takes the last cup of coffee from the pot, without remaking some. That's even more infuriating than his sloth-like drawl.

Henry grins. All of a sudden, I realize it's the movie star Clint Eastwood he looks like. Craggy and sculpted, they could have been separated at birth. "They're just dangerous. Take my word on that."

"Will do," I reply, relieved when he climbs to his feet as slowly and deliberately as he talks.

He tips his hat towards me, taking a few steps and then pausing. He digs his hands into his pockets, his lithe body illuminated by the warm golden glow of the fading afternoon light. Even though he's older, he's pretty muscled, I realize. I guess he's been using the weights in the dorm workout room—though I never see him in there when I do my daily lifting—because I'd never even seen him pick up a hose or a tray of seedlings.

Spring is beginning to bloom, quite literally, but the nights still get chilly and in late afternoon, you can feel a trace of coolness in the air. It wraps around me, making me shiver, but Henry still looks warm and comfortable. Without turning around to look at me, he continues speaking.

"The reason they wear that ridiculous outfit is because it hides things that are better off hidden, my boy. Because once you pull that veil away, there's no going back."

My eyebrows lift slowly towards my hairline, but Henry just gives a faint cackle of a laugh and roots in his pockets for more cigarettes.

"What?" I mutter slowly, brow furrowing over my nose, but Henry has lost all interest in the conversation and doesn't say a thing in response. I shouldn't put much stock in what he's saying anyway—they're just the ramblings of a crazy old coot.

Whistling, he saunters away with his back to me. It takes ten or so minutes to walk back to the staff living quarters, but going at his pace it may take him the better part of an hour.

I watch him leave, suddenly finding my appetite replaced by pure bewilderment; I toss the rest of the ham sandwich into the small backpack I tote around with me while I'm working. There's nothing remarkable in my bag except a bottle of water and a bound notebook that I keep private. I lean down, brushing my fingers over the faded leather of the cover and considering taking it out, but then change my mind and zip up the bag instead. Even though now would be a perfect time, I'll save that for later.

"Hey, kid," Henry abruptly yells, cupping his tanned and weathered hands around his mouth to shout over at me from the dusty road leading towards the door. I'm glad I left my notebook concealed now; I hadn't realized he was watching me again. "Before you head home for the night, go in through those big double doors there and then make an immediate right. I left some seeds in the pantry there that I'll need later."

I just give him a thumbs up, not willing to raise my voice

to shout back at him. Only once I'm sure that he's finally leaving for good do I climb to my feet, stretching out a bit more before walking towards the doors of the convent.

I brush a hand over the wall as I pass, letting my palm drag over the rough stone wall. The place is so big that sometimes it feels like if I step inside, it'll swallow me whole. I'd rather be swallowed up by the massive building than face Henry's aggravation, however, and so I push open the doors and step hesitantly inside.

Inside the building it's surprisingly cool, which I chalk up to the stone exterior. I inhale, tasting the dank coolness of the air, and then obediently turn down the hall and move towards the nearby door. It's so quiet inside the nunnery that each of my tentative, careful steps echoes loudly. I come to a small, nondescript door, one with a small cross chiseled into the mahogany wood. I pull it open and step inside, almost reeling back out the door when my eyes lock with the eyes of Jesus on a large wooden crucifix.

He hangs on the opposite wall, his body so masterfully constructed that his bleeding flesh could be real. Even his mouth is open in a twisted cry of agony I can almost hear. Every hair on my body stands on edge, and my jaw clenches abruptly.

What the hell was this place?

I turn around, taking in the desk and another wooden cross resting on its corner. Goosebumps drift slowly over my arms, leaving my entire body prickling. This creepy place definitely isn't a random side room pantry, and I definitely don't see any seeds.

Had I heard Henry wrong? Or was this some kind of hazing prank? With Henry, I couldn't be too sure.

With a grunt and a final shudder, I hurriedly whip back

towards the door, only to come face to face with someone even more terrifying than the dead Jesus pinned to the wall.

"What in the name of our Heavenly Father are you doing in my office?" barks Mother Superior Antonia Humilitas. She scowls at me, hands on her hips. "Are you snooping around, young man?"

"Hell no," I exclaim before I can help it, still completely freaked out by the crucifix on the wall behind me. I can feel him watching me even when I've turned away.

"Excuse me?" the mother superior gasps, cheeks going red. In her shock, spit flies from her mouth, peppering my cheek.

I wipe it away roughly and clear my throat. "I'm sorry, ma'am. Mother. Ma'am Mother. I just got ... lost."

Though I considered explaining that it was Henry who'd sent me here, it made more sense to just brush it all under the rug. Hopefully she'd accept the excuse and move on. But I should've known I wasn't going to be that lucky.

"Lost?" Mother Antonia says, moving so that she's blocking my way out of the room.

I glance desperately at the door, contemplating how to escape. But she'd just chase me, probably waving that crucifix on her desk all the way. But if I get fired from this job, I'll have to go to jail. Suppressing a groan, I focus back on the mother superior.

Though she's shorter than me, she's squat and rotund; if I wanted, I could probably roll her right down the hall. I try to edge around her, but she moves in front of me so that escape is no longer an option. It doesn't help that this room has no windows and the only light is a fading candle. I have to squint to see the woman clearly.

"If you were so lost, then why were you trying random

doors?" she asks. "And who are you? I haven't seen you around here."

"My name is Trevor. I only just started here under Henry a few weeks ago. I was told to collect seeds from a pantry and I thought this door was the one he was speaking of. I apologize for stumbling into your office."

I hope I at least sound sincere, because all I really want is to get the hell out of this room. The mother superior here has gray eyes that are colder than ice and breath that smells faintly of dead flowers—a sickeningly sweet fragrance that makes me want to retch. If I don't escape her presence soon, her polished black shoes are going to be in need of cleaning.

She huffs and puffs up like an irritated bird, then gives me the once-over with those frightening, lifeless eyes. But after what seems like an eternity, she nods and waves me away. "So be it, Trevor. But I never forget a name or a face. If I see you poking around in official Catholic business like what goes on within these doors of my office, you're going to be in deep trouble. The kind of trouble you won't find so easy to escape."

Even as someone who has seen their fair share of trouble, I got the feeling that Mother Antonia meant business.

"Yes, ma'am," I mutter, finally edging around her. But before I can get far, she catches me, her icy cold claws curling around my wrist. Another long shudder crawls up my spine.

"Call me Mother," she hisses softly, eyes narrowing on my own. Her tone has changed, going from self-righteous to almost ... territorial? Whatever the inflection may be, it's odd.

I give a curt nod, eager to be free of her hold, but she refuses to let me go. She just leans in closer, her nauseating, stale breath on my cheek.

"Yes … Mother," I finally whisper back, skin crawling by the time she releases me.

I pinwheel backward, rubbing the reddened skin where she was grasping me tight.

Without looking back, I shoot through the halls to find my way to the large double doors leading outside, but now that I've been so distracted, I can't remember which way is which. All the halls seem to be the same as I race around them, desperate to get outside before the mother superior discovers me still inside the building, and assumes I've been trying to cause more trouble.

I take one sharp corner before my body collides with something supple and soft that gives a faint yelp before we both collapse on the hard, stony floor of the convent.

"God, I'm so sorry," I grumble, pushing myself up to my feet only to realize that I'm staring at long, white legs protruding from under a twisted black skirt.

My eyes widen and my mouth goes dry as I take in the lacy white underwear revealed.

The nun gives a squeal before grabbing her robe, covering up and forcefully righting herself, pushing herself up onto her knees in front of me. It's none other than the beautiful, dark-eyed Sister Margaret.

"It's you," I whisper, sucking in a breath.

Even in that brief second, my eyes had mapped the shapely contours of the woman's milky thighs, and the tantalizing triangle of white lace above them. I'd always assumed nuns wore straitjackets or chastity belts or grannie underwear under their cloaks, but not Margaret. She'd been wearing simple white lace panties, a look so perfectly feminine and virginal, it made a feral growl almost creep up in my throat.

I'd seen plenty of women before; I was no stranger to

feminine charm. But there was something so pure about those white lacy panties, I felt my stomach knotting in on itself. All I could think about was what hid behind the thin cotton lace—it would be so easy to rip aside.

"What are you doing here?" she cries, still collecting herself as she tries to stumble to her feet. I climb instantly to my own and grab her, lifting her up with ease.

"Have you been eating?" I ask, before I can help it. She seemed so light and even more pale than normal.

She pulls away from me, glancing up and down the hall desperately as though looking for someone. "I'm fine. But I asked what you're doing all the way in here. No man is allowed this far into the convent."

Margaret gazes at me from under thick, black lashes that dust the tops of her cheeks. She's so pretty, like a painting. Her embarrassed flush from me seeing her panties has only made her more gorgeous. Rosy and ripe, like a tempting piece of fruit.

"I got lost," I answer, my heart thumping so, I could barely concentrate.

She frowns at me, lips pursed hard. Now her cheeks have begun to go even redder, the crimson flush creeping down her long neck. Her eyes dart over my jaw to where my shirt meets my collarbone and then firmly back to my eyes again.

"Just go back the way you came and you'll find yourself at the main doors," she offers in a strained tone.

"But that's what I was trying to do. I'm really bad with directions, Margaret. Won't you show me?" I ask, digging my hands into my pockets to show I'm not a threat.

"It's *Sister* Margaret," she scolds, eagerly putting another step of distance between us. "And I'm afraid I can't. I've lost track of one of my sisters and I have more I need to discuss with her. Just go back exactly as you came."

"I'll try. I hope you have a nice evening, Maggie," I answer, dodging her request to call her "Sister." It just felt so foreign—it doesn't suit her. Not the way it fit Sister Ruth or even the mother superior.

She sucks in a startled breath at the casual use of her nickname, cheeks flaming even brighter. There's a cherubic sweetness to her face that makes me want to corrupt her, even if it's by the subtle way of using a nickname instead of a formal title.

"I heard one of the other nuns calling you that. It suits you, you know. You have dark, beautiful eyes like a magpie," I whisper, before turning and slowly walking back down the hallway with my hands still in my pockets.

She doesn't respond to that, her eyes still wide.

She doesn't move, her gaze following me as I slip around the hall. I can feel her staring at me. Or into me—that's how intense it is.

Only when I get outside do I press the doors shut, one hand clapping over my heart. I bite back a groan, thinking of Margaret sprawled on the ground, back arched, body laid bare to me.

Why would God make a woman so beautiful, if she wasn't meant to be ravished?

6

Mother Superior Antonia circles her office, inspecting the nooks and crannies of the small space for any hint of a male's touch. She didn't trust the young man who'd broken into her office, no matter how seemingly innocent he was.

In fact, the mother superior didn't trust men at all.

Though most of the Catholic Church put the weight of mortal sin squarely on Eve's shoulders alone, Mother Antonia believed it was Adam's fault at the root of it all. She'd always loathed men and the way they demanded things with their raw, brute strength. It was appalling. An abomination, even.

Finally, only when she is convinced that the gardener hadn't brushed a single soil-flecked finger on any of her possessions, does she retreat to her desk and slide into her chair. The chair is hard and rough no matter how plush of a cushion was set atop it, and the reverend mother has to shift about in order to get comfortable. Her black skirt hangs in sheets around her plump legs as she rifles through her lower drawer and takes out a pack of crisp, chocolate covered cookies. She wets her lips, all but salivating as she peels back the thin wrapper and lifts one sweet morsel to her lips. She'd already picked through the gift basket that had been delivered to her office from the school in town, plucking out the tastiest of treats including these cookies and the chocolates that someone had dared steal.

It wasn't she who was disobedient to the Lord, after all. It was the young nuns and their wandering eyes. There is no need for the mother superior to fast—or so she believes. She's already closer to godliness than anyone else here, especially Sister Ruth.

Mother Antonia despises Ruth.

She'd tried a thousand times to get Ruth relocated to a different convent, or kicked out of the church entirely, but much to her disappointment, all of her attempts had failed. Ruth had been here longer than anyone else, and to remove her was going to take more than a false accusation or two. But Mother Antonia saw a bit of hope in young Sister Eva. That girl would most surely be of use, and she intended to exploit Eva's child-like eagerness to please to the fullest potential.

There may have to be some sacrifices along the way, but eternal purity was worth any cost. With a slow grin, Mother Antonia lets the cookie melt on her tongue before she crushes it beneath her molars.

Only when she hears the clack of noisy footsteps outside does she carefully place the cookies back in the drawer. Closing it, she summarily locks it with a key dangling from the same chain as the cross around her neck.

Then she calmly flips open her Bible and skims a random page while waiting for Sister Ruth to open the door.

Mother Antonia could easily recognize the noisy shuffle of the older woman. In fact, she has memorized most of the gaits of the women here. It's only Sister Grace's that is diffi-cult. The girl moves lightly and even Mother Antonia can rarely guess her delicate approach.

"Good evening, Mother Superior," Ruth announces as the door is pushed open.

The elderly nun gives a bow that makes her hip ache and then sidles forward to sit in the chair before the mother superior's desk. But etiquette dictated that Ruth wait for acknowledgement before sitting, and now Mother Antonia ignores such manners. Ruth winces, patting her hip, but refuses to let her expression melt into anything less than a pleasant smile. She felt her continually composed demeanor was one of the only ways to irritate the mother superior, without using her words. Ruth knew better than to use words that could be documented or heard and used against her.

"Good evening, Sister," Mother Antonia replies coolly, still refusing to look up and greet Ruth so she could rest her aging bones on the other chair. If the reverend mother allowed Ruth to sit, that would mean the woman was staying for a while, and the mother superior had no interest in that: she had more cookies to enjoy. "What brings you to my office? I have important things that must be done and no time for interruptions."

"Of course," Ruth says. "I was just hoping you and I could discuss that important matter I've been trying to tell you about."

Mother Antonia sharply lifts her head, the Bible slam-ming shut. Her eyes shift swiftly towards the closed door and then back at Ruth.

"You're bringing this up again?" she hisses, venom all but dripping from her mouth.

Sister Ruth stiffens before giving a faint nod. "It's of great importance. For weeks now I've been wanting to talk to you."

"Listen to me, Sister. We will discuss whatever it is when I deem it appropriate and not one second sooner—" Mother Antonia cuts herself off when she hears the hasty skip of shoes skittering down the hall.

The mother superior tries to place which nun the halting step belongs to, but finds it impossible. A moment later, Sister Catherine Mary bursts in through the door with red-rimmed eyes and shaking hands.

Both the mother superior and older nun gasp faintly in surprise, unused to seeing Catherine in such a state. The young woman stumbles forward, collapsing at Mother Antonia's side and burying her face into the mother superior's skirt. Catherine clings to the mother superior, tears soaking through the fabric until Mother Antonia pushes away the young nun to look her in the face.

"What in His blessed name is going on, child?" snarls the reverend mother, grabbing a tissue not for the weeping nun, but to dab at her own black skirt.

"Oh, Mother, I've been praying for hours and I've found no relief!" wails Catherine, who slumps backward so she's knelt on the cold floor. Her skirt surrounds her, her cape seeming to swallow her whole. "What am I to do if confiding in the Lord above doesn't help what ails me?" Catherine's voice cracks as plump tears roll down her cheeks.

Catherine, who was normally cool and often downright patronizing, is in a complete state of disarray. Her hair falls disheveled from her veil, her face shines wet from tears, her voice is strangled with despair. Even the mother superior doesn't know how to react to such a violent shift in behavior.

Mother Antonia casts a bewildered look at Sister Ruth, who shrugs but wrings worried hands.

"You must confess what's going on to your mother superior, Sister Catherine," Ruth encourages softly. "She will surely be able to guide you back to the light."

Mother Superior could be described as many things, but gentle and compassionate and understanding she was not—she was fighting the urge to roll her chair across the room away from the sobbing woman. Mother Antonia had never understood tears. She couldn't recall the last time any slipped down her own cheeks. It was a waste of time and energy as far as she was concerned. It was always for such silly things, too, at least when it came to Sister Eva. Had Mother Antonia not been so sure Eva would be beneficial to keep close, she would've banned the weepy nun from her office entirely.

"Yes, Sister Catherine. Tell me what's weighing on you," Mother Antonia finally huffs, still a full foot from the blue-eyed girl and her streaming tears.

Catherine pushes up onto her hands and knees and crawls forward, groping again at the mother superior's skirts as she stares desolately up into the older nun's eyes.

"As I'm sure you're aware, Mother, I was sent here to escape a life of devilish delights, yet I feel it following me. I might act condescending at times, but that's only because I'm so worried about slipping back into Satan's grasp. Still, I feel his crimson claws digging into my heart, Mother."

"How so?" Mother Antonia prods quietly, now interested.

"I've been having ..." Catherine sucks in a breath, pink lips forming a pursed circle, eyes rounding, "...thoughts."

"Thoughts?" whispers Ruth, both hands now finished wringing and clutching at the cross she wore on a silver chain.

Catherine swallows, fresh tears springing to her eyes,

and looks at Ruth for a moment before Mother Antonia. "Wicked thoughts. I feel as though I'm being pulled back to the secular world little by little, no matter how hard I struggle against the allure of an errant lifestyle."

"And that is not what you want?" Mother Antonia asks, her tone mirroring the stark surprise on Ruth's face. The mother superior would've guessed Sister Catherine would be the first one to escape the nunnery, given the chance.

Slowly, Catherine shakes her head. "No. I want to be here, Mother. I want to learn to be good and pious like the other sisters. I want to ..." she pauses as though thinking, her face crinkling for only a second before recollection lights her eyes, "I want to be free of plight and temptation and focus on establishing a love of the Holy Spirit!"

"Oh, my!" Ruth gasps, clutching her heart now. "Yes, Sister Catherine, we can certainly help you!"

"The best place to start such a journey is by focusing on the mission that I have told you all to plan for yourselves," Mother Antonia says, sounding much less gleeful about Catherine's confessions than Ruth, who has happy tears in her own eyes. "Have you been adhering to your fast as well?"

Catherine bows her head, biting her lip so hard that red lines appear in the supple flesh. "I have sinned, Mother. I stole hardened bread from the kitchen's garbage when I felt I could take no more hunger. I see now that I was led astray by temptation."

Ruth gasps. "Oh, Sister Catherine, surely it didn't come to that."

"I'm so sorry. Will I be forgiven, Mother Superior?" Catherine wails, more tears streaming down her face.

Mother Antonia awkwardly pats the girls head and smooths her black veil. "Of course. I will come up with a suitable punishment that redeems you in the eyes of the

Lord. Have you given any thought to your personal mission, however?"

Catherine slumps now, head lolling to the side. "I feel as though any task I come up with will be inferior to the other sisters. Perhaps I could join in with another of them and learn from their holy devotion?"

"... I assume that it is Sister Margaret whom you're trying to pair up with?" sighs the mother superior dryly.

"Sister Margaret is a good influence on me," Catherine agrees, rousing slightly as the tears clear from her glass blue eyes. "She was the one who encouraged me to come to see you with the things tormenting me lately. And she's also the one who's been making sure I do my evening prayers thoroughly!"

"That is good of your sister," agrees Sister Ruth with a happy nod.

Mother Antonia shoots her a look that tells the elderly nun to be quiet. "And what would Sister Margaret's focus be?"

"Well ..." Sister Catherine says, her face scrunching up again. "She only mentioned it briefly, but she so took to heart what you said about how connecting with the convent would also connect her with God above. I think she wants to start a garden so that the fresh vegetables can be used in our kitchen to nourish us, as well as being donated to the town soup kitchen. Isn't that lovely of her, Sister Ruth?" Catherine adds proudly, twisting to look at the older woman, who nods again eagerly.

"Such a labor-intensive project would certainly require some assistance," Ruth acknowledges with a pensive nod. "It would be good for you girls to cultivate a respect for the nature that our Father has bestowed upon us. I think this would be an exemplary mission. Don't you, Mother?"

Mother Antonia fidgets, gnawing at the inside of her lip. She can smell a scheme a thousand miles away, and this one is putrid.

"What do you girls even know about gardens?" she asks gruffly.

"We don't, unfortunately, but we will surely be able to ask some of the groundskeepers to point us in the right direction," Catherine explains with a respectful bow of her head. "Please, Mother Superior Antonia, allow me to help Sister Margaret with such a worthy endeavor. I feel as though if I can hold the earth in my hands, I may be able to better anchor myself here at the convent, and keep those wicked thoughts at bay."

"Fine, child," spits out the reverend mother, waving Sister Catherine away. Her head was beginning to ache, and she no longer wanted any part of this conversation that had already exhausted any patience she may have had. "It is approved; go and tell Sister Margaret that I expect you to start working on this garden tomorrow."

"Thank you, Mother!" gushes Catherine, springing to her feet. Her eyes are suddenly completely clear, all traces of tears evaporated.

Mother Antonia ignores the girl and shifts her focus to Ruth, who had showed no sign of leaving yet. "And you, Sister Ruth. Go do your rounds and make sure the girls are retiring for the evening."

"But, Mother Superior—" Ruth begins, clamming up when Mother Antonia gives her a firm glower. "Yes," she relents, deflated.

Catherine bows one more time and then skips from the room, a buoyant grin on her face and a conniving twinkle in her eye. Once out the door and safely down the hall, she claps her palms together with impudent glee. Though she'd been a desolate mess not minutes ago, she seems to be walking on air now.

Sister Ruth follows after the young woman, though with much less eagerness, her footsteps slow and tired, as though the gravity around her had grown ten times stronger than anywhere else in the convent looming around them.

A few minutes go by and then the mother superior slowly rouses herself, brushing a crumb of a cookie she hadn't noticed off her chest before approaching the door that neither Catherine nor Ruth had bothered to shut.

She closes it firmly and then leans against the hard wood, a smug smirk of her own tugging at her lips.

7

MARGARET

"You want to pray with me?" I ask blankly, gazing up into Sister Eva's icy countenance.

I'd just been fervently praying for a distraction from my humiliation, after the handsome gardener saw me sprawled out on the convent floor. Eva suddenly waltzed into view with a request that was rather odd coming from the willowy, disagreeable nun.

After Trevor had knocked me over in the hall, able to see only God knows what underneath my modest black and white habit, I'd been racing around in circles with my hands to my burning cheeks, trying to calm myself down.

Had I accidentally gone against my holy vows in allowing him to see me in such a shameful state? I couldn't very well ask Catherine, who would tease me incessantly, or the mother superior, who might very well whip me again. Perhaps I could find a way to ask Sister Ruth, who would probably give my shoulder a comforting pat and laugh over my concerns as though they were no big deal at all.

But Sister Ruth wouldn't know the whole picture. I wouldn't be able to tell her the way Catherine's naughty words from the library still whisper at the back of my mind, making prickles creep up and down me like lightly scratching fingernails.

I'd been almost ready to join Sister Grace in a meditative silence, with the hope it would still the whirling hurricane of my thoughts. Then Eva appeared. If anyone can distract me from these mortal temptations, it's her severe presence.

Even now under her gaze, I feel Cat's words receding slowly, leaving me joyously alone. The tingling sensation that flowed through my veins from my heart, through my stomach, to the strange burning warmth between my legs begins to fade; I was glad for that most of all. The forbidden area of my crotch is one of earthly desires, and I'd been told my entire life that it was a place only for naughty, ungodly girls to consider.

But the sensation was so overwhelming—a mix of tingling and prickling and the oddest, most compelling thrill I'd ever felt—it was hard to ignore. I don't know what it means, but when I think of Trevor, I start to throb there and my fingers twitch as though they want to drift between my legs and discover what is hidden there.

Thankfully, Eva interrupted me before I could give in to such enticements.

Plain Sister Eva is taller than I am and slim as a board, her nun's robe hanging around her like a sheet. The length of the fabric hanging around her arms dangles past her long fingertips.

When she opened her mouth to ask something of me, I certainly didn't expect her to request a joint prayer session.

It wasn't unusual for all of us sisters to pray together, or rather, it wasn't unusual for all of us sisters *except* Eva to pray together. Whenever I wanted someone to sit with me while I lost myself in the pages of my devotions, even Catherine was frequently up for the task, if I allowed her to gossip a little between pages. But never cold, distant Eva.

Eva liked to do her own thing and go her own way; that had never bothered me. In fact, I rather admired her for being able to commit to our faith in such total isolation and peacefulness. But now I couldn't figure out why she would suddenly be interested in spending time with me.

With a personality as unattractive as her looks, Sister Eva did not like any of us. She had no use at all for the twins Sister Lucy and Sister Genevieve. And it made sense that she avoided Sister Monica, who loved to play tricks and pranks often focused on her, as well as Catherine, because Eva and Catherine are both hotheaded and tended to combust when they got too near one another. But harsh Eva did not even like Grace, who was so mousy she wouldn't talk back to a buzzing mosquito. And as for me, even though I gave Eva a wide berth, her lips always curved into a snarl whenever our eyes locked during dinner.

My stomach rumbles at the thought of dinner: food. Surely our fast would be broken soon?

As was usual at this time, I'd heard the cooks in the kitchen, their pots banging. Now the scent of dinner was wafting through the halls of the convent. Right now I'd get on my knees and beg for just a spoonful of oatmeal.

"Are you rejecting me?" Eva asks in her dry, incessantly irked tone. "Would you really rebuff your own sister this way?"

"Of course not!" I answer with a gasp, one hand flying to the rosary around my neck and giving it an apologetic squeeze. "I'm just wondering what prompted this. You usually stay so …" What was the right word here? Aloof? Snooty? Condescending? "Independent."

Yes. That sounded like a compliment. Hopefully.

Eva's face gives nothing away. I don't think she's even blinked since she took her spot in front of me. She reminds me of a lizard sunbathing on a desert patio. Those creatures just stare ever onward, their expression never changing, no matter what happens around them.

"I just don't want to be alone," she shrugs. Her eyes avert mine for the quickest of seconds, the action happening so fast that, had I blinked I would've missed it in its entirety. My heart warms slightly for her.

Loneliness. I know it well.

It's one of the costs of following the dream of joining the convent and pledging yourself to your faith forever. Your vow is one of chastity and isolation. You can only go so long at it alone; eventually, you must depend on your sisters for company.

"Okay," I answer, making the mistake of patting her arm.

Eva recoils from me like I've just spit in her face, her mouth contorting into that same snarl once more. I keep my face pleasant, even though I want to roll my eyes. I'd noticed she always does this when touched before she can prepare herself for it, so it doesn't hurt my feelings. Living between these high, stone walls, you get used to not being touched. I'd forget what a hug even feels like if Catherine weren't so adamant on embracing me whenever the mood strikes her.

It occurs to me then that Eva could use a friend like Cat, even if neither of them would ever admit such a thing. Maybe, one day, they'll finally see the good in one another. I know there's good in Eva, no matter how much she tries to pretend she looks down on all of us and wants to squash us under her heel like the bugs she thinks we are.

After I collect my things from the room I share with Cat, I walk with Eva down towards the main hall of the church. We move along in silence, our figures casting shadows against the cobbled gray floor as we pass under the electric lights. I can only imagine the battle that had to happen to convince Mother Antonia to allow such technology under the roof of the nunnery. If it were up to her, we'd still be washing our clothes in basins and cooking our meals on a simple hearth, all by candlelight. While I know certain simplicities can be nice on occasion, too much would make life here at the convent unbearable.

Eva's long legs march like a toy soldier's, her arms unmoving at her side. I watch her from the corner of my eye, her gaze focused straight ahead in grim determination. Like Mother Superior, she doesn't often smile. In fact, Eva reminds me a lot of Mother Antonia Humilitas, but just on the surface. Underneath all that, I believe Eva still has a beating heart and life in her veins, unlike our reverend mother, who is cold and dead through and through.

"What?" the brunette nun grunts when she catches me staring at her. Her long fingers brush her high, gaunt cheekbones. "Do I have something on my face?"

"No," I answer, almost proud to have been the one to catch the vigilant nun off guard for once, instead of the other way around. A sigh escapes Eva's tight lips. "Then stop staring, Sister Margaret."

I do as she asks, focusing my eyes ahead. We pass by tall arches and marvelous stained glass windows that peer out onto the blue sky. Below the convent, rolling green fields and hills lead out to the surrounding forests. I try to remember what it felt like to walk on city streets, talk on telephones, watch tv and play games on my laptop before I came to the convent. But now I can hardly remember what a keyboard feels like under my fingers or the soft comfort of my denim jeans, let alone a ponytail curling against the back of my neck without being squashed by a veil. That all feels like such a distant, foreign world now. If I ever did want to leave this nunnery, I'd be so behind. I know how fast the modern world revolves, and it would've kept on spinning without me.

But, then again, it's not like I'm going anywhere. I'm safe here in my cloistered shell, and safety is all one could ask for, isn't it?

Once we reach the main chamber of the church, Sister Eva slows to a stop. Sometimes our priest is here, but today he's tucked away in one of his back offices working on his sermons. Or perhaps Sister Grace has begged him to show her his private library again. He has the most sacred of works back there, and Grace adores just gazing at them. She knows she mustn't touch any of the ancient, sacred texts, but just being near them leaves her glowing for days.

We settle side by side in a pew near one of the faceted windows.

Unsure if Eva is ready for me to look at her, I stare instead out the glass. The colors seem to swirl together as the sun shifts outside, the splendid rainbow of shades making me dizzy. It's so beautiful I almost want to cry. This is why I'm here, I remind myself silently. To marvel at the Lord's wonder and to dedicate myself to him. I can't be led away from this path I've chosen.

"Your face when I showed up ... you looked like something was bothering you," Eva remarks abruptly.

I turn back towards her, head tilting. I can only imagine what my face looked like, all flushed cheeks and dilated pupils.

Eva isn't looking at me, still focused ahead on the priest's pulpit. I stare down at my clasped hands instead. My fingernails are digging into the back of my other palm, red crescents starting to form. I can't tell her—I can't tell anyone.

I try to get Trevor out of my mind but he remains, his eyes glowing against the backs of my eyelids.

Again that heat begins to swell inside of me, as it does every time my mind wanders towards Trevor. The broadness of his shoulders, the green pools of his eyes ... what is it about him that makes my blood seem to simmer? Heat warms my crotch again and I'm aware of an inner craving, an emptiness that cries out to be filled, *now*. I shift back and forth, biting my lip.

I can't feel this now. Not here in the church. It's wrong.

I close my eyes, willing away the overwhelming sensation, but that seems to only make it swell inside of me. It builds further, making me gasp and clench my knees hard together.

Eva cocks her head, eyes narrowing on me. I hate the way she stares at me as though she can see right through my cloak and veil. I can hardly breathe, the boiling of my veins making my temperature rise and sweat form on my brow.

Desperate to get away from her prying eyes, I jump out of the pew and dash back towards the doors of the church. My feet click the entire way, the sound bouncing from wall to wall as Jesus looks on from the stained glass and from his spot on a crucifix above the pulpit. I run faster and faster, willing the heat of the exertion to replace the heat inside my core, but it all seems to slither and twist together until everything is spinning wildly around me.

As soon as I'm outside the church, I gulp in greedy mouthfuls of air, but find no relief until I grab my veil in both hands and tear it back off my forehead. My long, dark hair springs forth, slick from sweat, and I collapse on the sidewalk outside the convent in a damp, trembling heap. My hands press against my lower stomach, trying to figure out the source of those bewildering feelings, hoping they aren't rooted in the naughtiness I suspect.

Perhaps I should go see the doctor, just to make sure. Maybe there's something wrong with me ... this type of burning in my veins, it can't possibly be normal, can it?

Suddenly, I'm aware of eyes on me from somewhere around the convent grounds. I can feel someone watching me, their eyes taking in my hair uncovered by the veil. Expecting to see Eva smirking from the shadows behind me, instead my gaze collides roughly with that of the very gardener I'd been trying to avoid.

Trevor stares at me from over the handle of his shovel, which has plunged partially into the earth under his feet. But though he says nothing, his face is not a frozen mask like Eva's. Quite the contrary. There's something in his eyes, something hungry, something tempting, something dangerous.

The heat that I feel, he can sense it. Because he can feel it, too. I can see it in every line of his focused face, as he gazes at me fixedly.

Muttering a prayer, I grab my veil and rush back inside, comforted only when I hear the slam of the heavy door behind me.

What is happening to me? And why is it Trevor who causes these confusing—and thrilling—sensations?

8

———

TREVOR

In the half second it takes me to throw my shovel down on the green bed of grass beneath me, Margaret is already gone.

She was there for only a moment, like a mirage or a mystical illusion, just long enough to make me certain that angels do walk this world.

Her hair was not at all what I expected it to be. Though I could tell by her complexion and brows that her locks would be dark, I'd been expecting glossy, smooth hair that frames her pretty face. But her hair was a wild, cascading mane that went way down her back. I found I liked her hair better untamed than I ever would have if it was as smooth as I imagined.

Under that veil and that wild hair there is a wild heart, I'm sure of it. I can tell.

Abandoning my task, whatever it might have been—I sure as hell can't remember now— I bend over and dig through my bag. My fingers brush that weathered, old notebook I always have with me. Tugging it free from the bottom of my bag, I collapse down on the soft ground and lay it on my lap.

After looking carefully up and down the grounds to make sure no one was watching me, I stretch my legs in front of me and thumb open the book. If somebody sees me I could get scolded for not doing my duties.

Though the list of things I could bring with me when I joined the convent staff was extremely limited, I'd managed to keep this one special item hidden. I'd had this notebook for a year and a half, having picked it up back home when I started getting my act together. I'd had art therapy to help me through crises growing up, and been singled out more than once as a budding artist with professional potential. Unfortunately, I hadn't fulfilled that promise—at least yet— but I still enjoyed drawing whenever I could. On each of the pages, I've drawn various people in my life, or strangers in a restaurant or on a bus, or scenes, even objects like cars that I love. I draw whatever I feel like, and I find it helps calm me and keep me out of trouble.

On the most recent page is the face of a beautiful woman. Plump, delicately curved lips are set in a pale face sketched by my pencil: Margaret's face. Over the last few days, I'd spent hours hunched over this page working on getting it right, but it wasn't as good as I'd like it to be yet. Her eyes weren't quite the right almond shape and the bridge of her nose was just a little too strong, but I would get it there, and then I would show her.

I've drawn many things over the last year and a half, but nothing quite as lovely as she.

I flick my pencil carefully over the page, just beginning to mark the wispy, wild curls so that when I'm alone in my room later, I'll be able to remember just the way they danced across her forehead and down her back. But with a chuckle I realize I'm not going to forget that sight anytime soon. I can still see her perfectly in my mind's eye, her expression marked with shock as our gazes locked. She'd blushed and run away the moment she realized she'd been caught without her veil by male eyes, but what a sight she was to behold.

I'd never experienced anything as surprisingly gorgeous as the sight of her without her veil. There's no other woman like her on this planet, I'm sure of it now. It's totally unfair that I won't be able to hold her hand in my own or taste her lips. Or other parts.

She's so tantalizingly close, yet so far, unattainable behind the strict barriers of religion and equally impenetrable walls of a convent fortress that keeps her locked away. I still don't understand any of it.

I'd thumbed through the small bookcase we had in the living room of the male dormitory to see if I could find any literature about the nuns and their oaths, but the books had been boring and there isn't much there, anyway. Most titles had been about the architecture of the convent, while others had been on notable people who've passed through the halls. Then there was the odd Tom Clancy or John Grisham thriller.

In the living room, the handful of groundskeepers never talked much among ourselves. Nobody was outright unfriendly, it was just like we all mostly wanted to be left alone. I suppose we all have reasons for coming out here, and they're as unwilling to share theirs as I am mine. Because some things are better left unsaid. Though I do wonder if I'm the only one whose eyes wander towards the nuns sometimes. Not just any nun, however. Only my nun. My Margaret.

"You, boy," a voice calls.

I snap the notebook shut and tilt my face upwards to see the mother superior of the convent trundling towards me. Her eyes are cast down at the earth around us so as to avoid stepping on any errant rocks or sharp twigs, and so I have just enough time to shove my notebook back into hiding.

"Are you really taking your break so early?" she asks with a frown.

"My hands were starting to ache so I thought I'd give them a quick rest, Mother," I answer with a taut smile.

I'd made sure my bag was safely secured and she wouldn't be able to spy into it. I'm glad I did so, because she takes her time scraping her eyes across my backpack, as though looking for contraband. I don't have anything illicit in there except for the drawing of Sister Margaret, but I don't think that would go over well with the mother superior. Aside from the occasional lusty thought towards that beautiful nun, I have followed every rule as closely as possible. I don't want to get into any more trouble.

I really do want to make the best life that I can. Sure, before I may have been somewhat of a lowlife, but I want to prove that people can change; I want to one day be worthy of someone as beautiful inside and out as Margaret, though I doubt I'll ever meet someone who matches her perfection.

Before I can wonder if the mother superior had come all the way out over the grass just to scold me for sitting still for a moment, she huffs and looks back at me with those narrowed, cold eyes that match the shade of the stone walls rising behind her. The hair on the back of my neck goes up, the same way it always does when she gives me a look like this.

I don't like the woman, and I certainly don't trust her. She has the eyes of a rabid dog and the expression of a hunting wolf. I've seen many faces like that in my trouble-making days. It's never good.

I'm struck with the sudden urge to grab Margaret, hurl her over my shoulder, and take both of us as far and as fast from this place as I can run, but I know that's ridiculous. For one thing, Margaret would never allow such a thing, and besides, where would I go? Would I just return to the streets so I could get jailed again?

Mother Antonia gazes levelly at me for a moment, her eyes boring into mine before she finally begins to speak in that growling tenor of hers. Her voice is deep for a woman, the kind that gets its edge from constant yelling.

"Since you're going to be more involved with the nuns here, I wanted to make sure that you completely understand your task here at the convent, Trevor," she declares frostily.

She stares down at me, her black habit flapping around her black socks and masculine black shoes, as her hands are planted firmly on her big hips. Though far shorter than I, in this position above me Mother Antonia reminds me of an ominous, looming building, the kind that would never fall no matter what storm or earthquake or tidal wave should ever barrage its walls. I can't help but shudder.

When it comes to "being more involved with the nuns," I have no idea what she's talking about. Hopefully she hasn't caught me eyeing Margaret, because I think that'd be bad for everyone. Really bad.

I clear my throat awkwardly and tug at my collar, but Mother Antonia grimly purses her lips. She stops talking and gazes at me expectantly.

"I think I understand what I'm doing here, for the most part," I manage to respond. "To be honest, the instructions have been a little lacking, but I've been able to figure things out. I know where the seeds are now so I won't be wandering into your office again anytime soon. And I know that my duties, in particular, are the daisies and roses and not giving any nuns leaves to make tea."

Hoping to ease the intense tension between the reverend mother and myself, I crack a wry smile at my joke, but she remains impassive. The mother superior's eyebrow arches up so high it's almost at her gray hairline, though of course I can't see that under the veil. She blinks her eyes a few times as though I hadn't made any sense whatsoever, and then ruffles up like an irritated pigeon.

"What? Young man, no. I'm not talking about seeds or daisies or even tea. I'm talking about the virtue of the sisters here. Just as it is your responsibility to guard the grounds, it is your duty to guard their morals. If you see or experience anything of less than holy standards, you must report it immediately to me. Are we clear?"

Her words soak slowly into my skin, leaving me feeling repulsed.

Oh, we're clear, alright.

She's asking me to be a snitch, to come running to cling to her skirts if I see anything scandalous like Margaret's sudden removal of her veil. She may have worded it as guarding the girls' morals, but I can see right through Mother Antonia's carefully chosen words. The mother would surely love to know about Margaret's reckless behavior, but like hell I'm going to say anything: giving Mother Antonia news of the nuns would be like feeding a helpless bunny to the predatory wolf this vile woman is.

"Well?" she presses, teeth gritted in irritation that it took me longer than a second to compose an answer.

I grab my shovel again, tossing it over my shoulder as I gaze at the stocky woman with the stormy eyes. She'd like nothing more than to crush everyone here under her thumb in the name of her faith, but I'm not going to help her do that. I'd *never* help her do that—not even if it cost me my job here and sent me to jail.

Mother Antonia may have thought I would be another eager pawn in her game, but she has another thing coming. I'll play her game, but I'll play it right back at her.

A smile brightens my face and I dip my chin a single time.

"I understand what you're asking completely," I assure her, promising her nothing.

9

Sister Catherine walks—or better, wafts—on Cloud Nine through the darkened halls of the convent, inhaling the dank air and beaming from ear to ear. Occasionally, she does a perky little spin which reveals fishnet thigh-high stockings under her habit—her own personal form of rebellion, among other things.

She'd never been more proud of her ability to play-act then she is right now. This wasn't the first time she'd pulled one over on the mother superior, but this had been by far her best performance.

Earlier, Catherine had paced up and down the halls outside Mother Antonia's office for a full fifteen minutes trying to work up those tears, before she ran inside that office. She'd thought of everything from her childhood dog dying, to her parents kicking her out when she was just sixteen, to her first lover breaking her heart.

But she hadn't been able to work up a single teardrop until she thought about a very painful, old memory, one she usually avoided thinking about at all costs.

Just that thought had sent shivers rolling through her

entire body, and before she could even help herself, she was sobbing hysterically. Sister Catherine doesn't know how she feels about faith or even the vows she took as a nun, but she does know that, when it comes down to it, Mother Antonia is no match for her strength. Sure, the mother superior has her intimidating moments, but Catherine didn't fear her at all.

The strawberry blonde pauses at one of the upper windows, her fingers trailing across the dusty pane. The sky today is a perfect shade of blue, the kind that you would think comes from a tube of paint instead of nature.

Some people must love this weather, she muses to herself. She knows Maggie does. To Catherine, that girl was like a flower. Maggie needed to be outside, warm and nurtured, to bloom. Maggie hadn't flowered yet, but she would with Catherine's help, at least. Beautiful people like Maggie deserved as much.

"Cat!" cries Maggie's voice abruptly from the hall, quietly echoing from wall to wall.

Catherine turns to grin at the slightly disheveled woman whose dark veil was completely askew. Catherine walks up to Maggie and fixes the veil, carefully tucking unruly dark curls away, just the way she knew Maggie liked it.

"What's going on with you?" Catherine asks curiously, eyeing her with interest.

Maggie was usually much more composed than she is right now, and so Catherine was eager to hear what had put her in such an unsettled state. Things could be rather dull in the Convent of the Blessed Virgin, and Catherine loves gossip. Maggie gulps and stares at her friend, taking in her own panicked expression in the reflection of Catherine's blue eyes.

"He saw me," she whispers hoarsely, clutching at her

flushed red throat with horror. "He saw me without my veil. He saw my *hair!*"

"He?" Catherine prompts, nodding when Maggie shrieks out the gardener's name and buries her face in her hands.

"That's hardly the end of the world," Catherine responds with typical nonchalance. Nothing was ever a big deal as far as unflappable Sister Catherine Mary was concerned. "A lot of other nunneries allow nuns to show their hair now, you know."

"But we're not a lot of other nunneries!" whispers Maggie, clutching her best friend's hand tightly.

Catherine notices her hand shaking and her detachment gives way to compassion. She wraps her friend in a hug and pats her back. Maggie trembles in her arms and Catherine concludes that the other woman wasn't trembling solely because of humiliation, but something else, something more torrid and visceral. The way Maggie's hands and knees were trembling so ferociously, Catherine knew that feeling well.

"Okay, so Trevor saw you. What can be done now?" Catherine asks gently, rocking Maggie back and forth like a mother soothing her child. "You can't go back in time, Mags, so you have to just accept it—it is what it is. Anyway, it's really alright. There's no way he was shocked, we know that. And what's more, he won't tell anyone. We may not know him well, but I can tell he can keep a secret."

Catherine's words seem to have the desired effect, because Maggie relaxes against Catherine, her head on her friend's slender shoulder.

"I suppose it's true, nothing can really be done," Maggie relents. "But I'll have to tell the priest at confession."

"And he'll give you twelve 'Hail Mary's' and an hour of deep prayer and that will be that. Mother Superior won't even find out." Catherine steps back and places her hands lightly on Maggie's shoulders. Her blue eyes shimmer eagerly. "I have news. It's something that'll definitely take your mind off this."

"Oh?" asks Maggie, brightening slightly, like a wildflower peeking through the crack of concrete.

Catherine gives a tight-lipped nod, her eyes wide and excited.

Maggie slips away from Catherine and slides up so she's sitting on a window sill just barely wide enough for her to fit. Sister Grace would be able to lay sideways along the sill and stare up at a night full of stars if she wanted to, though Maggie had the feeling Grace would consider that disrespectful to the building. Grace walked with her arms tucked close against her tiny body and her feet just barely drifting over the floors, as though she wasn't worthy of touching even the dust on the walls.

"Are you going to tell me what it is?" Maggie presses with a faint laugh.

Feeling a bit more rejuvenated, Maggie frowns impatiently at Catherine while adjusting her veil to make sure her hair was thoroughly in place.

"Well ... I had a meeting with Mother Antonia," Catherine begins leisurely.

"*Mother* Antonia, Cat," chides Maggie before shaking her head and reminding herself to focus on what was important right now—that being Catherine's story, of course. Even Maggie was drawn to gossip. "What about?"

"Our homework assignments," continues Catherine, stretching it out. She's clearly enjoying feeding Maggie crumbs of her tale and making her work for the details.

"It's not a school assignment, it's a moral mission," Maggie says with a sigh.

She rests her hands on the window sill beside her and lets her back rest against the warm glass, which she can feel through the cotton of her habit. When Catherine responds by dramatically rolling her eyes, Maggie lightly kicks at her shin to beg for more information.

"You and I get to work together!" Catherine cries joyously, throwing up her hands in celebration. "Isn't that great! You wouldn't believe what I had to do to convince Mother Antonia. I had to pretend to cry, ugh, it was such a pain."

Maggie groans, not joining in on her friend's delight. "That's great for you, but that means I'm going to be doing double the work. You really want to transcribe manuscripts with me?"

"Oh, God, no," Catherine grimaces, as though the very thought is repulsive.

Maggie sucks in a breath and almost yells at her friend not to use the Lord's name in vain, but decides she's corrected Catherine too much in the last five minutes and yet another would risk Catherine not continuing her story. Maggie knew Catherine well enough to know that there was more left to share that Catherine was still withholding. So, instead, Maggie keeps silent.

"Maggie, I told you I was going to find you something more interesting to work on ..." Catherine says, leaning towards Margaret and planting both her palms on either side of Maggie's knees.

The two girls are close together, Catherine leaning over Maggie, who was pressed against the stained glass.

Maggie narrows her eyes suspiciously. "And what might that be?"

She racks her brain, trying to figure out just what

Catherine could be up to, but she could come up with nothing. You never knew with Cat, after all.

"You and I are going to be doing work around the gardens. Imagine that, you and I outside in the sun day in and day out nourishing our souls and the land and taking in God's bounty ... yadda, yadda, blah, blah, you get the point," Catherine trails off with a dismissive wave of her hand and a roll of her eyes.

"But ...." Margaret gulps, "but Trevor works in the gardens ..."

"And he is surely going to be able to help us with our demanding tasks. Won't that be kind of him?" Catherine muses with feigned nonchalance, though her eyes have turned to sly slits. "We'll have to ask him tomorrow, of course. But I'm sure he'll be eager."

"I can't, Cat. I can't be around him. He makes me feel ..." Maggie trips over her words, stumbling to a clumsy halt.

"Feel what, Maggie?" Catherine asks, one hand lazily tapping piano keys over Maggie's knee.

Maggie shifts away from her, sliding free of the window sill.

"Nothing. Nothing at all," she whispers hoarsely, her eyes darting up and down the hall to make sure there were no prying ears nearby.

"If he makes you feel nothing at all, then this shouldn't be an issue," Catherine chirps breezily. "I'm glad to hear that you're up for the task. Gardening is hard work, I hear. We start in the morning. You should make sure you get some rest tonight."

Maggie could only shake her head, watching as Catherine descended down a nearby set of stairs. Only then did she slump back against the window pane, desperately looking out over the wildflower-dotted hills around the convent.

She has no idea what tomorrow will bring, but she's sure it will be trouble.

Slowly, she lifts one palm to place it over her heart, feeling the rapid pace of it throbbing against ribs which by now must surely be bruised. Even just thinking about the gardener made her feel as though she was going to burst. How would she be able to work *near* him? Briefly, she considers going to Mother Superior and asking for a change of project, but she also knew that would only bring Catherine's wrath upon her; there's no way she'd ever disappoint her best friend.

In the end, she closes her eyes and hopes that something good would come of this task. For example, perhaps this was a trial of her faith, and she would have to show her devotion to the Lord by refraining from her own desires. Or maybe this would be her chance to bring Trevor into the holy light. Yes, that's what she would focus on for now. She could surely help him.

She opens her eyes, feeling refreshed, and hopes to make her sisters and her mother superior proud. She will use this temptation to better herself ... or at least that's what she's telling herself right now.

Catherine, meanwhile, continues to prance down the stairs, completely overjoyed with the way things had worked out. She hops with almost juvenile glee from one slick step to the next, humming some Top 40 song she remembered from before the convent—one that had a fair share of deliciously sinful words in its lyrics.

When she rounds the corner, however, all that delight melts clean off her face when she almost runs headlong into

Sister Eva, who had a habit of appearing exactly when she was unwanted most.

"Watch your step," mutters Sister Catherine, despite the fact that she had been the one not looking where she was going. "You wouldn't want to hurt one of your dear sisters, would you?" she adds, venom on her tongue.

Cat and Eva stare at one another, the tension thick.

The two women are vipers circling each other carefully, waiting for a moment to strike. "I have no sisters," Eva barks back, just as venomous, "only competition."

10

MARGARET

earty chicken noodle soup, just-baked crusty French bread and fresh spinach salad had never smelled as scrumptious as they did when placed in front of us fifteen minutes ago, marking the break from our blessed fast. We hadn't been sure how much longer we'd be forced to go without food, but thankfully the fast had finally come to an end, whether or not Mother Antonia approved. I could tell she was less than thrilled that we were finally being fed, because her eyes are set like smoldering, gray stones above her scowling mouth.

We'd all already eaten at least three bowls of the soup, only stopping when Mother Antonia rose from her own table near the front of the dining room, reminding us that gluttony was a sin. Twins Lucy and Genevieve sat beside each other with Sister Isabelle across the table, begging for their leftovers.

The only one who'd shown any amount of restraint after our forced fast was Sister Grace, who delicately sipped from her bowl as though she hadn't been starving. Her eyes, however, were much less grim than they had been in the library before, and it was nice to see some color back in her cheeks.

Next to Grace, Sister Monica's face is practically in her bowl inhaling the remaining soup she has, and when she lifts her face some of the broth clings to the corners of her mouth. When I indicate for her to wipe it away, she gives a faint giggle and does so. Though a bit of a trickster, Sister Monica did have a heart of gold. She just despised feeling bored more than she enjoyed peace and quiet; I couldn't fault her there.

Monica then rose to her feet, collecting everyone's bowls when supper ended. She even took Sister Eva's without "accidentally" spilling any of the remaining broth on the brunette nun's habit, though probably because Monica intended to slurp up the rest in the kitchen. After all, you could never be too sure when Mother Antonia would order another fast in the name of our faith. We each took turns helping clean up after dinner once the cooks were finished in there for the night.

The rest of us would retire to our rooms for our evening prayers.

Once we were released by Mother Antonia, Catherine and I walk side by side up the stairs towards our shared room. Catherine is a little more quiet than normal, brooding over something or other. I saw her shooting glares at Eva all through dinner, the expression quite forcefully returned. I'd have asked what was causing the tension, but there was always something going on between Eva and Catherine. It was like they enjoyed being at odds with one another. Tonight, among the rest of my prayers, I'd pray for both of them to find peace and harmony. It would surely lead to more peace and harmony for the rest of us as well.

Inside our room, Catherine and I begin to slowly strip away our habits and veils before getting ready for bed.

Catherine flings off her clothes and dives stark naked between her sheets. I slip into a modest, virginal white nightgown that hangs down to my ankles, then promptly climb into my own little cot. The beds themselves are not remarkable in any way. They're small, lumpy, and the quilts were stitched by nuns that came before us generations ago. I notice it's time to wash the quilt that's on my bed.

All of us sisters take turns sorting the dirty linens and clothes and sending them down the massive laundry chute that's in the hallway wall. They're loaded onto the big white truck every Saturday evening to take into town for washing. Sometimes, when it's Catherine's turn, she even convinces the driver to request fabric softener, so that for a week we can enjoy sheets that aren't stiff and scratchy.

Outside, the moon has risen, dangling from somewhere high up in the evening sky.

Our room has two barred windows, one above Catherine's bed and one above mine. They're set high up on the wall so that I have to sit up in bed to gaze out of it, but I don't mind. Then when I'm lying sideways on my mattress, I can see stars twinkling through the thick, iron bars that protect the window. And moonlight too, if the moon is in the right place.

When I first arrived, I'd asked Mother Superior why the bars were there. She'd claimed it was to keep anyone from breaking into our consecrated rooms, but I have a feeling it's more to keep us inside.

"Are you excited for tomorrow?" Catherine asks, her voice drifting from her bed where she's curled like a nude cat between her sheets.

She doesn't seem to care that the sheets and quilts are

scratchy and old and might bother her milky white skin—
it's being naked and free that she loves, after being caged all
day in her nun's habit.

"Why?" I ask, though my voice is quivering and gives
away the fact that I know exactly what Catherine is referring
to.

Tomorrow, I get to see Trevor.

Not only that, but I also get to talk to him ... to spend
time with him ... to watch his broad shoulders as he digs
through the earth and helps Catherine and me garden for
the first time.

I get to see the delicate way he handles the pretty plants,
and I get to feel the earth under my hands. I think of his
fingernails, which were brown from soil and dirt, and lift
one of my own hands to inspect. My palms are now healed
smooth, the welts where Mother Antonia had punished me
no longer painful or swollen; the aloe Trevor had given me
had worked wonders. I wonder if these hands are capable of
doing such work as Trevor does. I've never really had to do
anything with my hands; I've never had to work so hard my
back ached or my muscles throbbed. The only time I felt
that sort of discomfort was during long prayer sessions with
Grace, when my legs would go numb as I kneeled and I
would lose feeling in my clasped hands.

Catherine ignores my feeble attempt at coyness and
draws in a slow, long yawn.

Her mattress creaks beneath her as she changes posi-
tions in an attempt to get comfortable, and then rolls over.
It's funny with Catherine, that when she falls asleep nothing
about her changes. She thrashes about, moving back and
forth as though she's still running and roaming the castle
grounds. Even awake she can't sit still, and that remains the
same story when her eyes close and her dreams steal her

away. I, on the other hand, sleep like the dead. At least, that's what she'd said after the first night we shared this room together. I woke to find her staring down at me, eyes wide and pink lips pursed, her nose barely a centimeter from mine.

She said she hadn't been sure I was even breathing.

I tend to fall asleep right after my prayers, which I do lying on my back with my hands folded above my breast by my heart. After my last "Amen," I slip directly into sleep without moving an inch until sunlight warms my face the next morning.

I'm not sure whether it's because of the food or the prospect of tomorrow, but now I find sleep does not take me as easily as it has before tonight.

Forcing my eyes shut, I try to remember my typical prayers, but I find my mind wandering towards Trevor and the sight of him this afternoon. What had been churning in his mind when he caught me without my veil shielding me? I'd never once seen a look like *that* before.

He'd been shirtless, I realize now, beads of sweat dripping down the lines of his huge, muscled body. I'd only seen a body like that on the sculptures and artwork around the convent, but he was chiseled just as if he could have been from stone.

A shiver rolls slowly through me, that same fervent blossom of heat igniting my crotch. I press my knees hard together to try and still the growing heat, but that only seems to kindle it more. The sensation keeps growing down there and I press one of my palms hard against my night-gown, as though trying to squish the feeling away, like it was a bug.

I don't understand what this sensation is. It's nothing

like what I've experienced during my prayers. It only happens when my mind wanders to Trevor.

Again I see him against my eyelids, those piercing green eyes locked only on me, as though I was the only person in the world, and he'd never seen anything like me before. His naked chest, the sweat, the sharp curve of his jaw ... I bite back a gasp when the tingling between my thighs grows stronger. I wiggle slightly underneath my blanket to edge up my nightgown so that I can prod at my lower stomach just below my bellybutton, and find the source of this throbbing but pleasurable sensation. I can't describe the feeling entirely, just that it is hot like I have a fever, only in one forbidden area, and tingles like the tip of a long feather is being slowly dusted between my thighs.

My fingers trail lower, seeking the source of this odd feeling with increasing desperation; then my hand bumps into the hem of my white panties. I finger the edge of the fabric for a moment before my hand tentatively slips under the white lace.

What would it feel like if Trevor did this? I wonder. His calloused, rough hand stroking me where even I have never touched ...

Is this wrong?

But as my hand moves on its own, I don't pause to mull this question. One brave finger extends, trembling, the velvet pad slowly stroking over the soft thrush of dark curls growing between my legs. The hair is coiled and soft just like the hair on my scalp; I'd never been brave enough to touch it before. Even when showering, I clean that secret, forbidden place as quickly as possible, just to get it over with.

The feeling of my finger over the outer lips sends shockwaves through me, my back arching sharply towards the ceiling as I bite back another yelp.

I suck in a shallow breath and hold it, ears straining for any sound from Catherine, but she continues to quietly snore and thrash across the room.

Through flared nostrils, I let my breath slowly escape, my palm still pressed against those mysterious, throbbing lips between my thighs. I'd always been told it was naughty to touch myself here, but just touching near it feels so good that the room seems to spin.

Why would we be denied something pleasurable like this?

That brave finger again slowly moves, slipping between the outer lips to find something startlingly hot and damp. I bite my lower lip as electricity surges through my veins, and my finger glides over something small and round like a pearl, multiplying the intense sensation. I stroke over it a few times until I start writhing across my mattress just like Catherine does all night long.

Something inside of me grows hotter and hotter, a feeling like a rubber band stretching in my core. That's how Catherine had put it, and it was true.

As the sensation swells, my back arches and my breathing becomes short, my eyes snapping open to peer through the intense darkness of the bedroom. Across the room, one ray of moonlight shines on the crucifix dangling over our doorway.

Just the sight of Jesus makes me snatch my hand from between my legs and shove my nightgown back down over my thighs. Yet, my chest still heaves and my whole body tingles. The rubber band is still stretched deep inside me, begging to be snapped and to send my body over the precipice of something terrifying and unknown, but I resist the urge now.

Even as my knees continue to tremble, the heat of my body threatening to swallow me whole, I close my eyes as tightly as I can and whisper out a muted chain of desperate prayers. I need to take my mind off this intense sensation, and fast.

I don't know what that was, but I do know it was far too fun to be holy.

11

———

TREVOR

I wake early, stretching slowly out on the lumpy bed.

The flimsy mattress is so short, my feet hang off the edge. I'm taller than the average man working on these grounds, but I can't help but wonder how a couple of the other guys, like the nunnery doctor who's even taller than I, sleep comfortably on these old beds with their old mattresses. Come to think of it, maybe just like me they actually don't, and the uncomfortable, spartan beds are just our way of showing solidarity with the nuns and the harsh experience they're having at the convent. I try not to think too much about how many people have slept in this bed before me, because the smells that drift from the mattress are gross and vaguely sour. Until I can get to town and buy air freshener, to ward off the unpleasant smells I've been bringing some of the flowers I tend during the day into my room.

I'd been trying to convince someone to take me into town so I could buy some new sheets, too, but so far it appeared that once you came to this place, you didn't readily leave. At least my bank account was steadily growing; I'd have a nice nest egg by the time I departed.

When I was ordered to come out here, I was informed I only had to work here for a year— of which three weeks has already passed—and after that, I'm a free man. Once I've completed my time here, as long as I continue to stay out of trouble, I'll be able to follow my heart wherever it wants to go.

I have no idea where I'll go or what I'll do after I've served my time here, but I know I won't be returning home: with my old crowd still there, there's too big a chance of disaster. Instead, I'll go somewhere new. Maybe somewhere near water, like a sandy beach or bay. Somewhere I can still feel the sun on my shoulders like I do here. Maybe I'll even continue to do gardening work, considering how I've really taken to the flowers and shrubs. I didn't expect to love working with my hands so much, but I find I'm truly at peace when I'm watering my flowers and helping them thrive.

What would life have been like had I discovered the joy of a fulfilling job well done in my youth, before I wound up in trouble? I wonder what type of man I'd be today. Certainly not the type who works at a convent ... but then I suppose had my life taken any other path, I never would've met Sister Margaret. It's so strange to think about the fickleness of life; one different step, no matter how tiny, and your entire trajectory changes completely.

With a healthy yawn that echoes off the walls, I climb to my feet and walk to the nearby window to gaze out over the grounds.

A few of the other gardeners, Henry included, have already taken up their hoes and shovels and are milling about the convent. He pauses as though he can sense me staring, turning slowly to peer back over his shoulder, his eyes not quite catching mine at the third-floor dingy window where I stand. I make my bed, giving thanks that though my room is small, at least it's a private one: other workers aren't as lucky. Still, the walls are so thin I can hear the others talking or moving about in their own rooms, but I've always been a heavy sleeper so it doesn't bother me much.

I dress slowly, taking my time pulling on a clean, white shirt that clings to the lines of my hardened torso. Working here has at least been great for my body. I'd always been somewhat jacked from lifting a couple times a week, but now I like the way my arms and thighs have gotten bigger lately from full days of bending, squatting and digging. I tug on a pair of jeans that only have a small hole in the knee, cinching them around my waist with my old leather belt before walking down to the kitchen on the first floor of the dorm.

Dark-haired Doctor Cliff Clarke is slouched in a rickety wooden chair, his ankle crossed over his strong knee, his nose in the newspaper. He doesn't seem to notice me as I roam about the kitchen looking for a granola bar, but when I find one and turn around, he's lowered his paper to watch me with his storm cloud gray eyes, eyes that would remind me of Mother Antonia's were those steely orbs not much younger and infinitely warmer. He's been the doctor here for two years or so. From his clinic at the corner of the convent, besides the nuns and the convent staff, he also serves a number of locals who live closer to the convent than to the hospital in the town forty-five minutes away.

"Are you settled into your apartment?" he asks, folding the paper and laying it neatly before him. All of his movements are precise, which shouldn't surprise me since his profession depends on his steady hands.

Huh. While this place seems like a dorm to me, I guess calling it an apartment makes it less like college.

"Getting there," I answer with a smile, grateful to communicate with anyone who wasn't laconic Henry. I don't like to draw attention to myself—years in the foster system and escaping trouble on the streets had conditioned me that way—so I rarely go out of my way to talk to anyone here. But this guy seemed okay.

The doctor chuckles good-naturedly and climbs to his feet. He taps his white coat pockets, making sure he has everything he needs, and then his eyes widen just a hair. He glances around, steps closer to me, and withdraws a very familiar notebook from the inside pocket of his white coat. The second I lay eyes on my notebook, my stomach drops. I swallow hard, thinking of my drawing of Sister Margaret, and clamp my hand so hard down on the granola bar that it breaks in half, crumbs scattering at my feet.

Cliff discretely holds it out to me, a frown tugging at his mouth. "I wouldn't be so careless with this, Trevor," he says quietly. "I found it in the living room this morning. I don't think anyone else has come across it. I wasn't sure whose it was at first, but I recognized your handwriting."

"Thank you," I fumble, grabbing at the notebook a little too eagerly and with a little too much haste, then shoving it into my backpack so it was firmly out of sight.

Doctor Cliff doesn't say anything more, but just gives a small nod and walks out the door of the building. Now without an appetite, I wrap my granola bar in a napkin to save for later and lumber out after him, my head still spinning from the interaction.

It's a beautiful, warm day in early spring, but most days

at the convent have been mild and pleasant. It beats Boston, which was often cold and gray and frequently rainy. But though normally I found solace in the sun's rays, today I can't focus on anything but my mortification.

In fact, the thought of my embarrassment has increased my blood pressure and made me sweat. I unbutton my shirt and open my torso to the welcome balmy breeze.

How could I have been so careless with my notebook?

I'd been alone in the living room late into the evening, working on my drawings, but I'd been so sure that I had put my notebook away ...

I'm ripped from my thoughts when I hear two sets of delicate footsteps trotting over the damp morning grass. In a few hours, the dew will have dried and each perfectly trimmed green blade will gleam, but for now, everything is covered in a thin veil of mist that almost makes the convent grounds look like they're shimmering beneath crushed pearls.

I try to relax, but it's hard. What would happen if someone other than kind Doctor Cliff had found my notebook? With the drawing of Sister Margaret in it flagging me as what, a stalker? For sure I'd get dismissed, then go to jail.

Over the fields of green, two young nuns walk towards me, one looking much happier than the other.

Catherine walks slightly ahead of Margaret, a buoyant smile on her pale face. Sister Catherine strikes me as a Cheshire Cat type. When she's smiling, you should be half afraid of the reason why. Her eyes are locked on me and I can tell they're seeking me out, though I don't have any idea what the reason for this may be.

"Sisters," I muse in surprise, exploring Margaret's shifty-eyed countenance.

The dark-haired nun is doing her best not to look at me,

but her cheeks have flushed the faintest shade of pink, like the buds of a carnation. I want to brush my hand over her face and see if her skin is as plump as that delicate flower, but I dig my hands into my pockets and think of her dark, wild curls billowing against her cheeks, instead.

"Good morning, Trevor," Catherine, the braver of the pair, says lightly. She talks as though she's biting back laughter, her eyes occasionally flitting in delight towards her best friend.

"Maggie, don't be rude. Say hello," she adds with a gentle nudge at Sister Margaret.

I love the way Maggie fits her so much better than Margaret.

"Hello, Maggie," I say when she just bites her lip and shyly casts her eyes downward.

Her eyes widen just a hair, eyes shooting back towards me at the sound of her name on my tongue. The pink flush of her face deepens to that of a garden rose.

"Hel-lo," she answers faintly, tripping over the simple word.

It's then that I realize her chest is rising and falling as if she'd been running, her breath coming in shallow pants. Her dilated pupils remain locked on mine until, with a slight gasp, she forcefully tears them away.

Something stirs in my core when her eyes meet mine, a recognition of some mysterious force behind her gaze; there's more than shyness in that lovely face. Heat simmers in my veins and I feel electric sparks igniting me. Now, my own face is flushing. What was it in the depths of her beautiful, dark eyes that awakened this feeling?

Something about her has changed. Something is less ... innocent?

Whatever it is, it makes me hungry for a taste of her

ruby red lips and to see her beautiful white legs once more, while arousing other desires beyond those. My eyes tear across her habit, desperately seeking any trace of her body underneath—her heaving chest obliges my wish. I can imagine her breasts beneath the thick fabric, her pink nipples hard as rosebuds. I wonder what her skin would taste like under my tongue as it mapped every naked curve of her.

My eyes trail slowly up her long neck to her plump lips to her eyes, which are boring into mine once again. Her breath catches, her lower lip catching under her front teeth as she bites down hard on the supple flesh. I recognize the odd look in her eyes then.

It's desire. Raw, carnal lust.

My little nun is horny, and she's horny for me.

Before I can help myself, I take a step towards her, my fingers itching to grab hold of her hips and drag her towards me. But the movement seems to have broken the spell of her attraction. She staggers back, slightly hidden behind Catherine, who was watching all of this with amusement dancing in her own eyes. I clear my throat hard and try to remind myself to behave. I can't act like this. Not towards a nun. Not towards Maggie.

"Mags has something to tell you," Catherine continues, her voice still cool and amused. She moves out of the way of her sister so that Maggie is no longer concealed behind her, though Maggie looks like she's fighting the urge to hide once more.

She shoots Catherine a withering look before drawing herself up slowly and turning back to face me, staring intently at her feet.

"We were told by the mother superior to pick a mission," she says slowly, her voice strained and peculiarly pitched. "A sort of project that will bring us closer to God, while being of use to the convent. Some of our sisters are transcribing old edicts or cleaning stained glass ..."

"And we want to work in the gardens!" cries Catherine exuberantly, clapping her hands together. "We just need some help here and there. We want to cultivate nature and our bond with our vows, or whatever. You think you're up to the task?"

I arch an eyebrow, shoving my hands deeper into my pockets.

Is Catherine suggesting that we're all going to be hanging out and working in the fields together? It seems a little odd to imagine nuns digging through soil and plucking bugs off leaves.

But ... if it brings Maggie and me closer ...

When I don't answer right away, Catherine starts to pout. "Come on, Trevor. It took Maggie so long to think of this project, and now you're going to be coy about accepting the proposal?"

Maggie flushes brightly once more and shakes her head. "Cat, I'm not the one who came up with this—"

Catherine, however, brushes away the claim, cutting her off, "Oh, hush, you modest girl. This was a genius plan. Own it, Mags."

Maggie turns scarlet and tucks her chin against her chest.

"Well ..." I say slowly, eyes drifting up and down the woman once more. It's impossible to disguise my hunger. "Maggie, since this was your idea, I'd be happy to help. When should we start?"

"How about tomorrow?" Catherine answers for Margaret, whose head shoots up to look at me in surprise and a bit of eager delight, before she remembers not to look so enthusiastic. "Today we have prayers for hours and a meeting with Mother Antonia, but tomorrow we'll have more free time."

"Great. I'll see you two then," I answer lightly, still watching Margaret.

I just can't take my eyes off of her. Her own eyes slowly glide down over my sculpted chest, settling on my hard six-pack abs; she bites down on her lip once more. I'd forgotten to button my shirt when they came over, but apparently they didn't mind that at all, no sir.

Catherine nods and starts to traipse away, looping an arm around Maggie's and tugging her after, but Margaret stops and whips back towards me abruptly.

"I'm looking forward to ... to ... trying to save your soul, Trevor," she says after a moment, lifting her chin and gazing directly at me, as though she actually believed what she was saying. Her voice vibrates as she talks, trembling with subdued longing.

I just grin back at her, trying not to look too entertained by the claim. Because her dilated pupils are making a totally *different* claim.

"Sure, Maggie," I answer, though I'm no less captivated and can't even pull my eyes away from her as she begins to walk away.

That wasn't the desire to save someone's soul that I saw shining in her eyes, it was the desire to peel off every layer of clothing separating our bodies and run her hands over my tanned, hard body.

A happy expression forms on my face. Perhaps with time life here at the convent will get better and better. For sure, it's definitely going to get more interesting.

12

Despite her reputation for mischief, Sister Monica was typically a devout nun and a good listener. She enjoyed the sermons that she and the rest of her sisters regularly attended in the convent church and private devotionals, and could feel the hymns they passionately sang in her very soul. She even thrived off the lessons she was taught here at the nunnery. But what Monica just could not stand was the crawling, twisting feeling of boredom that crept through her, and far too often for her own good.

But while Sister Ruth, who preached ardently during some of the nuns' private meetings, generally captured Monica's entire attention, Mother Antonia was an entirely different story. Whenever she started preaching, or lecturing really, redheaded Monica would stare blankly down at her Bible and pretend to listen, while desperately trying to figure out how to sleep with her eyes open. She had yet to acquire this useful talent, however, and her eyes would become heavy and eventually drift shut. Then her chin sharply dropped towards her chest and she would lurch forward from where she was bent on her knees in front of the mother superior, earning a wicked, vengeful scowl from the woman.

But in general, Monica loved her faith and she loved her life at the convent of the Blessed Virgin just as much as she loved to learn. Faith and knowledge went hand in hand as far as she was concerned, and she soaked up all she could from the church teachings like a sponge.

She could often be found with virtuous Sister Grace quietly praying and clutching her rosary, though it wouldn't be uncommon for Monica's thoughts to eventually wander towards pranks.

Because while she enjoyed life as a nun, it was frankly a bit dull at times and she did believe everyone needs a laugh here and there, even if you're living at a convent. She did feel terribly guilty for Sister Margaret getting punished—and cruelly—for the stolen box of chocolates, however. She didn't mean to get anyone physically harmed, but you could never tell how viciously the crotchety mother superior would react to tricks.

All Monica *really* wanted was to make the perpetually-furious mother superior laugh, but she had been trying for over a year and had made little progress on that challenging front. There was one time that she skillfully tucked a trail of toilet paper into the back of Eva's habit, and thought she saw the smallest hint of a grin around the mother superior's mouth, but other than that, Mother Antonia constantly looked aggravated to the tenth degree.

Today, Monica would soon realize, was no different.

"Sister Monica Rosula," scolds the reverend mother with tangible fury in her words. Monica winces at the use of her full name, as though it was her own mother calling her out for punishment. Monica gulps and looks tentatively up at the irate woman, as Mother Antonia continues to scowl. "What on earth have you done to your holy text? You've desecrated it, you abhorrent girl!"

The flock of nuns gathered around Monica look over towards her curiously, trying to keep their heads bowed as though they were still deep in prayer.

The mother gestures at Monica's worn black Bible, the margins covered in colorful doodles of stars and hearts and ocean waves. Monica had never been to the ocean, but she loved to imagine it.

Monica swallows hard yet again. While she adored attention, she didn't like this kind. She always tried to angle her Bible away from the mother while Mother Antonia was circling them like a shark looking for prey, but she'd been fighting falling asleep so hard that her Bible, with its scribbled-over pages, had fallen open in her lap.

"Well?" Mother Antonia prods, jowls aquiver at the thought of anyone placing an errant pen on the pages of the Bible. She hated when Sister Grace would even dare underline certain passages she adored.

Monica pales, thinking of poor Sister Margaret's hands. Monica's own hands were surely more delicate than Maggie's, and how painful it would be to get smacked by that wooden cross. Though she couldn't resist the urge to play her silly pranks, she was still terrified of the consequences, should she be caught. Though that has never swayed her from her mischievous ways, of course.

"I ..." Monica begins, her brain scrambling to come up with some excuse that would send the mother back to her lecture, instead of glaring at the auburn tressed nun.

"Sister Monica is clearly just trying to display her faith through art, Mother," Sister Catherine interrupts sagely, her hands still perfectly folded to her chest, eyes closed in reverent respect.

Monica shoots Catherine a relieved look of gratitude, not at all surprised that it was Catherine who came to her aid. Catherine was most protective of Maggie, everyone knew they were all but inseparable, but Catherine was also protective of the rest of the girls as well—minus Eva. But Monica had a feeling this intervention was less caused by compassion than by Catherine just looking to irk the mother superior any way she could.

"You call this art?" Mother Antonia says doubtfully, scowling now at Catherine, who finally opens her eyes to inspect Monica's Bible. Monica dutifully passes the doodled book over to Catherine's waiting palm so she could take a look at it more closely. Catherine turns a few of the pages and then gives a devout nod.

"Who are we to judge what is holy art and what is not, Mother?" Catherine asks.

However, as usual, Mother Antonia was not placated by Catherine's attempt at rescuing Monica from punishment. In fact, whenever Catherine got involved, the punishments seemed to only grow even worse.

Mother Antonia sucks in a low, thunderous breath that makes Sister Catherine's eye twitch. She hastily hands back Monica's now-closed Bible as the young women wait to hear what their latest punishment will be. Grace presses her hands to her stomach, uncertain she could make it through another week-long fast.

"I thought that by giving you all purposeful missions around the convent, you would cease these idle sins, sisters," the mother superior growls.

She turns in a slow circle, inspecting every single pair of eyes that met her own gray ones. Sister Ruth, who was again back in a far corner of the room as though she had been banished there, straightens slightly and looks on with concern, scrunching her already wrinkled brow.

"But clearly that is not the case. You all only continue to let your worldly desires spur you on towards sin. Sister Monica, tell me what you've been doing the past few days," Mother Antonia demands.

"The usual," Monica answers, visibly perplexed. She nibbles her lower lip when she realizes that answer won't suffice. "I start my mornings with prayer and devote myself to the needs of the convent until noon. Then I just recently started assisting Doctor Cliff in his clinic for my mission—"

"So it's the work of this *man* that has you distracted from your sacred teachings?" Mother Antonia interrupts accusingly, enunciating the word "man" as though it sickened her.

While beside her Sister Margaret blushes crimson and clears her throat, Monica just looks ever more bewildered. "I don't think so," she says slowly, contemplating the question with more sincerity than the mother expected. "I mean, I don't even have my Bible out around him."

"You don't even have your Bible when you're around this man?" shrieks the mother superior, as though the roof of the convent had just been blown off. There was an underlying accusation to the tone, but Monica couldn't figure out what it could possibly be. "I did not approve this project of yours. Who did?"

Sister Monica doesn't say anything, but her eyes shift just slightly towards Sister Ruth. Mother Antonia scowls at the elderly sister.

"I find it hard to believe that you're doing any good at all when you're around that man," the mother superior continues gravely. "Do you two even pray together?"

Unsure what should be said, Monica only continues to

look between Sister Ruth and the superior mother; she wasn't sure what the reverend mother was trying to insinuate with her peculiar tone. Monica didn't even particularly like the doctor, she found him awfully dull and he was not the least bit interested in small talk or the planning of pranks. In fact, she was just as distracted in his presence as she was during the mother superior's sermons. Had she had her Bible with her during the times when she was working as Cliff's assistant, she would've been doodling in it just as much.

Monica looks around at the watching faces of her sisters, hoping one of them would point her in the direction that Mother Antonia wanted her to follow, but she can find no clues in any of their expressions. Sister Catherine looks irritated and rolls her eyes every time the mother superior spoke, Sister Eva looks as frozen in the face as ever, and Sister Margaret stares down at her tightly folded hands as though she wanted to become invisible. Sister Grace looks just as bewildered as Monica.

"Well, no," Sister Monica finally admits after looking back at Mother Antonia. "It's hard to hold a Bible and follow a devotional and work in the clinic at the same time."

"You will respect me, child," seethes the mother superior. "How dare you talk to me with such freshness."

"I wasn't ..." Monica begins to feebly whisper, but she could tell when she was losing this battle. Shuddering again at the thought of Margaret's bleeding palms, she bites back her complaints and nods instead. "Of course, Mother. I deeply regret my tone now."

Monica deflates like a balloon with a hole pricked in it, suddenly exhausted and overwhelmed from this conversation with the mother superior. As ever, the reverend mother had a way of sucking the life from everyone, even ones as drawn to fun as Sister Monica.

Mother Antonia's chin juts out. "It's become apparent to me that some of you are using these projects as an excuse to slack off. This wasn't the purpose of our missions, Sisters. If you recall, I told you that you were to help strengthen the convent and your bond with the Lord. Clinical busywork does nothing to strengthen your faith, Sister Monica, now does it?"

The freckle-faced nun frowns at Mother Antonia, debating her answer for a moment even though she knows it is useless. She had found herself disagreeing with the mother superior but wasn't sure if this was a test or not. Did Mother Antonia want an actual answer?

While Monica did not enjoy the doctor's dull company, she did quite enjoy the paperwork and the small number of nursing duties she got to do in his office. Doctor Cliff's medical office was slightly separated from the convent, and so she got to meet people from the nearby farms who would come in for issues and checkups. She would converse with them while they waited for the doctor, and even sanitize and treat small wounds if they were minor enough. The people had a lot of questions about life in the convent, and Monica was eager to answer. She even prayed with many of these people and she did feel like she was growing closer to her faith because of it.

"That's what I thought," Mother Antonia answers for her when Monica opts to say nothing at all, eyes blazing and daring the redhead to argue further. "How stupid do you all think I am?" she continues, scowling at her young nuns. "You take what I give you and turn it into something to be ashamed of. You are full of sin, sisters, every single one of you." She pauses between each gasping syllable so that her eyes can lock on each one of the young women kneeling before her.

Each one is left trembling, aside from Sister Catherine, who doesn't seem piqued in the slightest except for the waste of time she perceptibly considered this meeting. Mother Antonia glowers when she notices Catherine's lack of reaction.

"That's it," the mother superior snarls, "I have clearly given you all too much freedom here. I have allowed you to roam the grounds and to communicate with the workers here at the convent, but there will be no more of that from this day on. You will interact with one another, with me, and with your texts—that is it."

"Mother Superior Antonia," interrupts Sister Ruth with a faint gasp. "You can't be serious. You're going to keep these girls locked inside?"

Mother Antonia's bitter, gray eyes shoot to the elderly nun. "That's exactly what I plan to do. How else are we going to keep these women safe from the vile hands of the men working here? Clearly they are being led astray by temptation."

"You judge that by innocent, thoughtless doodles?" Ruth continues, frowning deeply. "To live in a nunnery is one thing, but to be completely cloistered and isolated is another entirely. You can't lock these girls away like princesses in a tower."

Mother Antonia laughs a long and bitter laugh, her head thrown back, her chest heaving. "These are no princesses. These are creatures of depravity. I see it in their eyes, each one of them. They may be able to fool you, Sister Ruth, but I am much more aware of what goes on in these hallowed halls. I hear things that would make the Pope weep."

Sister Ruth clearly wants to continue arguing, as her

eyes are narrowed and angry, but she clamps her thin lips together and says nothing more. Like many of the younger women, she knows that any furthered disagreement with the mother will only make the situation even worse.

Mother Antonia looks back at the young nuns, scowling at them. "From this moment on, no one will be allowed outside. If I catch you even glancing in the direction of the men at this convent, you will be forced into isolation."

A chill rolls through the room as the young women take in what has been presented to them.

Mother Antonia, they realized, was talking about solitary confinement, and after starving the girls for a week, none were sure just how long the mother superior would keep the misbehaving nun she catches locked away. It could be an hour, it could be a month. Maybe more.

Once her decree has been given out, Mother Antonia seems to relax a little. She feels lighter, her breath coming easier. She is certain that she has pleased the Lord and she is happy. After all, she is here to protect the young sinners who are here above all to bond with their faith, and she will do whatever she has to so that none of them make even the smallest of mistakes. If they deserve to be completely cloistered and shut away for the sake of their purity, the mother superior is eager to make sure that this happens.

The young nuns look back at her, each one wearing an expression of shock and extreme resentment. Only Eva feigns looking content, though her sole intention is to avoid bringing the mother superior's wrath down upon her.

"Go, Sisters," Mother Antonia says smugly, a satisfied smirk on her face as she waves the girls away to bed for the night, "and let the Lord guide your righteous path back to Him."

13
___

MARGARET

I sit cross-legged on Catherine's bed, gnawing at my lower lip and hugging my nightgowned knees to my chest. Outside the barred windows, the moon swells in the sky, beaming between shimmering stars. The silver moonlight spills into our darkened room, scaring shadows from the corners of the room. Catherine gazes at me levelly, her blanket hugged to her bare chest. Over the edge of her quilt, the tops of her milky white breasts strain. We've already gotten ready for bed and she is naked as usual, though her body is concealed.

Her strawberry blonde hair is loose and falls silkily down her back, while my curly, dark hair has been painstakingly brushed yet still remains a mess of chaotic curls, even though I've tried to pin it back into a bun at the nape of my neck. A few tendrils have sprung free, brushing the side of my neck. When I move, it almost feels like someone's fingertips are brushing over the sensitive flesh, until my skin feels as though it's tingling; electricity seems to randomly spark through my veins. I have to marvel at the strangeness of this:

I don't understand these new sensations that have erupted in me since meeting Trevor.

What is it about the handsome gardener that makes me feel like a fire has been lit in my core?

"Cat ..." I say suddenly, before my brain can catch up with my tongue.

We've had a long day and Mother Antonia's recent decree seems to have brought a desolate, black cloud down on all of us. It's not even that which concerns me right now, but more the odd sensations that have been swirling around inside of me, the urgent throbbing of those burning lips I'd discovered between my inner thighs. Since I'd tentatively touched myself, I haven't been able to get my mind off what it might feel like to do that again.

Catherine straightens up, her head tilting so her hair falls in a glossy sheet over her shoulder.

"Yeah, Mags?" she asks, the blanket slipping lower down the curve of her full breast.

I'd asked her once why she sleeps naked, but she'd just given me a rueful smile and told me to use my imagination. At the time I'd thought perhaps she just enjoys the scratchy quilt for some reason, but after last night when my hands had to fight through the fabric of my nightgown to stroke across my body, I couldn't help but wonder whether or not there was a more scandalous reason for her nudity.

"Have you ever—?" I start to ask, before cutting myself off and biting my lip.

How would I word this? Just what was I going to ask her? What had happened last night, it was a mistake, it had to be. I'd allowed my physical desire to overwhelm me. I touched places on my body that I never should have. I'd allowed Trevor to get under my skin and make me wonder what it would be like to be stroked by a man like him with his rough, muscular hands.

But that goes against everything I've dedicated my life to. I'm a nun, living by the veil, and I won't give that up. I'd chosen to follow this life because of my deep devotion to my faith. Would I be shaken so easily?

I'd been warned of temptation, but I'd never had any idea temptation would come in such a strong, tan, inviting package. "Package"—in high school I'd heard what that was the nickname for. That bulge in his pants, that's what it meant. That bulge ... oh my God, how can I be thinking these thoughts now? What kind of sinner had I become?

"Have I ever what, Maggie?" Catherine presses, eyeing me.

She reaches over, lightly hooking one finger under a sleeve of my nightgown that's tumbled off my shoulder and lazily dragging it back up in place. The sudden touch makes me forcefully bite back a soft moan, that electricity still sparking around in me. Every touch seems amplified, and all I can think is what it would be like to sink into Trevor's arms and have him touch me all over.

At the throaty sound, Catherine's head tilts even further. Her eyes skim the red flush creeping over my neck and the way I can't seem to draw more than a shallow pant as a breath. "Are you feeling okay?"

"I'm fine," I murmur, mind reeling for an excuse for my inexplicable behavior. "I was just going to ask if you've ever heard anything as ridiculous as Mother Antonia's rule from today."

Catherine rolls her eyes and flops backward on the bed, the sheet falling free so that her bare upper torso is illuminated by the moonlight. I can't help but stare at her, taking in the shadows of her ribs and the glow around her perky, full breasts. Despite the fact that Cat habitually sleeps in the buff, I've never seen her body up until today. I've never seen an adult's naked body, for that matter, and Catherine's is as flawless and beautiful as any in a Renaissance painting.

My eyes finally meet hers, a faint smile on her face.

She doesn't say anything, but I can tell she's enjoying the way I look at her, as though she's flaunting a rare treasure that's only hers to possess. She smirks when I blush and look away. Thankfully, she's feeling gracious and she doesn't bring it up again, instead returning to the discussion at hand.

"I know, that lady is on a serious power trip. She's acting like we're schoolgirls to be harangued, instead of women. Giving us homework, throwing a fit when it's not done perfectly, then putting us all in detention. There's no way we're all going to stay locked up in the walls of this prison."

"What else will we do?" I ask honestly, forgetting her nudity and staring at her in mystification. "She has eyes that follow you everywhere, like that crucifix in her office. She'll know if we go outside. Our project is over; we won't be able to work in the gardens after all."

It pained me that I wouldn't be able to see Trevor anymore, but it also brought me a measure of relief. Perhaps it was for the best. The way he'd captivated my mind lately surely couldn't be beneficial to my bond with my faith. Maybe in her own way, Mother Antonia sensed my trials and had decided to help me stick to my holy vows.

Sensing that her body had lost its shock value and was no longer being admired, Catherine draws her blanket back up to her pale chin so she's completely tucked away. She bites down on the inside corner of her cheek, the same thing she does every time she's deep in thought. For a whole thirty seconds she's silent, which is the longest period of quiet I've observed from her since arriving at this place.

Then she blinks and relaxes once more, reclining like a cat on the lumpy mattress.

"Do you remember what you said earlier? You know, when we were telling Trevor about our project and asking for him to assist us?" she asks, folding her arms behind her head and gazing at me down the length of her nose.

I remember perfectly: I told Trevor that I was looking forward to saving his soul. In truth, I hadn't been thinking about his soul at all when I spoke those words, though I *was* trying to convince myself that was the cause of the enthusiasm I felt about the project.

I had shyly hidden behind Cat while we spoke, because I didn't want him to pick up on the unclean thoughts whirling through my head. I'd thought if I had anything separating us, maybe my head would stop churning so wildly for at least a moment. But that had not been the case. Every time the wind blew, it was laced with his scent. It wasn't even a cologne or anything, it was just this masculine, strong fragrance combined with earth and sun and sweat; it made my entire body prickle.

"You said you were going to save his soul, Maggie," Cat reminds me gently, lifting her knee and drawing the blanket down towards her collarbone, so that she can nudge me with one of her small feet.

She prods my leg, almost tipping me over, but I grab her ankle to steady myself while stifling laughter so that no one would hear us out in the hall. We're already carefully making sure to whisper so that our voices aren't carried down the passageways of the nunnery, as you never know where Mother Antonia—or her spy, Eva—is lurking.

Catherine grins at me, jerking me again and threatening

to topple me onto the carpet, but eventually relents and lets me sit still.

"Are you really going to let Mother Antonia stop you from bringing Trevor closer to Christ?" Catherine asks.

I've known Catherine for long enough to know her tricks. While she may not glory in the Bible like the rest of us do, all the same, she knows it from front to back. She's able to pull out any Scripture she needs to make you doubt yourself, and she can be so manipulative, at times she even cut-maneuvers uber-manipulator Mother Antonia.

With a deft ability to instantly change her expression—from innocent cherub to tearful wretch—chameleon Catherine would've made a wonderful actress in another life.

Despite this, there's a real curiosity in Cat's face as she poses the question.

Maybe she's not as sure I'm devoted to my Bible as she's previously thought. Then again, I've been wondering that lately, too.

Still, I'm not sure what the right answer is.

Disobey my mother superior and try to preach to someone who isn't one of God's children, who needs to be brought into the flock? Or obey her and allow Trevor to slip further and further from his holy light. Neither one was an exactly perfect choice, but neither one felt strictly wrong either. It would certainly be easier to obey Mother Antonia and close my eyes and plug my ears and pretend like Trevor doesn't exist. But then, would a part of me always wonder, what if ...?

Catherine shifts and slowly pushes herself up to her knees, wrapping her arms around me in one swift, elegant motion. I'm captured against her naked chest, our bodies separated only by the thin cotton of my nightgown.

I can feel every inch of her against me, her heartbeat calm against my own rapid one, her naked arms smooth as silk. The embrace is so cozy, warmer than any separated by habits, and my head instinctively nestles against her shoulder.

"Maybe you should pray on this a while," Cat suggests, her breath hot in my ear. She strokes my back before releasing me, her hands lightly on my shoulders. "But, I promise I'll do whatever I can to help you if you decide to continue to aid Trevor. I think you two have a special bond, Mags. I think that if anyone is going to help him, it'll be you. You may be the gardener's one and only shot at eternal salvation."

I can't tell if Catherine is playing her little mind games with me or if she's being genuine, but there's a certain look of sincerity in her eyes that's startling.

Catherine is compassionate in her own way, like when she stood up for Monica during the meeting between us sisters and the mother superior this afternoon, but she is rarely sincere.

"I'll pray tonight and let you know what decision I've made tomorrow," I eventually say with a nod, before climbing off of Cat's bed and making my way back to my own.

She rolls onto her side, the blanket cast lightly over her hip, and props her head up on one of her hands while she watches me climb between my sheets. Even when a cloud rolls slowly in front of the moon and blocks out the silver light, I can still feel her eyes piercing through the shadowed room, watching me.

Obediently, I close my eyes and fold my hands over my chest, running through my usual prayers and thanks before

I allow my mind to once again wander towards Trevor and what I should do to help him.

It wouldn't be right to turn my back on him just because it was the easier choice. I'm sure Mother Antonia has her reasons for increasing the confinement of our cloistered lives here at the nunnery, but I won't be persuaded to close my heart like she wants to close the convent doors.

Trevor needs me, and so I will be his key to heaven in any way that I can. If I have to break a few rules here and there to do it, surely it will be worth it in the end.

14

————

TREVOR

The morning had come and gone, and there was no sight of either of the nuns who'd come the day before asking for my help with their convent mission.

Though I kept an eye out for the sisters, they never came out to see me or tend to the gardens like I'd assumed they would. I know nothing about a nun's life or what it must be like inside the convent, so I just assume that they ended up having some affairs they needed to deal with, and they'd come out to me whenever they had a few minutes to spare. Still, I found myself impatiently staring at the convent doors, just wishing Maggie would emerge.

Eagerness to see Maggie again has all but consumed me, especially after the way she'd been looking at me when we spoke yesterday. I know nothing can happen between us. I know she has her vows. But a man can't help but hope for even the smallest of sparks to ignite and be shared.

All night long I'd been thinking about her. Every time I closed my eyes I could see her face on the backs of my eyelids, her lip caught roughly between her teeth, her dark eyes wide, her cheeks flushed.

In the shower this morning, I'd tipped my head back under the hot spray of water and welcomed it as it poured down me, heating me to the bone. The warmth only made it harder to keep my mind clear of the beautiful nun, and desire had rippled through me, surging through my veins like a firestorm—wild and uncontrollable. As I thought about her, lust seared through me 'til the desire was almost unbearable. I felt my erection swelling between my thighs until my cock was so hard I could barely breathe. It was a mix of pleasure and pain unlike anything I'd ever felt before, and it's all because of her.

It felt wrong to jack off to the face of a nun, or those long, shapely legs crowned by that triangular mound of white lace I'd seen underneath her habit, so I'd done every-thing I could to not wrap my hand around my long, thick shaft—think of baseball, things I had to do on the grounds that morning, where I'd like to live after getting out of here —but it was all for naught, I couldn't resist.

Even after I'd pushed the faucet to the other side, making the water as cold as it could possibly get, my erec-tion wouldn't fade. It throbbed so much that I had little choice but to grip it, gritting my teeth and grunting with the intense sensation I got from touching it. Up and down I'd stroked, thinking of her face, her legs, that sweet pussy covered with virginal, white lace.

Then my eyes rolled back in my head and Maggie's name combined with moans that were just barely concealed by the surge of water deluging the shower stall. I imagined what it would be like to strip the veil from her head and cradle her face in my hands. I imagined what her lips would taste like against mine, and what it would feel like to roll between bed sheets with her legs wrapped around my waist, her hands intertwined with my own as I thrust deep inside her. To the hilt.

I could already picture what her beautiful curves would look like, the way she'd gaze up at me shyly through her long eyelashes, when she stood naked before me in all her divine glory.

When at last I came, it had been so intense and long that I'd slipped in the shower and come crashing down on the floor, but the incredible bliss of the orgasm had been such that it didn't bother me. I lay there grinning like a fool, while somebody banged on the door to make sure I was okay, ice-cold water pouring over me.

Even just thinking about it now had me grinning like a fool again as I returned to the staff apartment for lunch. I'd tried to go by the convent kitchen but the doors were locked. I thought perhaps it was another forced period of starvation for the nuns, and I told myself I would stick two extra sandwiches for Catherine and Maggie in my bag just in case.

The incident of the other day—when I'd accidentally misplaced my notebook—has already completely slipped from my mind. I'd been worried someone saw what was in the pages, but so far it seems only Cliff had been privy to the drawings and he hadn't mentioned them at all since he gave the notebook back to me. Since then, I'd been far more careful, double checking that I still had it everywhere I went. I couldn't risk anyone seeing those drawings of Maggie's unruly curls: that picture was just for me.

Henry is in the kitchen when I shamble in through the front doors, which were propped open to allow the cool spring air to drift inside the building.

I can tell a storm is on the horizon, even though the sky

is still cloudless and blue as a sapphire, because the breeze is more chilly than it has been for a week.

The older gardener glances over when I enter, slathering so much mayo on his sliced bread that he might as well not even bother with any other condiment. It's layered so thickly that it looks like a coat of whipped white icing; it makes my stomach turn.

"Want a mayonnaise sandwich?" he asks. When I wrinkle my nose in disgust and shake my head, he adds a gruff, "Suit yourself," and slathers some more mayo on the bread before stacking another piece of bread on top of it.

He grabs it with his hands and takes a huge bite, globs of white goo dripping from the bread onto the counter. When he's finished, he doesn't even bother to clean up the mess he made, instead licking his dirty fingers and frowning at me while I rip into another granola bar. I savor the sweetness of honey and oats as I eat it slowly, glad Henry isn't in charge of any of the meals for the rest of us workers. I would rather starve for a week like the nuns than eat a single one of those gross concoctions.

"So did you hear?" he asks, gazing at me as he continues sucking on his fingers.

"Hear what?" I mutter, wishing someone else would walk into the kitchen and take Henry's attention off me. I really just want to be alone and thinking about Maggie.

"About the nuns," he offers unhelpfully.

I just wish he'd get to the point. An irked vein pulses in my temple, but I keep my face calm. I can't tell if his slow speech is difficult on purpose, or if he's just naturally maddening.

"Did something happen?" I press, slightly worried that something had happened to Catherine or Maggie, and that was why they'd been mysteriously absent all morning.

Come to think of it, I hadn't seen any of the younger nuns today, only the older ones had been outside. Usually at least one of the young ones would wander outside to pick a few flowers, or to soak up a few minutes of sun between their devotionals. Or that elder one, Sister Ruth, occasionally trudged out to bring me a glass of cold water, but I hadn't even seen her today. The girls had better hurry if they wanted any chance of working in the garden before the storm rolled in.

When Henry just keeps staring at me, I realize he's going to make me drag the news out of him, inch by inch. The vein against my temple pulsates once more.

"Is anyone injured? I just figured Mother had ordered another fast," I say quietly.

"You call the mother superior 'Mother?'" chuckles Henry, distracted from our conversation like a train diverted onto the wrong tracks.

At least then I was pretty confident that none of the girls were hurt, or surely he would've shown some concern. With Henry, though, you never can tell.

"She asked me to," I answer dryly, "After you sent me into her office looking for seeds. Now, about the nuns—"

He barks out a laugh, one hand clapping against his chest. "Sorry about that, kid. It's a little prank I play on the newbie gardeners. Can't help myself."

I grit my jaw. "And the nuns?" I prod for what feels like the thousandth time.

"Ah, they're all fine. Fine as anyone could be, locked in that place, anyway," he mutters with a shrug.

He starts to shuffle past me, the scent of cigarettes clinging like a cloud around him.

"So what was the news?" I call after him, but he's already

ambled outside, giving no indication whatsoever of telling me what was on his mind.

I shake my head slowly back and forth, baffled by his odd presence, and then grab a napkin and quickly clean up the mayo covered counter Henry had left behind. He doesn't seem to care that anyone else would have to clean up his mess, but I don't want anyone else to return home after a long day to a filthy kitchen, one that I was in last.

Snagging another granola bar and tossing a few into my bag in case the girls need some sustenance, I sling my backpack over my shoulder and walk back outside. Against my back, my notebook thumps lightly, comforting me with its presence. I head towards the back of the convent where I'd chosen a sunny spot just under the back wall to start putting together a raised garden bed. I wasn't sure what types of fruits or vegetables or flowers Maggie and Catherine had in mind to cultivate, but this nice spot would give them plenty of options. They could grow peas or cucumbers or rosemary or raspberries, and it would all turn out great, as long as I was there to help them along, of course.

I gaze proudly down at my handiwork, which I'd been working on for the better part of the morning. I'd sawed all the wood myself from scraps we already had left over, then nailed them together to form the edges of the raised bed. It was a small plot of soil and it needed a bit more work, but it would do the job for now; if they wanted more space, all they had to do was ask and I would gladly build them another, grander garden bed.

Maggie and Catherine would surely be pleased ... this isn't really about Catherine, though. It's about Maggie.

It may be foolish, but I'd do anything she wanted. Anything. Even though I know we can never be together.

But until the day I leave this convent, she's going to be the one thing I won't get out of my head.

Chances are, even after I leave I'll take her with me—in imagination, only.

With a sigh, I bend down over the wooden ridges of the garden bed and start to work in the soil, sifting fertilizer carefully into the earth so that anything the nuns plant will bloom with ardor.

It's easy to lose myself in the work here, and behind me the sun slowly begins to drift lower in the sky, as gray clouds creep in with the approaching dusk.

By the time the moon should be just starting to peer curiously out onto the world, the sky has gone from robin's egg blue to a dark, stormy gray. I've still seen neither hide nor hair of a young nun.

Worry again begins to circulate through my mind—I've even been contemplating knocking on the closed double doors of the convent to make sure those girls are still alive in there. But all of a sudden, I see those very doors slip open and a woman in a flash of black fabric darts out like a rabbit from its den.

I can tell the figure hastily approaching is Margaret, even before she gets close enough for me to see the features of her face.

Her head is tucked low, her skirt gathered in one of her hands, but her gait is familiar. She isn't exactly elegant with the way she moves, but she isn't clumsy either; it's like every movement is wary. I settle down on the edge of the wood and wait for her to approach. When she finally reaches me, she's panting a bit and collapses at my side.

"Winded from that short run?" I tease, but she looks at me with a flushed face and I can see that the cause of her winded state is more fueled by alarm than exertion. I scoot instantly closer, one hand smoothing over hers and covering her elegant, pale fingers with my own dirty, weathered ones.

"What happened, Maggie?" I ask gently. "Where's Catherine?"

At my touch, she stiffens with a faint gasp, her eyes locked on our hands. I freeze, expecting her to pull away, but she doesn't. She just continues staring at the place where my palm meets the back of her smooth hand. Slowly, her face tips back to look at mine. There's an amazement in her eyes, a foreign sense of wonder. Her body trembles slightly under my touch but she doesn't pull away; she doesn't even look like she wants to. Instead, she looks as though she's reveling in the sensation. For my part, I know even just this small touch is making my entire body go hot, my heart rocketing against my ribs. The alarm in her face melts into yearning.

In the quiet evening, miles away from any city lights and with only the glow of the rising moon to light us, it feels as though we're alone in the middle of nowhere. The last two people on earth.

With my other hand, I reach slowly over, giving her time to shrink away from the movement, and brush a curl that's sprung loose from her veil, away from her cheek.

It's only then that she sucks in a huge breath, as though surfacing from the bottom of a deep lake. She pulls her hand away from mine, her body shifting slightly away from me.

"Are you okay?" I ask, scooting closer.

When I inhale, I can smell the fragrance of her shampoo even through the thick veil, and I watch her shoulders lift and fall.

"I'm fine," she answers. "Cat said she was right behind me, but I guess she may have stayed inside."

I bite my lip, tentatively resting one hand on her shoulder. She trembles again and then slowly leans back against my touch, my fingers dipping down over the ridge of her collarbone beneath her habit. I choke back a groan, delighted to even be touching her. Is this really happening?

"I got worried when I didn't see you today, Maggie," I whisper.

"You should call me Sister Margaret, Trevor," she answers, but her hand lifts and her fingers brush over the top of my hand, making sparks fly through my arm. Then she slowly pulls away and gestures at the garden bed. "Is this where we're going to be doing our work for the convent?"

I nod, my fingers still twitching to touch her, to take her hand and pull her to my chest so I can feel the comforting weight of her body, her breasts crushing against me. Instead, I just nod.

Her eyes search mine. She opens her mouth to say something, but then changes her mind and looks away. "Then we should get to work, don't you think?"

I want to beg her to tell me what the words she nearly spoke were, but I decide to show an ounce of restraint. I can still feel her soft body on my fingertips and all I know is, I'm absolutely dying to feel more.

Does she know how much she tortures me?

15

S ister Catherine slowly slumps down onto the window sill as she gazes out from within the fortress-like walls of the convent, one palm pressed to the glass. The night is growing cooler and gray storm clouds grow thick in the sky.

She shouldn't even be on this top floor of the nunnery, which was typically kept locked but that Catherine could easily find her way into. But this was the only spot where she could see the figures of Maggie and Trevor clearly. Trevor had chosen a good place for their rendezvous, even if he was unaware of it when he began building his garden box: the pair were hidden except from Catherine's vantage point up here.

This morning, Catherine had woken to the sound of Maggie dressing in her habit, her dark eyes deliberately focused on the cross on the wall. Catherine had known immediately that Maggie had made the right decision, and was proud of her for willingly disobeying the mother superior—she honestly hadn't been sure that Maggie would be able to do such a thing. While she wasn't as pious as Sister

Grace or as intrigued by faith as Sister Monica, Maggie was a "good girl" and a rule follower, so it was rather impressive that she was willing to risk everything for Trevor. Catherine had the feeling Maggie didn't even realize the significance of such a sacrifice, but she was sure Maggie would understand in time.

Of course, Catherine knew Maggie was not doing this out of the goodness of her holy heart. Maybe Maggie was still trying to foolishly convince herself that she was just trying to help Trevor get closer to the holy teachings, but Catherine knew the truth.

Catherine had been awake the other night, listening to the rustle of the sheets in the bedroom as Maggie writhed about and failed to bite back soft, kitten-like moans during her first exploration of her body. Catherine had fondled herself as she listened to the noises, her own body shaking with electric sensations of her own.

Catherine didn't understand why the female body was so condemned by the Catholic church. There was nothing sacrilegious about the hills and valleys of their breasts, nor was there anything sinful or unholy between their legs, no matter what the priest claimed.

That being said, she understood enough to know that it would be hard for Maggie to come to grips with the fact that she was a creature of desire, just like everyone else in the world. Catherine didn't often agree with Mother Antonia, but in this the old lady was right: temptation did live in this place and would continue, no matter how hard the mother superior attempted to keep it at bay within locked doors and stone walls. Catherine knew even pious, innocent Grace could be swayed given the right lure. No sister was exempt from this.

All day long, Catherine and Maggie had worked on their plan.

Naturally, Catherine told Maggie she would come out with her to the garden when Maggie went to meet Trevor, even though Catherine had no intention of going through with it. The two deserved to be alone, and she was eager to see what might happen out there if they were given the chance at privacy.

She and Maggie had just finished a nice dinner of clam linguini when Catherine told Maggie that now was her chance to rush out into the gardens. After dinner, Mother Antonia was known to retreat to her office for an hour or so of seclusion, and this would be Maggie's only chance to get out the doors without the mother superior seeing her. Catherine had herded Maggie through the halls, urging her to be as silent as possible, and then Catherine had flung open the door so Maggie could escape.

Once Maggie was outside, Catherine had whirled around, her back against the door to muffle the sound of it creaking closed, carefully looking up and down the hall to make sure there were no spies creeping about. She listened hard for Eva's quiet footsteps but had heard no such telling noise, so Catherine had rushed up the nearby stairs to the locked door that she knew how to force open, walking through the dusty room to the tall window to gaze down at Maggie and Trevor.

She'd told Maggie exactly where to go to find the young man, because Catherine had been up here earlier in the day and noticed him building the raised garden beds. He'd been toiling away under the sun, his shirt abandoned on the ground nearby, and his bronzed, Greek god body had shimmered in the sun.

Catherine was almost jealous of Maggie: of course her sweet face and beautiful eyes had captured the man's heart.

Though Maggie had the saintly demureness that Grace wished she had, she never failed to turn every head in the room. But actually, Catherine knew Maggie had no idea how beautiful she was. Catherine could tell that as she grew older, she'd been beaten down by her strict missionary parents, told her curves were temptations and sinful and anything but desirable. But Catherine hoped Trevor could make Maggie feel how truly gorgeous she was. It gave her hope that someday someone might find her beautiful, too.

With a sigh, Catherine leaned against the window and pressed her forehead against it.

Had anyone looked up, they would've thought a ghost was staring down over the grounds, but no one looked at the top floor of the convent anymore. It'd been closed off for decades—only God knows why—so the rooms were covered with dust.

When she would finish watching Trevor and Maggie's secret rendezvous, Catherine would leave the room and before heading downstairs, shake her habit off and knock dust from her shoes so no one would know where she'd been. She would leave behind a trail of footprints through the dust on the room's floor, but no one would know it was her. After all, she'd been coming up here for a long time, and even Mother Antonia had never questioned whether or not Catherine had been to the top floor of the nunnery. So Catherine felt rather safe up there. The dust didn't bother her and neither did the darkness. She liked having a spare moment to be alone where no one else would think to seek her out.

While Catherine was terrified of loneliness, she didn't mind the occasional bout of seclusion, as long as she could willingly leave it and rejoin her sisters. That was part of why she'd even agreed to coming here in the first place, when her parents told her they were shipping her to a nunnery so she could learn to control herself. She thought it would be nice to be surrounded by other women. She'd had no idea then she'd have to put up with "sisters" like Mother Antonia and Sister Eva—women more reptilian than human.

Below the window now, Maggie and Trevor were seated on one edge of the wooden box. Catherine could recognize the looks on both their faces even from where she was, so high above them. They both struggled with restraint. She wanted to grab them and push them together just so they would stop trying to pretend they didn't want to collapse into one another's arms.

Maggie was doing her best not to feel. She clearly wanted to pretend that the desire she felt surging through her was nothing more than the pure wish to help the godless young man, even though her fingers were digging into one of the sleeves of her habit so hard she would have marks on her flesh later.

Trevor was similarly marked by self-control.

His chest was close to Maggie and he breathed slowly, staring down at her the same way a powerful lion would gaze at his mate. Because there was something animalistic in the way he looked at Maggie, as though he would've laid his life down to protect her from anything, or anyone.

And, underneath it all, was that current of charged passion that they were so clearly trying to suppress.

But they wouldn't be able to ignore it for long—that's why Catherine had brought them together. She so wanted Maggie to experience the bliss of seduction, surrender, passion fulfilled. There was a whole other world that

Maggie would never know if she kept herself locked away in this convent.

Even if Maggie couldn't see the truth, Catherine could: Maggie wasn't meant for this nun's life. That wasn't to say she would have to give up her religion, but she just wasn't made for the convent, no matter how much she thought she was. Though she would miss her, Catherine desperately wanted to set Maggie free, like a songbird flying free from its cage.

Catherine pauses, contemplating the thought. She was a bird in a cage too, but she wasn't sure she'd ever find her own freedom. She rests her cheek on the glass, listening to the distant roll of thunder as a storm slowly crept closer and closer to the convent.

Catherine loved the rain, especially in early spring when the flowers were all in such fresh and fervent bloom. It would take all her might not to race right down to those doors and rush outside to dance from puddle to puddle, and let the cool spring raindrops soak her through. She would only hold back now because she didn't want to give away Maggie's clandestine meeting. Besides, Mother Antonia would probably know the second Catherine stepped outside.

Mother Antonia seemed to have a sixth sense when it came to Sister Catherine, and Catherine hated that.

Last time Catherine had danced in the rain, Mother Antonia had forced her to stand out there for over half an hour and Catherine was left shivering so hard, her teeth rattled in her skull and she bit her tongue. She'd almost come down with pneumonia. The mother superior had made her wait a week before seeing the doctor, telling the rest of the nuns to pray her illness away, even as Maggie had begged Mother Antonia to bring Doctor Cliff to Catherine's bedside.

Catherine almost wondered if the reverend mother wasn't trying to get rid of her somehow. Had she gotten ill enough, she would've been sent away from the convent. But there was part of Mother Antonia that liked keeping Catherine in a cage, Catherine could sense that, too. The mother superior liked to look at the younger nuns as her mice, while she was the cat batting at them and toying with them, and using their faith as the cheese to keep them close.

In general, Catherine was able to get a good read on people. She'd been through enough that she could tell when someone was good, and someone was bad, and when someone was just confused.

Catherine slowly lifts her hands and pushes back the veil of her habit, tugging it free and letting it fall behind her onto the dusty floor. How could something so light feel so heavy, she'd always wondered.

The second that veil was placed on her head, she'd felt like she was suffocating. Maybe that's why she likes to sleep completely naked, and there was something thrilling about being naked in a convent—she'd almost been hoping Mother Antonia would come to wake her one day, rip away the blankets and see her bare body exposed. It would be such a shock for the uptight lady that she would probably have a heart attack right then and there! She'd also give Catherine a hundred lashings the second she was well enough, but each one would be worth it and Catherine would grin through the pain.

Catherine's finger slowly toys with the neck of her habit, fiddling with the small straps there that keep it closed over her chest, as she watches Trevor and Maggie slowly move apart.

They stand on opposite sides of the wooden garden box now, gazing at each other. Occasionally, their mouths move as though they're talking, but it's their eyes that say the most. They keep looking one another over, skimming each other's bodies as though they're going to rip each other's clothes off using nothing more than their eyes.

Heat pulses through Catherine, thick and throbbing.

It's been so long since she felt those beginnings of lust, those beautiful first seconds where everything feels like the beginning of something, and you can't stop fantasizing about what their naked body would look like or feel like under your hands.

She gives up on the strings at her neck and instead leans hastily forward, the languid sense of desire suddenly replaced with urgent need. Biting down hard on her lip, she gathers her skirt roughly in her hand and drags it up over her hips so that her ass is exposed to the shadows of the darkened room, her fishnet stockings digging into her thighs. Her hand plunges between her legs; besides her scandalous stockings, there are no undergarments to get in the way of her eager fingers. Catherine rarely wore panties, her own naughty little secret just like this upper floor that no one else ever came to, where she escaped to when she needed release.

She strokes a finger over the drenched lips of her pussy, seeking the pearl of her clit with fervent determination.

There would be no light playing tonight, no stroking over her thighs or fondling of her nipples. She needs to feel the echoes of sweet release through her entire core, and right *now*. Harder and harder she strokes her clit, her finger circling and sweeping as carnal hunger rages through her.

She presses against the window, willing anyone to watch her, as her head tilts back and a shriek of a moan rises up in her throat. She clamps her other hand over her mouth as her eyes roll back and she screams with delight against her palm, sagging against the window until she falls to her knees. Her hand is still pressed to the quivering lips of her pussy as it throbs with ecstasy.

Her eyes drift shut as the aftershocks shudder through her, her body bent as though she were praying before the moonlit window.

Though she was too absorbed in her own ecstasy to notice, a shadow shifts behind her as someone vanishes through the door and into the hallway.

16

MARGARET

"I normally do this during the day when it's easier to see," Trevor chuckles, speaking so softly that I have to strain to hear him.

We crouch on different sides of the garden bed, working quietly, aside from the occasional bout of chatter. He seems so calm and relaxed, while my heart is in my throat, making every breath I take nearly painful. Does he really not feel any of this strange crackling inside of him? It's like pieces of myself are being slowly lit on fire one by one, going up in puffs of smoke that leave me feeling lightheaded and nervous.

I've never felt this way before.

"Well, Cat... I mean, Sister Catherine and I had to do some finagling because of Mother Antonia's new rule," I explain before digging my hands into the dirt.

It feels so good to feel the earth give way beneath my hands, like I'm actually in control of something.

I can already imagine what this little plot will look like with seedlings sprouting in it, their green leaves lifting towards the heavens and God's glory. Creation truly is remarkable, and that I may have a part in it is almost enough to distract me from the handsome man nearby—though not quite. I keep stealing looks at him, watching the muscles of his body move in the moonlight as he bends and digs to make little trenches for the seeds we'll plant soon.

He'd already assured me next time he'd bring with him an assortment of seeds and help me pick which plants were compatible with one another. It'd blown my mind that various plants may not get along in such close quarters, but Trevor hadn't made fun of me at all for not knowing. He'd been so careful and gentle while explaining the way dill loves cabbage but hates carrots. His eyes got tender as if he was talking about people he knew, rather than vegetables and herbs.

I wonder if he's lonely here. In overheard conversations between Sister Ruth and Mother Antonia, I'd heard bits and pieces about why he came to the Blessed Virgin convent. I know he was in trouble before, but I don't care about that. I may not be as perceptive as Catherine, but I know a good heart when I meet one.

"What rule?" he asks, leaning back on his haunches to look over at me.

He's slightly breathless from lifting the bags of soil and dumping them into the raised garden bed, and sweat sheens on his brow. The sight is distracting but I do my best to concentrate on my answer instead of his strong, slick body.

"The one Mother Antonia just made about how we're not supposed to interact with the male workers here anymore," I answer matter-of-factly, surprised that he wasn't aware of it. I'd heard the mother superior telling most of the other workers already that they needed to keep their distance, so I just assumed Trevor would've been aware as well.

"Oh," he says slowly, letting out a quiet whistle before stroking his chin in thought. "So that was what Henry was talking about earlier ..." He abruptly pauses, eyes shifting quickly back towards me with concern crinkling the lines of his forehead. "Wait, does that mean you shouldn't be here right now?"

I turn bright red, the same color as a lobster or a terrible sunburn, and I know that it's going to be visible even through the dark. I look away from Trevor, trying to conceal the blush, but he laughs before swallowing the noise so no one will hear, and creeps closer.

"You know, Maggie, I've been so curious about you since I first met you. I never would've pegged you as a rule breaker," he whispers intentionally now, his eyes scraping over the hills to make sure no one was looking over at us.

The only lights are from a few of the convent windows and from the apartment building far off down the hill where the male workers retire every night. Sometimes, when I would come out for an evening walk, I could hear music being played from their open windows and I would almost wish I could walk over and join them in their nighttime partying.

What must it be like to be able to dance whenever you felt like it?

"I'm not a rule breaker!" I insist, earning another muffled laugh from Trevor.

He bends down in front of where I'm resting on one of the wooden box ledges, and gazes up at me. The swirling gray clouds reflect in his green eyes, making them look like a kaleidoscope of colors. I'm entranced by it for a moment, my eyes skimming the length of his strong chin and broad shoulders. One of my hands lifts involuntarily, brushing over his hard bicep. His breath catches at the deliberate touch. I yank my hand back stammering out an apology, but he grabs my wrist gently in his hand and pulls it back towards him so that he can press my palm over his heart. His hand rests atop mine.

My eyes drift shut as I feel the rapid beat of his heart, echoing along at the same exact rhythm as my own.

Is he nervous like I am? Does he have these strange sensations like I do? Does he know what they mean? With his worldly knowledge, surely he could teach me ...

His hand continues to rest atop mine, capturing it as though he never wanted to let it go. His palms are calloused and rough, the scrape of his flesh over my soft skin making a shiver roll slowly up my spine. Heat blooms deep inside of me, the same way it had the other night when I lay in my bed and let my hands wander over my body. I'm struck suddenly with the desire to have *his* hands wander over my body, and I almost beg him to touch me everywhere. I manage to swallow those pleading words before they can break the silence between us.

My entire body starts to tremble. It's as though a thousand volts of electricity are shooting out from his fingertips over the back of my hand. I'm shaking so much that if I tried to stand, I'd surely crash to my knees because my legs would give out from under me. When I breathe, the wave of heat seems to spread, rising slowly from my core to reach even my fingertips and my toes. The lower pit of my stomach begins to tighten, just as it had when my fingers slowly dipped below the hem of my panties towards that place on my body that I had never touched before. Heat ripples from between my thighs as I remember how good it felt to touch myself even as tentatively as I had. Now I'm curious what would happen if I followed through and allowed my pleasure to overwhelm me, instead of getting frightened of the sensation.

Did Trevor know anything about that? Could he show me?

When my eyes crack open again, Trevor has crept closer. He's on his knees right before me, his other arm at his side, and now our faces are separated by mere inches.

I can barely see him through the dark, but I can see the swirling heat in his eyes. He feels this, too—he has to. It bounces between us back and forth, like a ball of electricity being passed between our bodies, growing stronger with every volley.

Overhead, a lone bolt of lightning cracks through the still night.

For just that piercing second, I could see my face reflected in his eyes, but it was a face I didn't recognize. I wouldn't have known that was me if I'd seen a picture of it, with those hooded eyes and desperately pursed lips.

What am I doing? Why am I sneaking out at night to visit this man?

I knew full well what I was getting myself into by coming out here, but I'd let Catherine talk me into believing my reasons were nothing but pious.

I'm a foolish, wicked sinner.

"We can't," I cry out too loudly, my voice rising above a rumble of thunder.

As I speak, I rip away from him, falling over the edge of the garden box and crushing the fresh soil below. It rises up around me in a dark cloud that will stain my robes. I scramble to be free of the box but everywhere I look, Trevor consumes me. He towers over me, scooping me into his arms and placing me on my feet. I wrench away from his touch, a touch which is all at once everywhere and making my flesh burn below my habit.

When I jerk away from him, he raises his hands with his palms flat towards me to show that he had no intention of grabbing at me, even though I almost want him to. Actually, I want him to argue with me, to drag me against him and hold me tight no matter how hard I struggle, but he does no such thing. All that he does is continue to stare at me with those mesmerizing eyes of his eyes, eyes I can't get enough of that will continue to haunt me even when I sleep.

"You're the one who came out to me," he says quietly, a frown contorting his handsome face. "I had no idea this was against the rules, but you did. You still chose to meet me here, Maggie." Even with that frown, why did he look so darn hot?

"Sister Margaret," I whisper beseechingly. "You have to call me Sister Margaret!"

I can't handle the way he says my name so fondly—lovingly, even. It seems to fit so perfectly between his lips, as though he'd been saying it his entire life. When Catherine says it, it ignites nothing in my soul, but when Trevor speaks my name out loud, it's suddenly hard to breathe. Even if the name is only whispered, the weight of it rests heavily atop my chest.

"You're not just some sister to me," he answers with a shake of his head. "It feels too weird to call you that. I don't want to. You're just Maggie to me. A woman."

"I made a vow," I continue desperately. "I pledged that I would remain pure and only devoted to my faith. You have to call me by my sacred name."

His arms slowly lower, and for a second I hope he's finally going to crush me in the tightest embrace. Instead, he just folds his arms across his broad, sculpted chest and narrows those gorgeous green eyes on me, searchingly.

"Are you trying to convince me or *you?*" he asks quietly, his words focused and firm. "None of this changes the fact that you sought me out tonight of your own free will. You knowingly broke whatever rule your tyrant of a mother superior issued. What did you want when you came out here?"

I reel back from him, almost tripping over the unlevel ground but managing to stay standing, somehow. "I came because I wanted to try to save you! Your lack of faith is clear in the impure way you regard me with those lusty eyes! I was hoping I would be able to bring you closer to Christ by coming out to see you."

Even though 'til now he's been hyper-conscious of their need for discretion, Trevor erupts in a spontaneous belly laugh, unable to contain his amusement. The sound of his mirth is carried by the whirling breeze as the storm above comes closer and closer, the wind gusty and cold and scented with wet earth.

"Okay, let me get this straight," he says when he's finally done laughing. "You broke the rule and snuck out at night. You snuck out at night to be alone with a man. Alone with a man in the shadows of your convent. So, you broke a rule and snuck out at night to be alone with a man in the shadows of your convent *because of your faith, Maggie?* That's a load of shit. Be honest with yourself, for once!"

Fat, warm drops of rain suddenly begin to barrel down over us, streaking down my face and soaking my body through. The dirt on my habit turns to mud and my robes feel heavy. Even though the air and the rain are both mild, my body starts to tremble. It's not the same pleasurable vibrations of before, but the kind that tells me that this conversation has gone completely off the rails into territory I never wanted or expected.

"Go on back now, Maggie," Trevor says, jerking his chin roughly towards the convent behind us. "Run back to your mother superior and claim that you were out here to save me. See what she has to say about those good, pure intentions of yours."

"You don't know me!" I cry back at him, hands curling into fists. I have to shout over the loud rumbles of thunder now ripping through the air.

"And you don't know *me,*" he answers back, eyes flashing through the dark. "Maybe you shouldn't be so quick to judge those around you."

I take one step backward, then two, struggling to figure out just how this conversation went south. I hadn't come out here to ruin everything. I hadn't come out here to leave in tears that he couldn't see because they were mixing with rain.

Unable to take any more of the storm or the equally stormy fury in Trevor's eyes, I turn and run as fast as my soaked habit will allow back to the convent, slipping in through the door. My chest heaves, tears stinging my eyes as droplets of rain fall from my habit, sprinkling the floor. There will be no hiding what happened now: Mother Antonia is going to know someone went outside during the storm.

I rush towards the stairs leading to the room I share with Catherine, slipping all the way, but as I round the corner I run nearly headlong into Sister Eva.

Eva just drifts to the side to allow me to pass, her eyes slightly unfocused, her lips parted, cheeks red. She looks as though she's seen a ghost.

Usually I would've taken longer to check on her and

make sure she was okay, but I knew if I lingered she would come back to her senses and dart straight to the mother superior, to tell her that I was the one who left the halls of the convent wet and muddy.

Instead, I rush to my room. Once I was safely hidden away from prying eyes and ears, I burst into the torrent of tears I'd been holding back since Trevor's scathing words had bitten through me.

Though my virtue is intact and I'm no longer in the vicinity of that tempting man who makes me tremble with sinful desire, why do I feel like I just made the biggest mistake of my life?

17

TREVOR

I have no choice but to watch as Maggie furiously climbs the back slope towards the convent, my heart struggling with the urge to chase after her and pull her into my arms and beg for her forgiveness. I really have no idea how the conversation took that unpleasant turn; all I know is I want to go back in time and replay the scene again to figure out where I went wrong. I totally blew it, and no way I'm going to do that ever again with her.

The last thing I ever wanted was to make Maggie cry. That's why I keep my desires to myself and I don't chase her, even though every fiber of my being is urging me to do just that. I won't ever trap her the same way she's trapped by her mother superior, ever force her to do anything she doesn't want to do.

Yet I so want to be near her, basking in the shining light that is her presence. I don't care if she preaches to me or if she never lets me touch her, all I want is to be close to her.

For a moment a sliver of yellow light from inside the convent walls shines before the door closes and it vanishes, along with the beautiful woman.

The emotional scene has totally spent me. My exhausted head falls into my hands, even as the storm continues to rage around me. I simply can't work up the energy to grab my bag and head back towards the waiting apartment, even though I'm probably going to be out past the men's curfew. Anyway, even with the curfew, I'm not sure anyone will even notice I'm gone. No one here cares about me, I don't matter. I'm invisible, a cog in the wheel. I do what I'm told, I eat, and I sleep. That's all that I am here.

The only one who I thought saw me as a person rather than an invisible nobody is furious with me ... now I really have no clue at all what Maggie thinks about me. Now to the dark-eyed nun, I might very well be a nobody, too.

Had I pushed her away as I had pushed away so many other people who'd bothered to care about me over the years? Or had this been her doing? I could no longer tell which one of us had sabotaged this; maybe, in fact, it was both of us. Anyway, I suppose who messed up doesn't matter, all that does matter is that I doubt she'll ever talk to me again. And she may not ever again be able to, with this rule of Mother Antonia's keeping the male workers and the nuns separated.

My heart is heavy from the words Maggie had said. What about me made her believe I am a man without morals or convictions? A man who needs to be "saved?" Do I have to believe in her religion and her version of God to be worthy of her time?

I don't even really know where I stand when it comes to faith, but to have her judge me like she did, it stung. I press a hand over my heart, the same place where her palm warmed my chest not long before. If I focus hard enough, I can still feel her touch lingering there. That moment had been so brief and yet so very intimate.

That look in her eyes as she'd touched me—for a moment I thought there was really something amazing growing between us. I've never been in love, but this new feeling sure felt like the beginning of that. At least, from what I've heard about how being in love feels.

But anyway, there really couldn't be anything between us, and this conversation was just the harshest of reminders that this was the case and would always be. She has chosen to devote her life to her religion and she would spend the rest of her days in the walls of her cloistered convent, while I would be free to do whatever I want, wherever I want.

I couldn't very well spend the rest of my life here just hoping to catch occasional glimpses of her. Yet, even with all these problems and obstacles keeping us apart, there is something so special about that woman, she keeps drawing me back to her—no matter how much I try to convince myself to let her go and put her lovely face behind me. I just wish she knew how I felt.

It would be pointless to tell her that she intrigued me or that I wanted to get to know her better: Mother Antonia had already laid down the law making that impossible. And though Maggie had broken the rule once supposedly to bring me her idea of salvation, I couldn't see her doing that again.

Would this be the last time Maggie and I stood face-to-face? Would she recall this painful, rain-drenched moment every time she thought of me from now on? That certainly wasn't how I wanted her to remember me.

I peer through the rain at the garden bed, replaying the conversation we'd had about what sorts of plants she wanted to see grow. She'd seemed so enthusiastic about it, eagerly listening as I went over various, easy-to-grow seedlings. I'd picked things she'd see quickly sprout, like corn or tomatoes or spinach. If I still planted those for her, would she see them through the windows of her convent and know that I'd planted them all especially for her?

Would it make her smile even if she and I would never have a chance to speak again? That's what I wanted. For her to be happy.

With a sudden stricken gasp, I spot my abandoned bag beside the garden bed and remember that I still had my notebook inside the now-waterlogged backpack.

I spring into action, scooping up the bag and holding it against my soaked chest as I dart back towards the apartment. My legs pump as fast as they can as soft, wet earth tugs at my shoes as I run, nearly tripping me and sending me hurtling headlong into the grass. I keep sprinting until I skid safely into the apartment foyer and welcoming shelter.

Cliff, who was reading a medical journal in the living room when I slid inside, looks up as I make my dramatic entrance and shakes his head slowly.

"You're going to catch your death, kid," he calls over, using the demeaning moniker, despite being only a few years older than myself. "Come see me tomorrow when you wake up with a fever."

I ignore him, storming up the stairs and to my room. I don't even bother stripping off my wet clothes, not caring about the puddle of water gathering underneath my body as I rip open the bag. Turning it upside down and shaking it, I watch in horror as water carrying my notebook and a few empty water bottles spills out onto the already soaked carpet.

With clumsy hands I lift the notebook. Grabbing a towel hanging from the corner of my room, I furiously rub the water off of the soaked cover. All my drawings, all my art, have got to be ruined inside.

When I flip it open, however, I'm shocked and beyond grateful to see that the pages are nearly completely dry.

All of my artwork is safe, including the beautiful drawing of Maggie with her wild mane of untamed curls and her Mona Lisa smile. I thumb through the pages, unable to believe what I'm seeing. Though the wet edges of the pages are a little worse for wear and will furl with water damage, tomorrow they'll be dry and the pages will still be intact.

Overwhelmed by relief, I collapse back on the now-wet carpet of my bedroom, staring up at the ceiling with my arms and legs extended and the notebook resting safely on the table.

If there is a God, He had surely saved those pictures for me. Because they may be the last remaining memory I have of that lovely woman who has captivated me so.

Eventually, I climb to my feet and pad out to the hall to get more towels, laying them down around my room on the puddles before I strip slowly out of my soaking wet clothes and hang them on furniture to dry. Later, I'll take them down to the laundry room to wash the dirt and mud out of them. Then I grab one of the dry towels and wrap it around my waist, heading to the bathroom to wash the chill from my bones.

I take my time showering, even though it's late and the rattle of water through ancient plumbing will keep everyone in the dorm awake. Once I'm warmed up, I ease out of the shower and dry off before pulling on a pair of flannel pajama pants and a white tee shirt.

When I pad back out into the hall, I hear my name being called in a gruff but quiet voice. It's coming from the kitchen, along with the sound of light clattering of dishes. Curious, I follow the sound, finding Henry standing at the stove stirring a saucepan. I clear my throat, wishing I'd just gone back to my room and closed the door. I'm exhausted from everything that happened and I just want to close my eyes and try not to think about Maggie for a while.

"Have a seat," he says quietly in his husky drawl. For a change he's not wearing his cowboy hat, and I take note of his full head of chestnut brown hair that's gone salt and pepper at the temples and sideburns—even though he's at least fifty, he's still a handsome man. Distinguished, even. Though rough around the edges, of course.

Sensing he's got something important to say, I do as I'm told and sink down into one of the uncomfortable chairs. A second later he plops a mug in front of me filled with steamed, hot milk. Tendrils of steam roll up from the chipped porcelain mug, licking my face as I inhale the comforting fragrance. He pours himself a cup and then sits opposite me at the table.

"I heard the doc say you're going to get sick so I figured this would help you avoid that," he explains with a shrug while watching me sip from the mug.

Each drop of the milk warms my throat all the way to my stomach, slowly calming me. For the first time since Maggie dashed off, I feel like I can finally take a breath and try to sort out the hurricane that is my thoughts. Outside the apartment building, the wind still roars, rain hurled against the roof so loudly that perhaps my shower wouldn't have woken anyone. Occasionally, the plink of hailstones peppers the windows. Hopefully, this terrible storm doesn't do too much damage to the plants, or we're all going to have a long day tomorrow.

"Thank you," I answer, surprised that Henry could actually think about someone other than himself—considering his typical aloofness, this loner could be surprisingly kind.

Before now, I'd had him pegged as a selfish lout who helped himself to the last cup of coffee and didn't make more; now I was grateful he at least didn't try to comfort me by making one of those gross mayo sandwiches he loved.

Henry just shrugs again, staring down at his cup of milk as though he could read the future from the small ripples in the steaming drink. Eventually, he sips it, slurping from the rim of his glass so noisily that I have to bite back a laugh. He may not be as selfish as I thought, but he was certainly just as loutish.

When he sets his mug back down, he's already gulped up all the milk like a starving cat, the remains of the drink clinging to the edge of the cup. I continue to sip at mine much more slowly, savoring the sweetened flavor. Apparently Henry had added honey and perhaps a bit of vanilla to the concoction. It made my eyes drowsy and I had to put my chin on the palm of my hand to focus on the man as he began to speak.

I keep one eye on him, wondering why he had summoned me down to the kitchen. Did he have something to say, or was he just feeling hospitable?

"I just want to tell you that I understand how confusing it can be to work at the convent," he explains quietly. He gazes off towards the corner of the room as if lost in his own thoughts, like he'd forgotten he was talking to someone; all the same, he continues. "The girls are beautiful. Unnaturally so. Blessedly so," he adds with a faint chuckle. "The Lord does shine on them, in their youth, at least."

"Have you been here long?" I ask, despite knowing the answer. I thought perhaps I would glean more information from him if I feigned ignorance.

"Since I was a tad older than you," he says with a nod, talking more glibly than I'd ever heard before. I wonder if perhaps he'd snuck a little rum into the drink mix. His eyes connect momentarily with mine, though the copper-colored orbs are still hidden behind a layer of what seems like distant foggy glass. "And there was one of the girls who caught my eye. She was so very beautiful. I wanted her."

"Did you get her?" I ask, despite realizing that Henry is now here at the convent with no bride and no home to go to. He's spent every day here, gardening endlessly until his face is tanned and weathered and his eyes are foggy with memories.

"No," he says grimly. "Take this to heart, Trevor. You will eventually have to make a choice. Her or you. It's that simple. You may believe you can have both, but you can't. These women don't give up their own lives, you just find yourself in a hopeless trap, unable to escape once they've snared you."

I don't say anything, pondering his words and letting them soak into my brain.

He blinks. Suddenly he's back on planet Earth and rises slightly in his chair.

"Do you want more?" he asks, gesturing to the still-simmering pot on the stove.

I push away the glass, letting it skid across the table even though I'd only drunk half of it and the sweet liquid still clung to my lips.

'No, thank you," I answer, getting up to wash the cup, then walking towards the stairs. "Thanks for the drink," I call over my wearily over my shoulder.

"Trevor," Henry calls. He waits for me to look at him, but I just stop at the bottom step, one hand on the rail, my shoulders slumped with exhaustion. With my back to him, I can't tell whether he's smiling or frowning as he looks at me. "I just thought you might find some use in that story. Sometimes I think the young boys need to hear it most of all. You won't be the last to fall for a holy temptress."

With a nod, I continue up the stairs and though my footsteps are heavy, I keep my chin lifted. When I enter the room, the notebook with my drawing of Maggie is still open on the table, her smiling face still etched on the page where I'd drawn her. I gaze at her, leaning against the door, more confused now than I've ever been before.

18

———

After supper, Mother Antonia makes her way slowly down to her office. For a woman who is frequently fierce, she seems rather at peace at the moment.

This is perhaps the only time of day she doesn't stomp about the halls looking for misbehaving young ladies to punish. She knows the younger nuns will all be finishing their dinners, and then roguish Sister Monica will be stuck in the kitchen cleaning for at least a half hour, so she has no one to worry about. Soon enough, the girls will gather in the small, dimly lit choir hall for their after-dinner hymns.

Today had been long and Mother Antonia is looking forward to finishing up her evening routine and retiring to her private chamber, a large but simple room with a mattress newer than those of the rest of the nuns, and far softer blankets. She listens to the sound of her feet clicking along the stone floor, absently counting the steps it takes to return to her office. She'd been on the phone for most of the day calling other convents and slowly working her way up the Catholic Church's bureaucratic ladder.

Things are finally starting to fall in place, and she's clearly pleased by this. Though Mother Antonia doesn't smile often, she's been delightedly giggling to herself for hours. Only a few more pawns need to move and then the way will be cleared.

Safely within the locked space of her office, the mother superior sinks down to her knees before the lifelike representation of Christ on his cross, her hands folded and pressed against her forehead as she whispers urgent prayers. Even though she wants to start with the matter at hand, which she considers the most important, she delicately pushes it aside for the moment so as not to appear too selfish to the good Lord above.

One's prayers should always be about others first. She'd been taught to do her litanies that way since she was old enough to whisper out the garbled devotionals as a toddler. Never start your prayers pleading for the things you want: it's selfish and won't do for a proper Catholic girl.

Just like weary Mother Antonia now, child Antonia would collapse to her knees and vehemently pray. Back then she would pray for simple things; she knew better than to pray for new toys or clothes, because she never received new things to begin with. She would pray for her schoolmates' salvation, especially the little boys who would tease her relentlessly and pull her pigtails 'til she cried, and she would pray for her teachers, even the ones who gave her bad grades, and she would pray for her parents, even when they were cross with her.

But most of all, young Antonia prayed for a purpose.

She always knew she wanted to be a nun. The calling had found her at a young and tender age. Or perhaps it was the incessant bullying of her schoolmates that pushed her towards a cloistered living, though she would never admit that out loud.

Today, Mother Antonia is glad that she had finally discovered her purpose: guiding her flock of young nuns to their faith, even if it required a heavy hand.

As far as the reverend mother was concerned, harsh and ruthless severity was the only way she would ever convince the wild-hearted young ladies to stick to their vows. She'd seen far too many other nuns fall by the wayside, one by one forgetting their sacred calling after being drawn towards the shiny allure of earthy pleasures.

This disgusts Mother Antonia, who had never once wavered in her own promise to the Lord ... as far as she would ever admit to herself.

The day she accepted her holy cloak and veil was the day she felt the most complete; she could still remember that momentous occasion with absolute clarity. The smell of starch as the old mother superior, who was far too kind, placed the veil upon young Antonia's dark hair. The weight of the rosary as it was tenderly placed around her neck, the rosary she still wore to this day. At that precise moment Antonia had gazed up at the previous mother superior and known that she was destined to replace her—and so she had.

But things had changed since Mother Antonia took over the head position at the Convent of the Blessed Virgin, and for the better, she was sure—she did not believe in the significance of laughter or importance of joyous devotion as the previous mother superior had. Mother Antonia is of the opinion that true dedication to the faith should be one of grim, austere commitment and nothing more.

She continues to pray, her hands clutching tighter and tighter, her fingers laced together. Her squeezed eyelids occasionally twitch from the vigor with which she appeals to the Lord.

Now she prays for those sinful young sisters gathering now to sing their evening hymns.

The newest group of nuns at her convent are beautiful—save plain but useful Eva—and that is a problem: it's the pretty ones Mother Antonia has to worry about most. She knows she mustn't covet what others have, but even in her prime years the mother superior was never beautiful, and it infuriates her that these lovely young things are as delicate and desirable as newly bloomed roses. That was why, despite having a multitude of older nuns to lead at her convent, on a daily basis she focused mostly on her young nuns, and had now ordered that their cloister be even more strict than previously. There was no way she'd risk any of the men working on the grounds plucking one of her beautiful flowers. They belonged to Mother Antonia and to her alone.

Besides, it was just more enjoyable to focus her attention on the younger nuns. Inexperienced, cowed by authority—both hers and the Church's edicts—and best of all, susceptible to threats of eternal damnation, they were easy to control and bend to her iron will. The icing on the cake was, how entertaining it was to punish them. What good would their beauty do them when a mere whim of mine could make them miserable?

Yet that beauty was still troubling. Because in the face of it, not one of the male staff around the convent was to be trusted.

Mother Antonia has always despised men, from young to old. She'd fought to have them all removed and replaced with an entirely female staff, but the convent headquarters hadn't been able to find any women willing to do the grueling work the convent required.

She was tired of her requests being denied.

Mother Antonia had tried to be rid of the men and of elderly Sister Ruth but she'd been stuck with them both, all the same. Still, she wouldn't give up. She would turn this convent into the perfectly sacred place she knows it can be. She just has to pray a little harder and the Lord will see her tasks through.

She's so very close now. She can tell that soon enough the pendulum will swing back in her favor; she must only be patient as the Bible commands.

Her head lifts as she hears a noise from out in the hall— a door swinging closed in the stone frame?

She abruptly silences herself mid-prayer and listens hard instead, straining her ears, but it's begun to storm outside and she can't hear anything beyond the whirl of the tempest, with its billowing wind gusts and sheets of heavy rain. Perhaps the door had been left ajar earlier, and it was only slamming now because of the air pressure.

From down the hall, she could hear the beginnings of a few sweet voices singing the holy hymns they'd been assigned for the week, and Mother Antonia forgets her momentary concern with the door. As infuriating as the redheaded sister was, even she has to admit that Sister Monica has the voice of an angel. It was devout Sister Grace who was the weakest singer of the group, though that was possibly because she was afraid to lift her voice higher than a squeak.

Mother Antonia climbs to her feet, rubbing at her creaking knees.

Though she was a nearly thirty years younger than Sister Ruth, lately it was getting harder and harder for her to pray while kneeling on the floor. She's considered laying a pillow down to cushion her knees, but that would seem to make her prayers too easy. Devotion, Mother Antonia believes, should hurt a little or what is it worth?

She hobbles over to the door, pushing it open and peering out into the darkened passage in the direction she'd heard the slamming noise.

Because she'd ordered those annoying, flickering electric lights to be turned off promptly as evening arrived at the convent, she could hardly see anything among the dark shadows in the hallway. She can just barely make out a few shimmering puddles near the convent doors, but she shrugs, assuming those are due to the door being thrown open and then closed by the storm. No one would be stupid enough to frolic outside in such a maelstrom, not even that irritating Sister Catherine, who pushes every boundary possible in order to get a rise out of the mother superior.

Thinking of Catherine, Mother Antonia shakes her head and closes her door once more, clicking the lock into place. She returns to her prayers, listening to the sweet sound of the hymns with distaste: she hates the song they're singing right now.

Meanwhile, down the hall from the mother superior's office the small group of sisters continue singing together in a back room of the convent which had been made into a little choir. Though there should be at least eight of them this evening, two are notably missing.

Sister Grace, squeaking along beside melodious Sister Monica, does her best not to assume that Sisters Catherine and Margaret are getting into trouble somewhere. She doesn't want to jump to unfair judgment as that would not be morally sound. Sisters Genevieve and Lucy share a role, their voices perfectly pitched for the supportive alto undertones to Monica's soprano solo. Monica, who took the lead of the song as she typically does, is too lost in the beautiful flow of her hymn to wish that she were out with her sisters instead of stuck in this dark room with only one flickering candle lighting the pages of the hymnal. Anyway, Monica knows the songs by heart, though Sister Eva was having more difficulty.

Their hymns were mostly written in Latin and despite their Latin lessons, Eva didn't have a good grasp of the language. She prides herself on being accomplished at most things, better than pious Grace, at least, but Latin was one of the skills that constantly evaded her. Because of her poor Latin, and the fact that she could hardly read the pages due to the flickering candle, Eva flounders as she sings, making their song sound flawed instead of elegant and smooth. She and Sister Isabelle fight over who's closer to the hymnal, neither one adept at reading the antiquated tongue.

It didn't help that Catherine and Margaret weren't there to sing their own parts. Eva did not know where Margaret was, but Sister Catherine was a different story.

Eva's eyes snap abruptly shut at the thought of Catherine's body pressed against the glass window upstairs, thinking she was alone, the milk-white flesh of her long legs shimmering in the silver light of the moon.

Eva had only followed Catherine up there because of the task the reverend mother had given her, to keep an eye on things around the nunnery. Eva hadn't been able to find Sister Margaret and so she'd followed Catherine instead, hoping to figure out where her dark-eyed best friend had suddenly vanished to after dinner.

What Eva had seen, however, she didn't even know how to process. All she really knew is that, for some reason, she felt no inclination to tell Mother Antonia about what she'd witnessed. And when she thought of what she'd seen, she'd felt the strangest heat swirling through her veins like the storm outside, unrelenting and powerful in its gale.

A sharp elbow digs into Eva's rib, making her jump as Monica nods her head towards the single hymnal book all three of the girls were sharing.

Eva rubs a hand at her throat, pretending that it's bothering her. Monica shrugs and turns her full attention back to the songbook, eyes drifting shut as she allows her voice to crescendo into a beautiful, high-pitched note that makes tears well in Grace's eyes, both because it's absolutely lovely and because Grace wishes she could sing like that. What Grace doesn't know is she has her own highly attractive attributes: every sister in the convent admires her exceptionally pretty features, from her cinched waist and rounded hips, to her pillowy pink lips that beg to be kissed.

Sometimes, before they were locked inside the convent and refused the right to go outside, Sister Grace would take her hymn book outside and walk as far into the trees as she felt safe going. Then where no one could hear her, she would sing her heart out. She knows she's not as talented as Sister Monica, but the birds seem to appreciate her songs. She doesn't mind when *they* listen; it's peoples' criticism and judgment that makes her knees quiver.

Suddenly, the heavy door is yanked open. Sister Margaret appears there, winded and flushed and shaking.

Taken by surprise, Monica stops singing and for a second Grace continues before she realizes the lull in the song and with a pink flush, snaps her mouth shut.

"I'm sorry," Margaret says hurriedly, her shoes squeaking across the floor and leaving a trail of what appeared to be mud streaks behind her. "I forgot that we were singing hymns tonight."

Eva takes note of this, one of her eyebrows lifting towards her severe widow's peak. Margaret's habit is dry but her shoes are caked in wet mud; her face looks damp as well.

Rousing herself, and knowing that if they're too quiet before the hour of their songs is finished, that Mother Antonia will come to admonish them, Monica resumes singing, instructing Grace to join her. The candle flickers as Margaret and Eva stare at one another. Margaret stumbles forward, taking her usual place beside slender Eva and avoiding her inquisitive eyes.

"You were outside," Eva whispers into the young woman's ear.

Margaret sucks in a trembling breath as Eva tries to decipher the dark-eyed nun's multifaceted expression.

There was pain, definitely, Sister Eva could see that clear as day. Margaret's eyes are red-rimmed and swollen and her voice sounded thick, as though she'd been crying. Catherine hadn't arrived yet, probably still upstairs in her hidden room looking out at the moon; Eva wondered if perhaps the two best friends hadn't had a disagreement ... but about what, Eva wonders. They were always attached at the hip, whispering and skulking about, and Eva had always been curious what things they murmured to one another when no one was listening.

At one point Eva had told Mother Antonia it wasn't a good idea to allow Catherine and Margaret to bunk together, because they were so close—who knew what scandalous things were going on in that room—but the mother superior had only dismissed the concerns without care.

Eva inspected Margaret's face, realizing that there was more to her expression than just sadness.

There was definitely something gnawing at Margaret,

but Eva did not know what it was. Though she looked deflated, there was a strange flush to her, an energy with which she moved, an erratic agitation that belied something more.

"I can't do this," Margaret suddenly says, her voice strained and breathless. "I've got to ... I need to get out of here."

She lifts her hands to her face and dashes back out the door of the small room, leaving the rest of the women staring after her in bewilderment. Again the hymns are cut short.

"She looked sick," Grace offers sympathetically, "like she might vomit."

"I hope it's not contagious," Monica says with a wince. She grabs Eva's sleeve before the young woman can chase after Margaret. "Not so fast, Sister Eva. You've got to at least try to sing this with me. If Margaret is sick, Catherine will take care of her."

Eva's hands curl into fists, a desperate yearning growing within her to get to the bottom of that mysterious look on Margaret's face. But she settles back at Monica's side, accepting the hymnal into her outstretched hands.

Even as Sister Eva sings, all she can think about are Sister Margaret's flushed face and maddeningly enigmatic behavior, and Sister Catherine's shuddering body in the moonlight. Too much in one day for any budding spy.

19

MARGARET

The door to the choir swings shut behind me and for a moment, I pause to see if Eva is going to chase after me.

She certainly knows something is going on, but it's nothing I can ever share with anyone except perhaps Cat, who I haven't been able to find since she disappeared after dinner.

My entire body shakes so violently that my knees ache and I stumble down the hall of the convent as though I'm drunk, even though in my entire life I've never had more than a sip of communion wine. My palms smack against the stone wall as I stagger forward towards the doors of the convent church, seeking salvation from the whirlwind of desire that boils inside my core.

An elder nun passing me in the hall stops to ask if I'm okay. With difficulty I respond, "Thanks, I'm fine," but I feel her turning to watch me as I lurch forward towards the church, her kindly face a map of concern. I pray that she doesn't follow me. I desperately want to be alone.

Even against the rough, cold wall all I can feel against

my palms is the thump of Trevor's heart under my hand. I'd never been that close to a man, his breath on my cheek and his calloused palm covering mine and squeezing my fingers as though it would pain him to ever let go.

He'd gazed at me with those mesmerizing green eyes of his and I'd completely stopped caring about my faith and my vows. I'd stopped caring about everything but the magnificent feeling of his heart under my hand, throbbing as though it beat only for me. I'd never wanted anything so much as I'd wanted then just to rip his shirt off, so I could see his naked chest under the stars and run my hands over his entire body.

And this yearning, burning, prickling sensation that fills me ... it's all-consuming.

My entire body feels as though it's on fire; the only thing that will douse the torrid flames is his mouth on my own. While we spoke idly about gardening, all I could think of was the way his lips might move against my own if he cradled me against him; the way I wanted to feel his fingers knot in my hair at the back of my head, twined in the curls.

Suddenly I wanted out of this habit, to be out of *everything* except for his arms.

But this is so very wrong. I can't feel these things when I've made the commitment to the Church that I have. The day I took this veil was the happiest I'd ever had ... until I laid eyes on Trevor, that is. Then it was as if a whole new world was opened up to me. There's no going back now—I know that earthly plane of raw temptation exists and, sinful or not, I crave his touch and my name on his lips.

My body heaves against the church door until it gives way and I stumble out into the empty aisle. Long before, the priest had left for the evening; I am completely alone.

Outside, lightning flashes, illuminating the stained glass.

Though earlier today I'd thought it was lovely, with the flickering and flaring rainbow lights, the faces and the art now seem only hauntingly twisted.

Do they scream inside like me for freedom, too? How do I silence this tempting call?

In my hurry towards the holy altar, I trip over the edge of my habit and spill roughly onto the floor, my robe coiled around my knees. I lay there in the aisle. I'd thought if I could just reach and touch the altar, perhaps I would be cleansed of my sinful thoughts and Trevor would release me from his hold.

The huge crucifix looms above me, Jesus staring down at me in disapproval. Even when I squeeze my eyes shut to block out the storm and the stained glass and the cross, I can feel his judgmental glare.

When I close my eyes, however, all I see is him. Trevor. Broad-shouldered and shirtless with his hand extended towards me. And how badly I do want to take that hand ... I want to roughly grab his wrist and thrust his big, calloused hand under my pure, virginal cloak so that he feels my warm body and beating heart beneath—a body that yearns to belong to him, and him alone.

I roll onto my back, tears streaming from my eyes, even though they're still squeezed shut as tightly as possible.

I wish our time together hadn't ended so disastrously. I wish I hadn't said what I had. I wish I could go back and take back every single cruel word. Because those hadn't been my own thoughts, they'd been Mother Antonia's—I'd just acted like a parrot regurgitating it all up, no matter how much it hurt Trevor. Clearly, I'd lashed out because I'm terrified of the way he makes me feel, the way he makes me question every vow I've ever taken.

There was no use, I had to stop pretending. Of *course* I

hadn't gone out there simply with the intention to save his godless heart, I'd gone out there because the thought of not seeing him again made me want to die.

But even now, the intense sadness I feel over my fight with Trevor is mixed with those electric sensations he gives me; it's almost too much for my heart and body to bear. It's like the sadness just amplifies my desire, making this craving inside me magnified so intensely, stars burst in front of my eyes.

It's like I'm no longer in possession of myself, like I've lost all sense of what is right or wrong, and all I know is that my body desperately needs something and I am finally at a loss to deny it anymore. I close my eyes, finally allowing my body to take control and do what it has wanted to do ever since I set eyes on Trevor.

As I long for Trevor's hands to, my hands stroke over the cotton of my habit that covers my chest. My soft fingertips move slowly, taking their time to reach the crest of my breasts. They linger there at the top of the swell, flicking and pinching lightly, then more roughly, until my nipples have hardened like beads under the fabric. One of my hands stays there, rubbing in a slow circle until my nipples stand at attention and intense tingles wash over me. Waves of desire build in me as I imagine Trevor touching my breasts, with his hands and his mouth.

Meanwhile, my other hand continues to move over my habit on a southward journey that I am powerless to stop. I'm too far gone, enraptured by physical lust. Lower and lower it moves, 'til it reaches the yearning mound between my legs and dances and swirls on top of it lightly, tantalizingly; I squirm and writhe until I can't wait another second to feel that sensation directly. Grabbing eagerly at my nun's cloak, I yank it up over my hips.

Laying in the aisle of the church, my habit is flung up over my body, revealing my navel and white lace panties and long legs. I don't even care that someone could look in and see me. I don't even care that if Mother Antonia found me, she would put me in the cellar for a week without food and water.

All I care about is this feeling and finally fulfilling this irresistible, intense longing for something that I don't understand.

Trevor flashes in front of my eyes. Him grinning, touching my hand, slowly pulling his shirt off over his head and letting it fall behind him. That handsome, tanned face setting off his flashing, white teeth. That manly, square jaw. Those broad shoulders. That sculpted chest. Those huge, powerful arms. That rock-hard abdomen.

What would he taste like? What would his eager mouth feel like as it crushed my own plump lips, his tongue searching hungrily for mine? And what would his tousled hair feel like if it brushed against my inner thigh, his breath hot as his tongue explored this forbidden place between my legs?

I bite back a moan, writhing as my hand rips my panties off one leg and my knee lifts towards the ceiling of the church. With my other hand I pull my habit up higher, gliding my fingers over my naked breasts, tweaking the nipples so roughly that the sensation both stings and makes my body twitch with pleasure.

Even though I know the sinful thing I'm doing goes against the teachings of the church, this time I don't stop. I can't stop. I *won't* stop.

The hand in my panties cups the mound between my legs, feeling it in its entirety and lightly caressing it. It throbs against my palm, begging for more. It's begging for Trevor, I realize.

I am not completely innocent. I know how a man and a woman couple together to create life, and now it all makes sense to me. Because all I can think about is Trevor wrenching apart my legs so that this secret place is completely bared to him, as my naked body sprawls out before him, aching for his touch.

With a moan that I can't suppress, my fingers spread out and begin to stroke between the wet outer lips of my pussy —my eyes crack open, startled by the naughty word that floated through my head. I'd heard Catherine say it a handful of times and it'd always sounded so crude, but in this moment, it sounds delicious and enticing.

I continue to play with my pussy, still shivering at the thought of the scandalous word, stroking up and down the lips. Shocks of pleasure ripple through me, growing more and more intense with every second that passes. I find that pearl of pleasure once more, the little bud that makes me gasp and twitch like mad every time I allow my finger to swirl around it.

Faster and faster my hand moves on its own, my back arching towards the ceiling, my eyes rolling back in my head. I allow one of my fingers to slip inside my hot, wet slit, biting back a scream of ecstasy as I explore myself there. It feels so good I put two more fingers in, now getting an idea of what it would feel like if Trevor were inside me, his thickness thrusting into me, over and over.

By now I've lost all control of my body, and my muscles are writhing and twitching on their own, ready to explode. Then the thought of Trevor, thick and hard and pounding inside me, takes me completely over the edge. A crack of lightning surges through the church, lighting up the cross;

my eyes lock on it just as my body is carried up in a wave of unimaginable ecstasy, my pussy throbbing now not with desire but with sweet release. I convulse in paroxysms of pleasure that go on for what seems like minutes, my almost inhuman shrieks of carnal pleasure ones I don't even recognize—I can't believe they're coming from me.

At long last the aftershocks are over and I'm left, spent and splayed on the floor, my body a heap of trembling, hot flesh.

Eventually, when the spasms of intense pleasure have ebbed, I roll onto my side. My habit remains hitched up around my waist as my eyes drift shut, soft pants parting my lips. I have sinned and I have loved every moment of it. I don't know what this means for me, but I know there's no going back.

It feels as though a door has opened for me now. I don't think I will ever be able to forget what it felt like to step over that threshold. Yet even now, though I just had what I'm pretty certain was an orgasm, my body has begun to beg for more and more, because when I flash once again on Trevor's handsome face, a familiar, insatiable desire swells inside of me, making a wave of goosebumps wash over my quivering flesh. What would an orgasm with Trevor inside of me be like?

Because as wonderful as that solo fantasy was, I still only desire Trevor, and I want him for real and in the flesh. And considering what happened between us, I need to see him soon. I need him to hold me, to reassure me that I haven't ruined everything after all.

If he hasn't forgiven me, this moment of ecstasy was as close to heaven as I will ever get.

20

TREVOR

Outside my window, rain cascades down the window pane in such a thick sheet, I can only see the swirling clouds when bolts of lightning and booming thunder crack the sky. The storm rumbles through the apartment building, too. The walls creak so violently I wonder how this place remains standing at all.

Henry still moves about in the kitchen. I can hear the occasional clink of dishes and smell something simmering on the stove. He's probably making more rum-laced milk drinks vaguely reminiscent of eggnog. It's almost tempting to go down there and have another cup, though that would mean chatting more with the old gardener, and that's much less appealing.

I roll onto my side on the mattress, gazing over again at where my notebook rests. I'd propped it up with paper towels between each of the pages so that they would dry more thoroughly. Hopefully by tomorrow it would be back to normal, if slightly more crinkled, and I could return to my drawing of beautiful Maggie.

She still haunts me. Even though I've tried to push that

conversation out of my head, I can't stop thinking about it, and about her.

At my very core, there's still a compelling part of me—my soul—begging me to run across the soaking wet grounds to those convent doors. I'd bang and bang on them until she answered; and if she didn't answer, I'd shove aside whoever did and run through those cold stone halls screaming her name until she finally came down to see me. Then I'd take her in my arms and I would kiss her and kiss her until she pleaded for me to stop.

And if she didn't beg me to stop, I'd pick her up in my arms and I'd carry her right out of there to be mine forever.

I don't care what would happen to me if I left my posting here early. I don't care if we'd be on the run for the rest of our lives. All I'd care about is being with Maggie and both of us being free and together at last.

Let's face it, this convent is more of a prison than a place of worship; clearly, Mother Antonia has no intention of this being a place where love and faith abound. I hadn't been sure what to expect of a convent, but I certainly hadn't been expecting a place so grim and strict. Mother Antonia runs it as if she's a jail warden instead of a heavenly mother—no way is this a place for anyone to exist, much less thrive. Obviously, her sole aim is to beat down the girls here until they are subservient zombies, and as dead in the eyes and cold in the heart as she is.

I won't let that happen to Maggie. All she'd have to do is say the word and I'd get her out of here, even if it cost me everything.

Because even after the harsh things Maggie said to me, I still want her, I absolutely *have* to have her. It's like she's water and I'm a parched, dying man crawling on his hands and knees towards her oasis. Every step may be torture, but it'll be worth it when I reach that lush paradise, and life. Maggie *is* life.

True, I may be acting like a complete fool right now. Maggie may not even want me the way I want her. But I've seen that hungry look when she stares at me, I've noticed that gleam in her eyes that I've never seen from any woman before, and I'm pretty sure it's love.

There's definitely something there; she has to know that, too. She's got to have this same unmistakable feeling that we belong together, like I do. It may be crazy to think that, yet I know somewhere deep in my heart that it's true.

Down in the sitting area of the dorm, the phone rings. The sudden sound makes me leap up in surprise.

The phone here in the staff dwelling is an old one that's been sitting on a side table near the radio for at least three decades, if not more. It's the vintage kind of phone with the confusing dial of single digits that you have to spin one at a time to call anyone, which I think is put there on purpose to make it harder than normal to place outside calls. I still haven't figured out how to use it. Its ringtone is chirpy and loud and vibrates loudly through the thin walls of the dorm. Fortunately, it rarely rings, especially this late.

The phone rings a few times before someone answers, their deep voice resonating all the way upstairs. It goes quiet for a few moments and then I hear the squeak of the stairs as someone ascends the steps. Then there's a knock on my door.

I slide out of bed and make my way to the door, cracking it open to peer out into the hall. Though I expect to see Henry, it's Cliff standing there with bags under his eyes, dressed in a tight pair of navy striped boxers that cling low on his hips. He yawns and jerks his chin back towards the stairs.

"For you," he mutters sleepily.

I blink in surprise. "The phone?"

Too weary for too much discussion, Cliff arches an eyebrow and nods before stumbling down the hall towards his own room. I stare after him, still startled, and then slowly go down the steps.

The phone is waiting patiently off the hook, set on the table where the base of the telephone is secured. I sink down into the overstuffed armchair beside it and lift the heavy receiver, pressing it to my ear.

"Uh, hello? This is Trevor," I start uncertainly.

"Hello, Trevor!" a pleasant feminine voice responds. The sound is vaguely familiar and I start trying to figure out where I might have heard the woman's voice before. "This is Anita Wells. I was part of your legal defense earlier in the year."

"Oh! Ms. Wells! Hello!" I sputter, startled.

My hands get clammy, clenching the receiver. Did she somehow know that I was considering throwing everything away and rescuing a nun from this horrible place? Or maybe Mother Antonia had actually caught me looking at Maggie and requested I be dismissed.

"I apologize if this is late," Anita continues smoothly. "Our meeting just finished and I didn't want to wait to call you with the news. How are things at the convent?"

"Fine," I answer stiffly, used to that being my typical answer. My upbringing made me into someone who doesn't give details unless specifically asked. But I was still nervous about what "the news" might be that she was referring to.

She laughs and I can all but see her shrugging across the line. "If you say so." Did she know everything wasn't fine, in fact, that everything was far from fine? Why the hell was she calling? I just want her to get on with it and deliver the bad news.

"I wanted to tell you right away that there's been some reorganizing of sentences like yours."

"Oh…?" I murmur, stomach dropping. Okay, she hadn't mentioned Maggie or Mother Antonia. But now I couldn't help wondering, was I going to jail?

"It's nothing to worry about, Trevor!" she exclaims, sensing my concern. "Just that we plan on relocating you Sunday morning. We're no longer going to be working with the convents, but with some nonprofit housing organizations instead. Think Habitat for Humanity, but with bigger condos down south in Florida. They're going to be needing a groundskeeper and I think you'll be perfect. I've already gotten the transfer approved. Good news, huh? I figured by this time you'd be itching to get away from that nunnery." Anita laughs joyfully. "Does that sound like a plan?"

My heart throbs in my chest.

I'd not only be leaving this place, but leaving Maggie as well. On one hand, I couldn't imagine not being with her; on the other, do I really want to spend the rest of my days here like Henry? Staring out on the grounds and longing for the woman the convent denied him years ago? I just couldn't see how a glimpse of Maggie now and then could sustain me for a lifetime. We *have* to be together.

"Trevor?" Anita inquires after a moment of long silence. "I know this is short notice. I do apologize if this is sudden and if it's inconvenient, but unfortunately there is no other option. Like I mentioned, we're no longer sending people to work at the convents and we're relocating all of the staff we've already placed in them. If you reject this offer, there will be no choice but to be jailed for the rest of your sentence."

"Of course," I answer throatily, the room spinning. My world has been turned upside down. "I understand completely."

"Good!" Anita answers buoyantly. "I'll have the paperwork sent over to the convent tomorrow, and Sunday morning you leave. Give me a call then—by that time I'll have the exact address for you. You can take the bus to Boston, then down to Florida—we'll expect you there by Wednesday. Have a great night, Trevor!"

Before I can say anything else, she hangs up the phone. The dial tone echoes in my ear, the beeps seeming to resound from one side of my skull to the other. Numbly, I hang up the phone and slouch down into my chair, my legs limply stretched out before me. So much to think about.

I should be happy about this: I get to leave the convent. I get to say goodbye to Mother Antonia forever. But how am I supposed to leave Maggie behind in this horrible place? It's not like I can force her to renege on the vows she took. It's not like I can be a total barbarian and carry her away from this god awful place, slung over my shoulder while she kicks and screams and clings to her rosary.

I can't even choose to stay here—that wasn't an option. It was either I go work at this nonprofit condo or I go to jail for the rest of the year. Clearly, my options are limited and my hands are tied, but I'm still not willing to give up on Maggie.

Slowly, I push myself to my feet, taking in the empty kitchen nearby with a pot still on the stove that Henry had forgotten. I turn my back on it and walk over to the window, gazing out over the rolling grounds. I'd enjoyed doing the gardening I'd done here, but I could do that anywhere. In this new job, I'd even get to continue doing that.

I try so hard to find any spark of joy inside of me at this new opportunity, but I can't find any. Instead, I continue to be haunted by the tragic inevitability of Maggie and me not being together, and really fearful of what may happen to Maggie if I leave.

Outside, the rain has slowed from a torrential deluge to a light drizzle, though the night is still thick with gray clouds and the moon and the stars are completely hidden from view. Not even bothering to put on shoes or a jacket over my pajamas, I walk back towards the front door of the dorm and push it open so that I can step outside. The air is fresh and chilly from the storm, and I can still feel the heavy static of lightning in the air.

I begin to walk over the sopping grass, every blade plump and thick from the rain and very soft under my feet, like green mush. By the time I make it to the raised garden bed I'd built for Maggie and Catherine, I'm shivering from the wet and cold, but I don't regret coming out here. The soil is black from the rain, and though I can barely see them in the light from the convent windows, earthworms have begun to peek their heads out from the dark earth. I watch them, contemplating.

Though I may not have any choice but to leave, the least I can do is finish this project for the girls before I go. Then, maybe one day, Maggie would be allowed out of the convent and she could come out here and garden to her heart's content and maybe, just maybe, think of me. I just wish I had the chance to tell her that I was leaving.

I turn back towards the convent and gaze at the austere walls. Most of the lights are out now, just a few small bulbs glowing in a handful of windows. I wonder which of those rooms Maggie calls her own.

Would I be able to sneak in there even for just a few minutes to tell her that I was leaving ... and to beg her to come with me? Or would that make me even more of a fool than I already was?

I almost laugh, but I can't—my heart is too heavy.

There's no way she would agree to run away with me, but I feel the compulsion to ask her, just the same. Because if I leave her with one last memory, let it be my heartfelt message that I adore her and always will, and want her to be by my side, forever. Sure, this rule of Mother Antonia's that the nuns were no longer allowed to associate with the male staff would make it difficult to get the news to her, but I would find a way. Even if she turned me down or laughed in my face at the thought of it, it would be worth it as long as she understood that I would always have her back, and I was ready to spirit her away under the cover of night if she'd just say the word.

I don't fully understand the way I've been so quickly swept away by her, or what it is exactly about Maggie that has so captivated me, but I'm glad that I met her. She makes me feel alive in a way that I have never felt before, like my heart is beating for the first time in my entire life. At just the thought of her, I feel the heat of aliveness surging through me. There's no way I can live without her.

Sopping wet again, I ponder all of this as I walk away from the convent towards the apartment building and another dry pair of pajamas. I'm quite a ways along when suddenly behind me there's the distant creak of a door cracking open. I turn around, eyes already adjusted to the dark, just in time to see a figure creeping out of the convent.

My breath hitches. It's her. It has to be. I'd know that figure anywhere.

21

Though the Sabbath is technically the holiest of days, Mother Antonia has a soft spot in her heart for Fridays as well.

What made it even better was that she could sit at her desk for a few minutes and relax, while the assistant mother superior, Sister Ruth was out wearing holes in the heels of her faded black shoes.

The elderly sister's duties around the convent had just been expanded, both to keep her busy and to keep her out of Mother Antonia's gray hair. Ruth not only was carrying the bulk of the young nuns' lessons now, but she also had a long list of clerical duties to fulfill as well. What made Mother Antonia even more giddy was that when Ruth protested that this was quite a few responsibilities for the older woman to handle alone, she had been able to laugh and tell her that it wasn't by her own order that Ruth be kept more busy, but the bishop's.

This situation came about because Bishop Frederick, who was the head of their string of convents and monasteries in this region, was under the impression that Sister

Ruth had been growing jaded and bored in her elderly years. It was possible he believed that because Mother Antonia may have hinted strongly at such a thing, but the mother superior felt no need to share all the details of her conversation with the bishop to Ruth.

Mother Antonia wets her lips, palms rubbing together as she bends her stout body down to unlock the bottom drawer of her desk and takes out the box of chocolate cookies. She'd made the mistake earlier of not locking away all the delicious delicacies from the gift basket, and one of the girls —Sister Monica, she now had no doubt—had snatched away her box of chocolates. Mother Antonia was not about to make that mistake twice. It seemed now that she had punished the wrong girl for the crime, but it was all good: she felt certain that sinner Maggie's palms had deserved the whipping they got, in any case.

Though the gift basket had been presented to all the young nuns, so the reverend mother was technically supposed to share it among them, Mother Antonia preferred to keep them to herself. She would make the noble sacrifice, preserving the other nuns' devoutness and keeping them safe from sin. Heaven forbid they be tempted by the delicious seductiveness of dark chocolate. Mother Antonia, of course, did not believe herself possible of being seduced by anything or anyone, and so the treats were safe with her.

Plus, this Friday evening was one of celebration. After her prayers an hour or so ago, she'd received a rather cheering phone call informing her that her plan was moving along quite well. All she needs now is for one more piece of this elaborate puzzle to fall into place. It was taking a bit longer than she would have liked, but patience was a virtue, after all.

When there's a faint knock at her door, Mother Antonia rolls her eyes and, after brushing crumbs from her ebony lapel, shoves the chocolate cookies back into the drawer. It's so irritating to be interrupted anytime, and she especially doesn't appreciate it at such a late hour.

Outside, she can still hear the heavy drum of rain on the heavy stone walls, but it's no longer storming as it had been during her prayers. The young sisters who'd been singing their hymns have now retired for the evening, and the mother superior wants nothing more than to snack in peace until every last crumb is gone that could possibly tempt her young, less-disciplined charges.

Mother Antonia walks to the entrance of her office and cracks open the door; the dim candlelit glow from within spills out into the cobbled stone of the hall, illuminating a tall man.

Henry stands there silently, hands shoved in his pockets, a half-smile on his twisted mouth. His pale, copper eyes seem to flame in the night.

The mother superior stiffens, her eyes flickering over him for half a second before returning to his craggy, tanned face. He's still handsome, she registers fleetingly in some primal place in her body not subject to her rigid beliefs.

"What do you want?" she asks impatiently.

The head gardener is drenched from the rain and his clothes stick to his body, revealing sculpted muscles from long hours of working outside. Mother Antonia's heart flutters and pulse quickens. Instinctively, she moves to slam the door, but Henry pushes his foot forward to block it.

She and Henry have known each other a very long time, and though she doesn't consider him a threat, he's not a friend, either. Yet despite her ambivalence towards him, and as much as she despises men, she feels a peculiar, baffling attraction to him—but thankfully, that feeling never lasts more than a split second. In any case, she isn't interested in speaking privately with him at this time of the evening, not when there are cookies to devour.

"A meeting, Mother," he coos in such a sweet voice that it turns Mother Antonia's stomach. He smells like rum. "Can't that be arranged?"

"Our convent is adhering to a strict cloister at the moment," Mother Antonia hisses, shoving at the man's boot with her own. "Under these conditions, it isn't proper for me to be alone with a man at such an hour."

Henry forces his foot further into the doorway, his fingers curling around the edge of the door. His fingernails are dirty, fresh soil smudging his fingertips. The mother superior swallows hard and gives the door one last push before Henry is able to overwhelm her and stride easily into the office. Water follows him, dripping on her floor and forming rivulets between the stones. Mother Antonia is visibly aggravated. She is going to have to get one of the girls to clean up in here later.

"That boy that you don't like, the young gardener," Henry begins, "He's leaving in a few days. I overheard him on the phone arranging for his departure. You should be receiving word of it soon."

Mother Antonia perks up, forgetting the water on the floor as she stares at the gardener in tepid surprise.

"Really?" she asks, practically preening with more contemptuous delight.

This isn't the puzzle piece she needs, but it's a nice bonus. She's going to have extra cookies tonight. She doesn't like Trevor—she can smell trouble on him. She has a sixth sense that way. It's like the vague feeling she gets from the head gardener in her office now, but more so.

Henry nods, abruptly closing the distance between the mother superior and his own body. The movement happens so fast that it catches Mother Antonia off guard and her eyes widen just slightly.

She does not back down or cower. Instead she puffs up her chest slightly and tips her head up towards his, eyes locking firmly on his own. His eyes pass over her habit in a way that makes her clutch at her robes, grateful for the covering because she can feel her neck and chest growing flushed. Henry has never been subtle.

His eyes linger either on the rosary dangling between the hills of her breasts or on her breasts themselves, and she's suddenly conscious of the way her body moves when she's breathing.

"Why did you come all the way out here to tell me this?" she questions coldly.

The reverend mother doesn't fold her arms, choosing instead to lift her chin higher as her eyes narrow to threatening slits. She's used to being obeyed in her convent, and Henry's intrusive assault has left her feeling unsettled, not that she would ever admit such a thing.

If the head gardener wasn't careful, he would be her target once she was rid of irritating Sister Ruth—Ruth who always tried to meddle in her disciplinary choices regarding the young nuns. Mother Antonia felt they need a strict, harsh hand of iron, while Ruth was prone to gentleness and mercy. The reverend mother did not approve of that. As for Henry, he never got in her way, exactly, but he still managed to be distracting at times. Mother Antonia does not approve of distractions, either.

The mother superior believes that she has been put at this convent by the Lord to carry out His will. As it is said in the Book of Psalms, "Whoever heeds discipline shows the way to life, but whoever ignores correction leads others astray."

Mother Antonia is going to be sure that none of her pretty, young charges are ever led astray.

Henry chuckles, the sound grating to her ears. The hair on Mother Antonia's neck prickles, her fingers curl into fists.

"Do you really have to ask me that?" he whispers, his breath warm on her cheek as he leans towards her to whisper in her ear.

His fingers barely brush the black fabric of her habit at her hip, when all of a sudden a crack rings out, disrupting the rhythmic peace of the rainy night.

Even as his cheek blooms an ugly crimson in the shape of a palm, Henry doesn't flinch. Mother Antonia's hand remains lifted up after she'd slapped him, her eyes still locked angrily on his. Her chest heaves, her lips pressed so hard together, they vanish into a thin line on her quivering face.

Henry just laughs again, his eyes smoldering.

"Thank you, Mother," he smirks, before being shoved towards the doorway.

22

MARGARET

ool droplets of rain snake down my forehead, streaming down my cheeks. I tip my head back and welcome it, allowing the dwindling storm to wash over my skin and make it new again.

I feel reborn, charged with electricity and a drive to do something I may very well regret later, yet that doesn't matter to me. I search my mind for verses on repentance and though there are many, at this moment I can remember the words to none—probably because I feel no need to repent. The convent rises behind me through the foggy dark, swallowed by shadows.

As I make my way over the grassy hills, my feet sink into the drenched earth, trampling wildflowers and the soft green blades of grass. The ground sucks at my shoes until I fling them off, toes welcoming the ice-cold water that immediately soaks my socks.

The rain still falls but I don't care. It drenches me through and weighs down my black cloak and veil until they feel like they must be fifty pounds. The fabric drags through the grass, collecting dirt and mud until it becomes almost impossible to walk. With a faint grunt of annoyance I rip my entire habit off of me, yanking it over my head and hurling it onto the grass. My curly, dark hair cascades down my back as a sudden chill sweeps over me. It feels bracing and welcome.

With all of this rain, the cotton of my white slip and white panties is going to be nearly translucent, but right now I could care less. I also don't care that this is the second habit I've gone through today because of this storm. At least the laundry is collected tomorrow and I'll be able to borrow one of Cat's habits, if need be.

As I walk away from my discarded clothes, my hands smooth over me, feeling for the first time the dips and curves of the body that I have only just begun to explore.

Tremors still ripple through me, making my breath come short and the cold rain seem to sizzle when it hits my hot, naked arms, lifting up like steam towards the night sky. My arms wrap around my body, clutching me hard the way I imagined Trevor doing. I can still feel the stone floor of the church on my back as my body writhed and shook with ecstasy there.

I'd never known a sensation like that could exist. Even now, as I move I feel like I'm dreaming, like my head is underwater and I'm lost in a foreign sea of bliss that goes against everything I once believed.

It's not that I no longer have my faith, it's just that I see everything differently now and I am at a loss where to go from here. I can't confide in anyone about this, not even Cat. This moment is so personal, it's all mine to savor forever, no matter what choice I end up making.

I'm glad the moon isn't out tonight, or the silver rays would glow on my flesh and someone could see me from inside the convent. Between the rain and the clouds, I feel invisible right now, like not even God can see me. I find myself grinning again, romping through the rain and grass like a forest nymph in a fairy tale.

Maybe that's why I've been suddenly struck by this strange bravery that I can barely comprehend. I'm not a brave girl, at least I don't think so. Cat is brave in her brazenness. Grace is brave in her piety. Even Monica is brave in her pranks. But me? Courage does not normally flow through my veins. Not until tonight, that is. And it may only last until the sun rises and the clouds clear and with them, my holy conscience.

But for now, I'm on my way to the staff apartment building and Trevor—I absolutely must see him before I have a chance to doubt myself again.

"Maggie," a voice calls, my head twisting towards the sound in surprise.

As though summoned by my desire for his presence, Trevor parts the rainy veil before me. His jaw goes slack as his gaze takes in my nearly naked figure, my white slip wet and clinging to every curve of my body. I watch him swallow at the sight of me, his Adam's apple bobbing.

No one has looked at me with such carnal hunger before. It makes my skin feel hot, trembling, and clammy, like electricity is pelting me along with the rain. Trevor's arms open wide, beckoning me to the embrace I've been craving. Like a moth to a flame he captivates me, and I'm unable to resist the thrall of his arms as they spread to welcome me.

I rush forward, throwing my arms around his neck. I crash roughly against his chest, sending him staggering back a step, but he holds me with ease so that the tips of my toes just barely brush the ground. My breasts crush against him as my heart heaves against my chest. I can feel his heart racing against his ribs as well.

When I close my eyes, I could mistake this for heaven.

Trevor's fingers knot in my long hair, his breath coming in hot and shallow pants as we hold one another. My clothes must be drenching through his own, but he doesn't loosen his grip in the slightest. My skin still feels electric, like jolts of energy are leaping from pore to pore, only made stronger by his passionate embrace.

"I knew it was you," Trevor murmurs, but he barely gets a chance to speak before I press my mouth hungrily on his.

He draws in a shocked breath and goes utterly, completely still as I savor the taste of his lips on mine. The clouds swirl slowly overhead, the rain falling now in a soft gray curtain, and I am more alive than I have ever been before.

I've never kissed a man, but Trevor makes my soul feel like it's on fire.

Though his work on the convent grounds has made his hands rough and calloused, his lips are plump and soft as satin, more delicious than any fruit I'd ever tasted. A hunger grows inside of me, not for food but for more of this handsome man. Ravenous for him, I cling to his strong body, cupping his cheeks and deepening the kiss until he gives a faint growl that is more animal than human.

The sweet tip of his tongue just brushes between my parting lips, the tantalizing taste abruptly bringing reality crashing back down on me. I wrench my mouth away from his, chest still heaving. My knees shake, every inch of my body begging me to explore more of him.

Had that kiss lasted a second longer, I would give everything I have to him, but the truth remains that I've already promised myself to my faith. If there's anything I keep, it's promises.

Trevor stares at me, smiling and clutching me against him, the heat of his body penetrating the thin fabric of my sopping dress. Even though I'm warm, I can't stop shivering.

"You're shaking," he breathes, his voice husky. "Are you cold?"

I am, but that isn't why I'm trembling. It's because when I'm in his arms, it makes me question every oath and vow I've taken. It fills me with doubt that the future I have planned for myself isn't the one I'm destined to follow. Yet I still don't know what the right choice is, or the right path. Even praying about it feels sacrilegious, like I'm questioning God himself.

When I don't answer, Trevor's arms abruptly tighten around me and his eyes get serious. "We ... we need to talk."

"We do," I answer, interrupting him with a quavering voice. If I don't say this now, I'll never be able to—I'm riding the high of my forbidden ecstasy and I'm already running out of time. "I was cruel to you earlier, but the sentiment that I shared with you then remains the same. You and I cannot be together. I belong to my church, to my faith, and it's not you that needs to be saved, it's me. I've let myself be led astray. That isn't your fault, it's mine."

"Maggie, no—" he cries sharply, but I silence him again with a single, chaste kiss that I do not let linger no matter how badly I want to savor him a while longer.

"I'm sorry," I whisper. I've made this vow and it's one that has to be obeyed." I pull away from him even though he tries to hang onto me. His fingers gently dig into my arms, but he reluctantly lets me go.

I shake my head and turn, racing towards the convent building. No longer do I feel like a dancing nymph, but a wretched creature. Which love and passion am I to follow? The one I've known my entire life, or the one that makes me feel alive?

As I run back to the convent, I can feel the blistering heat of his stare from behind. I grab my soaked habit from the ground and make my way to the church doors I'd escaped from. To my horror, the doors are now locked.

I can't go back around to the other doors by Mother Antonia's office. I'd gotten lucky the first time I'd passed through them, and there was no way I would get that lucky again. If I attempted to creep by once more, she'd find me out in a heartbeat.

Panicking, I round the corner of the convent only to collide with a soft body.

Claw-like fingers dig into my arms as Sister Eva's cold, dark eyes fix on my own. I try to twist and yank away from her, but she refuses to release me. She drags me against her, her embrace as hellish as the gardener's was heavenly .

"I saw you," she gloats, eyes shimmering with joy. "I saw you and that *man,* Sister Margaret!"

23

TREVOR

Against a hazy backdrop, Maggie stands in front of me. Her supple body is wrapped in a thin, almost invisible, layer of cotton. Her body is perfect, her pink nipples straining against the fabric, her curved hips just made for clutching, and her long, milky legs that seem to go on forever.

It's like experiencing a fantastic vision of heaven. One, beautiful moment she's in my arms, then the next she's out of my grasp, leaving only her sweet taste on my tongue. She turns around, body shimmering like a mirage, and leaves me behind.

No matter how much I shout or plead, she doesn't even look back. I try to run after her, but my legs seem suddenly fused to the ground beneath me, and I can't put one foot in front of the other.

Wrestling free of my invisible bonds, I finally charge forward, only to have the ground suddenly fall out from under me. A shocked cry gurgles up in my throat as I crash down into what must be the dark pits of hell, only to come to a sharp, rough halt.

My eyes spring open, cheerful, golden light spilling peacefully in through my window.

A dream.

For a second I lay there on my bed, panting and rubbing my eyes. I pull myself up slowly to my feet, wondering if last night was just a dream as well.

Had Maggie really said she didn't want me? That she was choosing life in this cursed prison over freedom with me? How could she kiss me like she had and then reject me? Damn, there had been such conviction in her eyes! I hadn't even gotten the chance to tell her I was leaving, but that doesn't seem to matter now. She's made her choice clear, and that choice is with the Church.

I can't deny it, I'm disappointed and depressed. But even though I want to wallow the day away, I still have a job to do, so I numbly pack my bag to head out to the grounds. If I took too long getting ready, Henry would come over and hassle me, and that would only make my already grim mood even worse.

I want Maggie. I want to hold her again in my arms and feel her soft lips against my own. She'd given me just a taste of what it would be like to have her, and that taste has left me yearning for more.

As I cross my room to pull on a shirt and jeans, I notice my notebook, the one with the picture of her beautiful face in it. Last night, unable to sleep, I'd added details to my drawing of her. I'd delicately traced the curve of her shoulders and the way the night's shadows lit her collarbones, the dimple of her bellybutton visible under her soaked slip. Under my pencil, Maggie had come to life, her animated eyes leaping from the page, alive.

I pick up the notebook and toss it into my bag. Today

there isn't a cloud in the sky, as though the torrential rains of yesterday had never happened, and I want to finish my drawing.

Perhaps I'll find a way to leave it with Maggie, so she can remember me after I'm gone from this place. Then again, she may not want it. She may want to forget I ever existed and that our passionate kiss had ever happened. I, however, will never be able to wipe her from my mind. She'll linger there always, a beautiful mirage, cruelly out of reach.

There's something about her that has left a permanent mark on my soul. I really care about her, more than just lustfully or because the way she says my name makes my flesh tingle. I care about her heart, her soul, her happiness. I don't know what love feels like, but if this isn't it, I doubt I'll ever be lucky enough to know. And I'm pretty sure this is it.

Even my footsteps sound glum as I tiredly shuffle down into the kitchen to find Cliff still in his boxers. His body is slick with a faint sheen of sweat as he messes around inside the old oven in the equally old kitchen. The windows are open and illuminate his chiseled body. He turns around at the sound of me, a frown on his face.

"The oven broke," he remarks irritably. "Can you go to the kitchen and get us all some food? I said I was going to make pancakes for everyone because I'm off for the morning — clearly, that's not happening."

Dr. Cliff, among many things, was an amazing cook. At least when he wasn't trying to turn tasty, traditional recipes into healthier versions of themselves. So I had no doubt his "pancakes" would be part protein powder, bananas, and Greek yogurt. The kitchen's food was way better, in my opinion.

I start to tell him that I have things I have to do, but one look from the ill-tempered man holding a wrench changes my mind. Cliff is usually more chipper, but maybe he was really craving those pancakes.

Besides, going into the kitchen at the side of the nunnery will give me the off chance of running into Maggie. I shake my head, silently lamenting that I'm acting like a lovestruck schoolboy, and then amble across the grass towards the convent. The walk doesn't take long and the sun warms my shoulders, comforting me. The earth is still soaking wet from the storms of yesterday and all the plants that survived it are standing tall on swollen stems, drying off. Thanks to the gales, we're going to have quite a bit of work to do around the grounds today. Some bushes are now lopsided and need to be re-pruned, a few young tree seedlings have fallen over, and the flowerbeds are in general disarray.

When I walk through the doors of the kitchen, the place is buzzing like a beehive. Though the inside of the convent is quiet and calm where the sisters pray and convene, in here it's loud and lively as pots and pans crash together and a staff of cooks rushes back and forth. A big, blond man a little older than I in a white chef's coat bellows out commands. A lurid tapestry of tattoos peaks out from under the sleeves pushed up around his muscled forearms. His eyes glow bright blue above a strong nose—he looks like a Viking lord.

His gruff eyes lock on me the second I step inside.

"What the hell do you want?" the chef barks, swiping his palms across the white coat straining against his toned body. "I've already begun making breakfast and I don't have enough for you and the women."

The scent of frying eggs and toast is thick in the air, as is coffee.

I'd only spoken to Erik, the head chef of the convent, a handful of times, but it had always been a rather … colorful conversation. He's broad and tall, built like an ox, but he can whip out some of the most delicate and beautiful dishes I'd ever seen or tasted. I have no idea how he wound up at a convent, and his salty language certainly didn't explain that choice, either.

Unlike the rest of the staff who stay in the apartment building on the outskirts of the convent, the cooks live in a side wing of the building that leads to the kitchen. This separation of the two groups of employees has led to some tension from what I gather, though I doubt the living conditions are any better here in the nunnery.

"Our oven broke—" I start.

"And do I look like a mechanic to you?" Erik interjects rudely, his face resting in its usual scowl.

"Um, no, but you look like a cook," I mutter through gritted teeth, "and we need breakfast at the dorm."

"I require all orders be placed the day before. You may be new here, but that's the rule. I have a menu to plan and over a hundred people to feed. You think I can just order my cooks to make you some breakfast because you can't make a bowl of cereal for yourself?" he growls, arms folding over his sculpted chest.

"Forget it," I mumble, and start to turn to leave, but Erik cups a hand around his mouth and turns back to his cooks.

"Our pretty flower boy here needs some grub for his friends in the staff apartment. Get it before he throws a tantrum!" he commands, as his fleet of assistants starts frying bacon, cracking eggs and cutting toast slices off huge loaves of bread.

He glowers at me before returning to his own task, making a special plate of French toast and fresh berries. I can smell the maple syrup and it makes my mouth water. When he catches me watching him, he pulls the plate closer, as though he's afraid I'm going to snatch it and run.

I roll my eyes and wait as patiently as possible, setting my bag down on the floor at my feet while I do so. I keep my ears alert, listening for any sign of Maggie or even Catherine, who might be able to point me her way. Occasionally, a nun pops in and out of a small side door leading into a passage that I'd never noticed before. It was usually kept closed, but today it was cracked open; I observe it curiously. Erik notices.

"That lets us serve the mother superior directly in her office," Erik mutters nonchalantly as he begins whisking a bowl. "So if you piss me off too much, just know I can have her in here in a heartbeat." He pauses, nose wrinkling. "Not that I would! Ugh!" he exclaims with disgust, a look of repulsion on his face.

"Chef," one of the other young men says, edging towards the bad-tempered man. "Uh, the laundry called. They're running late for their pickup again. They won't be here until about nine tonight."

"Are you kidding me?" growls the head chef. "Again? They leave that laundry cart out at the chute and it stinks up the entire kitchen. I swear, everyone else here is incompetent."

The breakfast I've been waiting for is now ready and packed. Erik furiously shoves several take-out boxes across the counter at me, then aggressively hustles me out of the kitchen while I juggle the tower of meals, glaring at me until he slams the door shut.

I linger there for a moment, looking up and down the quiet outside walkways of the convent, but there's only the swish of fabric from older passing nuns. Then I walk backwards for a few yards, facing the convent with hope in my heart, wishing that I could have just one more look at Maggie before I have to say goodbye forever.

24

"I'm so hungry!" Monica whines as she and twin sisters Genevieve and Lucy walk through the halls of the convent, heading towards their early morning devotionals with Sister Grace, who would've roused hours ago already.

Sister Monica had woken with the sunrise yearning for some French toast with fresh berries and maple syrup, which she knew was what Mother Superior Antonia routinely had on Saturday mornings. The rest of the nuns had to make do with the usual fare. There was nothing wrong with eggs and toast, but Monica would've preferred the luxury of eggy bread and syrup, especially when it was her turn to sort the dirty laundry this evening and someone had left piles of muddy clothes waiting for her.

Though the fast seemed to have shrunk the rest of the girls' appetites, it had only made Monica crave more food, or at least that was the case when there was anything sweet involved. That sweet tooth required regular attention, and that's why she had to pilfer the chocolates from Mother Antonia.

Sister Genevieve rolls her eyes and giggles faintly. "You're always hungry, Monica."

Sister Lucy eyes Monica critically, checking out the way the slender girl's habit drapes around her lovely body. Though Monica has a sweet tooth, she only seems to gain weight in her hips and breasts, which makes Lucy jealous despite the fact that envy was a sin. Reading her twin's mind, Genevieve gives her sister a disapproving look.

Trailing behind Monica, they pass some elderly nuns gathered in conversation, then come across two other young nuns standing under the stained glass of the main hall.

Sister Monica pauses, taken off guard by the strange expressions on both women before her. The twins similarly skid to a halt, though Lucy is much less interested in the situation and picks at her nails, while Genevieve curiously appraises what's going on. Genevieve and Lucy tend to keep to themselves, uninterested in the silly drama between some of the other girls. They keep away from Catherine and Isabelle, who like to imagine they run the place, as well as Grace, who is just boring and on whom Lucy feels a fine figure is wasted; Eva, who they find contemptible, is never worth their time.

But here on this lovely morning is typically-severe Sister Eva, now beaming from ear to ear and a walking evocation of the cheery day outside.

Lucy turns her critical eye to the slender woman, making the mental note that Eva is almost a little attractive when she bothers to look pleased, which is rare. The other woman in the room, pretty Sister Margaret, is the one who looks unusually somber. The two nuns stop talking the moment Monica and the twins enter the room. Margaret lowers her eyes, going pale. Genevieve notes the muddiness of her shoes with curiosity.

"Good morning, Sister Monica," Eva greets the auburn haired nun airily, still beaming. Even her voice is remarkably light.

Monica stiffens. She makes it a point not to judge anyone here in the convent, but Eva has always rubbed her the wrong way, and she doesn't trust this sudden gleefulness.

"Good morning, Sister ..." Eva adds, glancing at Genevieve and then Lucy and then back to Genevieve again, unsure which twin is which. She clears her throat and amends her greeting, "Good morning, Sisters."

Genevieve and Lucy exchange a glance and a suppressed smirk.

The only one in the convent who could tell them apart was Sister Monica, and that was only because the three of them shared a bedroom and spent most of their time together. That is, when Monica wasn't praying or doing her devotionals with Grace. Even Mother Antonia couldn't tell the pair apart. It helped that the holy cloaks they wore concealed every identifying feature beyond their matching faces.

The twins' mannerisms, however, were different when the two weren't purposely mimicking each other. Genevieve tended to laugh and smile much more easily than Lucy, who was prone to austerity. That being said, when they wanted, the two could switch personalities like a light switch. Like Monica, they enjoyed their tricks and employed their identical looks to that end. It was their only form of entertainment here at the convent.

"Is everything okay?" Monica asks worriedly, taking in the grim lines on Margaret's face.

Monica liked Margaret. She liked her even more now that Margaret had taken the blame for Monica's mischievous act a few days prior—seeing her so down now pained her, and she didn't want the nice girl to be in such sad spirits. Then again, the general mood within the convent had become bleaker now that the strictness of their isolation was being more forcefully imposed. Monica hoped that would be lifted soon since she missed interacting with the people of the nearby farms with Doctor Cliff. She enjoyed talking with the farmers and going into the village to sell the nuns' quilts and to volunteer at the local school. Monica adored children, with their sweet smiles and silly giggles and their appreciation for her playfulness.

Monica also missed having free rein of the kitchen, where she would go with the pretense of helping the grumpy chef, while stealing morsels of delicious food. She was no longer allowed to go in there at will, having been forbidden by the mother superior to interact with the male convent staff.

"Everything's fine," Eva answers for the dark-haired Sister Margaret, who only kept staring at her muddy shoes.

Monica purses her lips but nods, moving past them. As she and the twins step out into the hall, she casts a look back just in time to see Sister Eva's wide grin curl with cruelty. She'd have to find Sister Catherine later and make sure it was all okay. Monica wasn't sure how she felt about Catherine, but she did tend to take some of the heat off Monica where misconduct was concerned.

"That was weird," Sister Monica considers as they shuffle through the convent, her stomach abruptly growling. She gives a faint groan and presses her hands against her stomach.

"Let's sneak into the kitchen, Monica," Genevieve whispers, looping her arm through the redhead's own.

"Really?" gasps Monica. "But Mother Antonia said not to talk to the men here."

If there was anyone who was ready for a prank, it was Genevieve. Monica loved that about her, just as she loved Lucy's resigned acceptance of it. Though Lucy would've much rather stuck to the rules, she was capable of being cajoled into mischief as long as Genevieve was game.

With glittering eyes, Genevieve nods. "If she doesn't want us to talk to the men, then we won't talk. We've snuck into the kitchen before, we can do it again." Lucy groans and Genevieve pretends to pout. Eventually the trio is tiptoeing towards the kitchen.

The kitchen had two doors that Monica frequented: one went straight into the dining hall of the convent, while the other led to the outer grounds facing the staff apartment building. The three girls opted to sneak outside and use that door, because it tended not to squeak and also tended to blow open after being left ajar, so they would hopefully go unnoticed sneaking in.

Of course, it was against the rules to be outside, but Monica was just as keen to see the sun shimmering on dewy grass as she was to get some delicious food, and besides, they were already breaking one rule and might as well make it two.

As they creep out into the courtyard of the nunnery, Monica sees the young gardener in the distance walking back towards the dorm. He's carrying a mountain of carry out boxes.

Monica leads the trio and they gather in front of the doorway, listening inside as the chefs bustle back and forth getting breakfast ready. Besides the usual breakfast fare today there are scones, all made fresh that morning; the oven-fresh smell makes Monica's mouth water. When she hears the head chef's voice fade, she grabs the door and nudging it carefully, slowly opens it until they can slip in one by one. The door creaks shut, but by then, the girls are hidden beneath one of the counters.

Head chef Erik returns, clunking something down on top of the counter where the girls hide. He's talking to someone, his voice gruff and deep. Monica listens as he speaks, intrigued by the pitch of his voice. Though the way he speaks is cold, she can hear something in the layers of his voice, something sad that plucks at her heart.

Above them, they can smell the delicious food being cooked. But breakfast isn't due to be served for a while, and by the time it is, Monica is almost certain she will starve.

Genevieve, adjusting her position under the counter, bumps into a small backpack. It tips over and the flap opens. A notebook tumbles halfway out. She grabs it and thumbs through it inquisitively, her cheeks glowing red when she reaches the last page. Lucy watches, intrigued, but Genevieve tucks it under her arm before Lucy can get a peek. She frowns and pouts at her twin, while Monica slowly reaches up a hand to pilfer a bowl of fresh berries from the nearby plate of French toast.

As her fingers curl around the edge of the bowl, another big hand abruptly snatches her wrist and pulls her out from under the counter and up onto her feet. Genevieve and Lucy give a yelp and take off running, abandoning their friend as they hurtle back outside the kitchen and into the safety of the convent.

"Sister Monica," Erik grunts, glowering at her. "I should've guessed. It's always you stealing my damn plates."

Monica blushes faintly at the man's words and the way his rough fingers dig into her wrist before he lets her go. She clutches her wrist against her, not because it hurts, but because the heat of his touch made her body feel strangely tingly. His eyes lock on her, his head slowly shaking.

"I'm sorry!" she murmurs. "It just smelled so wonderful in here that I couldn't resist. You make the most amazing things, Erik."

Monica's eyes wander hungrily over the kitchen. The man's harsh eyes soften slightly. Dolloping on some freshly-made honey yogurt he'd stayed late in the kitchen to make the night before, he pushes the bowl of berries towards her: it wasn't often someone appreciated what he made. In fact, he couldn't even remember the last time anyone told him that they enjoyed his cooking.

"Take it, you silly girl," he sighs, "and then get the hell out of my sight." Erik waves her away but doesn't turn his back on her, watching instead as she glides a finger through the yogurt and passes it between her cherry pink lips. Her pretty green eyes roll back with pleasure, making Erik draw in a shallow breath.

"It's delicious," Sister Monica whispers delightedly, pink tongue licking her fingertip while her eyes lock on his for a heartbeat longer. The food has brought out her sensuality, and intentionally or not, she is flirting.

Then the young nun turns, sailing from the room with the fruit bowl tucked under her arm. Erik stares after her, distracted from whatever his previous task may have been, wondering if he truly knew anything at all about the nuns he feeds.

25

MARGARET

When the sound of Monica and the twins vanishes down the hall, Eva giggles a rather evil giggle and steps closer to me.

I can't even manage to lift my eyes from my shoes, noting the way my steps had left smudges of mud behind me. I should have known that my actions would leave traces. I'd given in to the allure of that handsome man, and now I was going to have to pay the ultimate consequence.

There was no telling what the reverend mother would do to me. She may whip me, she may lock me away, or she may very well ship me off to a convent on some isolated island where I'll never see another man again.

What would my parents think if they found out what I'd done? She'd surely tell them. She'd delight in saying that their daughter had utterly failed in her devotion to the veil. She was probably making that phone call now—that had to be the only reason why she hadn't already come to drag me away.

And what of Trevor? What would they do to him?

My heart sinks at the thought of anything cruel

happening to him. Mother Antonia can't torture him the way she can me, but she could still have him fired and maybe invent some charge or other to get him arrested, even.

I'd made so many mistakes. How could I have allowed myself to do such a thing that would not only hurt myself and my family, but the man that I care about so much?

Last night had been the longest night of my life. Not only was I mourning the loss of Trevor and closing that chapter in my story, but I was trembling with fright at what Sister Eva may do to me. She'd allowed me back into the convent, but not before telling me I should pray all night for forgiveness instead of resting for even a second. Then she'd skipped up to her room like a prancing mare. Today, she'd sought me out early and told me to walk with her for a spell.

I hadn't even had the chance to tell Catherine about all this, because she hadn't been in her room when I finally fell into a restless sleep, and had already vanished by the time I awoke. I only knew she'd been there because her bed was mussed and the pillows tossed aside as they always were in the morning. One of our daily duties was to make our bed, but Cat often disregarded that. As usual, I'd made it for her, and tried not to weep.

"You're a naughty girl, Sister Margaret," Eva scolds elatedly. "To kiss a *man* ... I can hardly believe it. Did you taste the devil on his lips?"

She doesn't whisper as she talks and her voice bounces down the hall, making me shudder. Anyone could hear her. She's probably hoping the reverend mother will be wandering by and she'll get to watch Mother Antonia punish me.

I'd tasted nothing on Trevor's mouth but a delicious,

honeyed taste that was somehow masculine and inviting, and made me want to taste more of him.

"It was a mistake," I whisper urgently. "Please, Sister Eva. Don't tell anyone. It won't happen again!" I don't even know why I'm bothering to try and reason with her—Eva isn't the type to *ever* see reason. She only calculates her own gain and how she can benefit from the information she unearths.

Eva sighs and clicks her tongue. "Oh, Sister Margaret, I won't tell anyone ... yet. But mark my words, I *will* tell. Someday, whether it's the near future or much, much later when you've all but forgotten it even happened, I will tell." She smirks, supremely satisfied with herself.

A chill rolls over me, a shudder moving up my spine, vertebra by vertebra. Eva's eyes glint, her vicious smile now so wide it reminds me of a puppet. That's all she is, Catherine likes to say, Mother Antonia's little puppet.

I won't ever forget that the kiss happened. It had been magnetic and beautiful and amazing, the best feeling I'd ever had. But it had also been wrong and it wasn't something I was going to repeat ever again. I'm glad that it happened, but of course Eva was there to catch me like the spying reptile that she is. And to hold it over my head like this when I'm grieving the loss of Trevor from my life for good ... she's such a monster.

"What's going on here?" Catherine's voice quietly snarls from behind us.

Relief replacing my apprehension, I whirl around to see my best friend. Eva snickers sand walks by Cat, slowing her stride.

"You should know," she whispers under her breath, giggling again before heading off down the hall.

Catherine watches Eva leave, her shoulders tense, before

she turns towards me. Her face is pinched with irritation. "What is she talking about?"

I rush over to Catherine, throwing my arms around her neck and hanging on as tears sting the corners of my eyes. Cat squeezes me, her heart fluttering against her chest. Though it's nice to be in my best friend's arms, I feel nowhere near as safe with her as I did with Trevor.

Why does my heart long for him so much, when it's so wrong? Why can't I be a good girl and obey the Church's doctrine? And why is it that when I think of him, heat pulses between my thighs and makes those naughty cravings ignite inside of me?

"What's going on, Mags?" Catherine presses earnestly. "What'd that bitch do to you?"

I'm so frazzled I don't even bother to correct her crude language, not that I have any right after all *I've* done in the past few days: I deserve this harsh cloister. In fact, I may be the only nun in this convent who appreciates it right now, since it's preventing my temptation to run back to Trevor again, this time perhaps for good.

I already miss him so much, it's like my soul has been stolen away and it will only be returned to me when I taste his lips again. So how can I devote my entire heart to my faith, when Trevor owns it already?

"Trevor and I kissed," I whisper hurriedly, body starting to tremble. I didn't even take a moment to look around and see if anyone else was listening. "Eva caught me."

Catherine exhales sharply, sitting down on a window sill and shaking her head. After a second she reaches out and pulls me towards her, hands grasping mine.

"How was it?" she whispers, biting her lip with excitement and even a slight envy in her eyes.

"It felt like I was outside of my body, tethered to the

earth only by his hands on me ...” I murmur, forgetting my fear for a moment and reliving the way his muscled arms cradled me lovingly and protectively, nearly crushing me against his chest. It would've been so easy for me to wrap my legs around his waist—now I wish I had.

Again I shiver, rubbing my tingling arms as if I were still standing in the cold rain. His body had been so hot against my own, his taste addictive, his hands strong and rough.

Catherine nods and then nibbles her thumbnail in pensive thought. “Well ... the bad news is that Eva is going to tell Mother Antonia, probably sooner rather than later, no matter what she says about holding it over your head. The good news is that it's her word against yours and there's no way she can prove it.”

I settle beside her, slumping over slightly. “But Mother Antonia will believe her; like you always say, Eva is her puppet. Besides, Mother Antonia dislikes me to begin with. We know from me getting punished for something I didn't do, she just has it in for me.”

“Well, Mother Antonia dislikes everyone. Even Sister Eva.” Catherine shrugs and then looks over at me, her brow furrowing again.

She tilts her head, her head against the glass of the window, and gazes at me silently, studying my eyes.

“Was it worth it?” she asks softly, searching for something in my expression that I'm uncertain of.

My throat goes tight, hands clammy. Involuntarily, my fingertips brush over my lower lip where Trevor's tongue had traced the curve.

“It was,” I answer honestly. “Every second.”

Catherine interlaces her fingers with my own, holding my hand against her chest and squeezing it hard. “I'm only going to say this once, Mags. You don't have to lock yourself away here. You don't have to live like a bird in a cage longing for the sky."

"But I made a vow!" I exclaim, yanking my hand from her own.

Eyes narrowing, Catherine continues to stare at me piercingly. "Do you think your God would want you to suffer through a broken heart? Deny you the opportunity for life-long happiness? Do you think He requires that great of a sacrifice?"

"Everyone has a cross to bear, and this, apparently, is mine," I murmur, startled by the sudden feebleness of my tone.

Catherine doesn't even blink. "It doesn't have to be that way. You can have your faith and have Trevor, too. All you need to do is to leave this place for that. You're the best person I know—that I've ever known—Mags. I don't know if I even believe in God, but He would see that in you, too."

I turn away from her, mind reeling and suddenly feeling very heavy. The stress of these endless conflicting ideas in me battling each other is exhausting. We sit in silence for a while before she stands up, pressing one hand comfortingly to my shoulder before leaving me to brood over all of this.

How can I have this doubt, anyway? How can one person entering my life suddenly make me question all of it, past and present? Isn't my faith everything to me, and hasn't it always been that way? And if it were true faith, how could it be shaken so easily by a pair of green eyes gazing lovingly into mine, and rippling biceps I only wanted to crush me forever in embrace?

But, come to think of it, there really isn't any conflict at all when I ask this final question: Why does the thought of being with Trevor make me feel happier than anything about this convent ever has?

26

TREVOR

Carrying the half dozen boxes of breakfast back to the apartment building, I kick open the door and set everything down on the kitchen table. A few more men have woken by now and are getting ready to go to work.

Cliff stands at the stove, a plate of perfectly stacked blueberry pancakes resting next to him. He glances over, grinning. He's in a much better mood than he was before, but now I'm the one that's gotten grumpy.

"Oh," the doctor announces casually, "I forgot I sent you out there, Trevor. You took so long, I figured you just went straight to the garden beds."

Grease leaks out from the boxes, staining the cracks in the wooden table. It's all over my hands and arms, too. I grab a paper towel to start cleaning myself off, meanwhile glaring at the gray-eyed man humming and flipping pancakes. Though he has a bunch of them on the plate ready to be eaten, no one else has touched them yet. This doesn't seem to bother Cliff in the slightest.

Henry walks by, silently snagging one box from the

lopsided pile I'd carried all the way back from the kitchen. Dr. Cliff glances over his shoulder, a frown tugging at his mouth. I look on silently, still trying to pat away the grease on my arms.

"You planning on sharing that, Henry?" Cliff chuckles, trying a little too hard to sound friendly.

My eyes shift immediately to Henry, curious of his reaction. I've never seen anyone else interact with the older gardener. I get the vibe most people aren't friendly with Henry, and go out of their way to avoid him when possible. I know I do, at least.

Henry doesn't even seem to register that the doctor said his name, and heads to his room to eat alone. I can't even begin to pretend to understand the head gardener.

Cliff just rolls his eyes and returns to his cooking. He attempts to offer me a pancake, but I hold up my hands and try not to grimace. He eyes me, still frowning, and I mutter that I'm not a fan of blueberries, even though I frequently ate blueberry yogurt at lunch.

I pop open one of the boxes and help myself to a thick slab of bacon. Chef Erik may be gruff, but his food is delicious; cooking clearly brings out his best.

"Is Henry always like that?" I ask, through a mouthful of breakfast.

Cliff nods. He's put on a shirt now, but his biceps strain against the fabric. Even though he's locked in his medical clinic all day long treating the nuns, staff, and nearby locals, he makes an effort to take care of himself as well. I've often seen him in the weight room, and besides that, Cliff runs several miles after work. In a few minutes he'll open his clinic doors. His white coat is tossed over the back of one of the kitchen table chairs.

"Yes. He's a prickly, old dude," Cliff sighs, back to feeling rather prickly himself now. The bad mood spreading over the grounds must be contagious. He devours three pancakes, then stares at the stack of leftovers with a slight frown before wrapping it in tin foil and chucking it into the fridge. Swiping some bacon from the kitchen boxes, he remarks, "I have to go into work earlier than I expected. There are a lot of patients today and the mother superior still isn't letting the sister that was helping me return to be my assistant."

I nod and watch him, eyes drifting out through the window. I have to get back to work, too. Though I can't imagine pretending to focus on the task at hand, when all I can think about is the way Maggie felt in my arms, and the fact that I have to leave her all too soon.

Even though I knew from the start that nothing could ever come of the attraction between us, somehow it ending like this feels even worse than anything I could've imagined.

Cliff grabs his coat and stuffs his muscled arms into the sleeves before his eyes lock on me. "Be careful with him," he whispers, chin jutting towards Henry's closed door and then back at me. Before I can question him, Cliff hurries out the door and slams it behind him. I stare after him dully, a frown tugging at my lips.

Whatever. I wasn't exactly planning on being best friends with Henry, anyway.

Turning, I go to grab my bag to head out to the garden, only to realize that the backpack was nowhere to be seen. I turn in a slow circle, eyes skimming over the short journey I made from the front door to the kitchen table, before my heart drops like a lead weight straight into my stomach: the kitchen. The convent kitchen. I put my bag down while I was waiting for the food, and in my hurry to return with all those take-out boxes, I must've forgotten to pick it back up.

Oh, hell, my notebook!

I take off like a rocket out of the building, passing Cliff and sprinting over the grass towards the convent looming up towards the sky.

When I burst into the kitchen, Erik is wiping down a counter. The side passageway is now closed off, and the rest of the staff is walking in and out of the dining hall, serving the nuns eating breakfast there.

Erik's patent scowl forms like a storm cloud over his face, his head shaking back and forth.

"You've got to be out of your damn mind," he growls. "You're not coming into my kitchen and begging me for *seconds!*"

"I'm not here for food," I gasp, one hand on my chest over my racing heart as I look wildly around.

The chef's brow furrows over his strong nose, head tilting to the side like a foulmouthed puppy. He almost looks offended that I hadn't come in here to ask for more food.

"Really?" he asks, a pout on his chiseled jaw, but I don't hear the question.

My bag, now toppled over, still sits at the base of the counter where I'd abandoned it. I breathe a sigh of relief and bend down to rifle quickly through it. I poke past some crumpled papers, a half-empty water bottle and some granola bars, only to realize with a sickening dread that the notebook is gone.

Erik leans over the counter, his buff arm resting on the shining wood; he notes my stricken face and reads my mind. "If you're looking for something that's gone missing, then that rascal Sister Monica is the one to track down. That girl is pretty, but she sure loves to get up to no good. She'll give it back though, usually, once she's bored of it."

"No, I need it back right now," I exclaim, dragging a

hand through my hair. "I'm leaving the convent tomorrow morning and I have to have it."

Even though I'd considered leaving the drawing with Maggie, I know I'm going to need it. There's no way I'll ever forget every perfect inch of her divine face, yet I want to keep that drawing of her with me always as a memento of our too-brief encounter. But how will I get it back before I'm set to leave the convent? Anita made it clear I only have 'til tomorrow.

"That's a shame," Erik says with a flippant shrug. "Guess you're shit out of luck."

27

Sister Catherine leans back against the outside wall of the kitchen just beside the door that's ajar, her throat going tight. She can easily hear the voices of the gardener and the tattooed head chef coming from inside. She tilts her head to the side, peering artfully in through the small window of the door, just to be sure.

Trevor stands there, tall and tan and pensive. Catherine's eyes wander down his body before she shakes her head and reminds herself that he belongs to her best friend. Then she concentrates on what to do now, pondering what she'd just heard and Maggie's tearful confession.

Trevor is leaving. This isn't good, Catherine thinks. Nor is it good that Monica has pilfered his naughty notebook.

Catherine already knew what was in the book. Because Catherine knew most things. Like Mother Antonia, she had her ways of finding out. Catherine could be charming when she wanted with either sex, and she knew how to flirt and flatter and bat her eyelashes with ease. Men were especially susceptible to her feminine wiles and she enjoyed that influence over them, especially when she snuck them a peek of her fishnet stockings under her habit. She had a string of cooks and laundry boys and townies who did whatever she wanted. She kept her flock small, though. The more people she had wrapped around her little finger, the more chance one would spring free and spill her secrets to Mother Antonia.

It had been a few days now since Catherine had found Trevor's notebook and then snuck it back to the doctor, whom Catherine trusted. Trevor was careless with his notebook, which irritated Catherine. She was always careful with her forbidden items, and life was always easier when others did the same. The sisters all had their own secrets, even Eva, perhaps most of all, and Catherine frequently found herself in the position of helping them remain hidden. She didn't consider herself a particularly good person for that, but she did consider Mother Antonia a *bad* person. Most of the sisters were Catherine's friends and she was happy to help them out from time to time. Plus, when you help someone, even without their knowledge, they're in your debt. At least that's how Catherine saw it, and so her list of debtors was a long one.

Maggie was perhaps the only girl for whom Catherine didn't keep a running tally, and right now Catherine has to try and clean up this mess before Mother Antonia gets a whiff of it. Maggie is already in enough trouble as it is, with Eva having seen the kiss the nun and the gardener shared.

Catherine throws open the kitchen door and storms inside. Trevor and Erik look at her, Trevor going pale and Erik faintly smirking.

Erik, with his steely blue stare, may be coarse as sandpaper, but he has a soft spot for the sisters. Or at least a few of them. He sees a lot of himself in feisty Sister Catherine and mischievous Sister Monica.

Earlier, Erik had seen Monica the second she crept into the kitchen, and had even pushed the bowl of berries to the edge so she could snatch it more easily. But then when he saw that pale hand and those long fingers emerge from behind the counter, he couldn't help himself. He'd just wanted to know if her hand was as silky as it looked.

It was.

Catherine notes that the side passage of the kitchen, with the door designed to be hidden among the patterns of the wallpaper, was closed while the kitchen staff was serving breakfast. This period of the day was the busiest at the convent and the best time for her to visit Erik, which she did almost daily. She hadn't expected to encounter Trevor as well.

Catherine was a frequent visitor to that concealed passage. She even had a key, one Erik had given to her himself. It made visiting her upstairs vantage point easier at times.

She supposes there could be worse things than Monica having Trevor's notebook with its seductive drawing of Maggie inside. Monica, at least, knew how to keep her mouth shut when it was important. She may be prone to tricks and pranks but she was trustworthy—most other people in this nunnery weren't.

"Paper," Catherine demands from Erik, who blinks surprised eyes.

"Excuse me?" the chef says.

When she repeats her request, this time holding out an expectant palm, Erik glowers, then rips a paper towel off a nearby holder before pushing it towards her. She wrinkles her nose but then shrugs and leans over to take it, along with a pen that was already on the counter.

"Show him to the room, Erik," she says, also a command.

She doesn't look at him, focused on writing something on the paper towel instead. "You know the one," she adds, with a pointed jerk of her head towards the side door.

"I'm not your damn slave, woman," the chef mutters irritably.

Trevor just looks on, surprised to see that anyone could boss the head chef around in such a way.

"It's *important,*" Catherine murmurs, her tone so sincere that both men give pause. She finishes writing and tucks the paper inside her habit above her breast.

Erik looks over at Trevor, frowning, and then shrugs. "Fine."

Catherine gives a sigh and then looks back at Trevor. "Where are you going?" she asks quietly. "Somewhere far?"

Trevor gives a faint nod and the strawberry blonde nun bites the corner of her mouth.

"Good," she murmurs after a moment of deep thought. "Go up to where Erik shows you and wait for me there."

The handsome gardener frowns, offended that Catherine would say it was good that he was going far away, but by then Erik has already cracked open the side passage door and is beckoning Trevor towards it.

Erik knew the little side passage led to a few different places in the convent, though only two mattered now. There was the upstairs path leading to a locked room high in the convent, and there was the path that went to the mother superior's office. That doorway was hidden behind a grotesque statue of a crucifix.

"You're going to head straight towards some stairs," Erik instructs. "Be quiet. Go all the way to the top and you'll see a small door with a lock on it. Use this key to get in. Got it?"

When Trevor nods, Catherine turns and races back into the convent, unwilling to waste any more time. It was easy to find Sister Monica where she was now kneeling with Sister Grace, doing her prayers.

"Where is it?" Catherine demands, earning a bewildered blink of Monica's eyes as Catherine kneels in front of the redheaded nun.

"What?" Monica asks, confused.

Grace clasps her hands, plump lips moving in prayer, her breaths short and shallow. She doesn't even appear to hear the other two girls conversing.

"Erik told me what you stole," Catherine shoots back sharply, grabbing the young nun by the shoulders. Monica pales and glances around shiftily.

"I'm sorry, Cat," she begins to sputter. "I didn't realize you would want berries, too. Next time I'll beg him for two bowls and I'll bring you some."

"Berries?" Catherine repeats irritably. "No, Monica. I'm talking about the gardener's notebook. What did you do with it?"

"Notebook?" Monica blinks. "I'm sorry, Cat. I have no idea what you're talking about. I never took a book."

Catherine eases back, staring at Monica in bewilderment. If she hadn't taken the book, then who had?

Sister Eva, who had been listening curiously to the exchange from around the corner, slips back into the shadows and makes her way down the hall. Though Catherine is usually more quick on the uptake, it's Eva who's figured this mystery out first.

She makes her way up the stairs towards the large convent library, where she can hear muffled voices from under the doors. Whenever anyone has something to hide, they come here first. Eva throws the doors open to find Sister Isabelle and the twin girls, hunched together on the floor and staring down at the pages of a crumpled book.

"I wish I had that kind of hair," Sister Lucy murmurs, appalled at her own flat, silky locks in contrast to Sister Margaret's thick, dark curls bouncing down over her shoulders.

Sister Genevieve rolls her eyes.

When the three women notice Eva's approach, the twins blanch and quickly gather themselves up, murmuring something about being late to breakfast. They rush off, avoiding Eva's scornful glare.

Isabelle remains, slapping the book shut and folding her hands on top of it.

"Hand it over," Eva demands, folding her arms across her chest.

Isabelle, the only one besides Catherine not afraid of Eva, stubbornly lifts her chin. Isabelle is the oldest of the young group of nuns, and she isn't afraid of making an enemy of treacherous Eva.

"No," Isabelle replies coolly.

Isabelle isn't particularly interested in protecting Sister Margaret, and it really was obvious it was Margaret's body drawn on the pages of the wrinkled paper. She didn't know who'd drawn the picture, but it was masterfully done. What Isabelle *is* interested in is depriving Eva of anything she wants.

"If you don't give the book to me now, I'm going to show Mother Antonia the sketches that you've made. Do remember how irate she was at Monica's little doodles. How do you think she would feel if she saw what *you* were drawing?" Eva replies smugly.

Isabelle's face falls, a fatal mistake when dealing with Eva. Eva wiggles her fingers, beckoning for the book as an expression of victory lights up her face.

"You'll still tell, won't you?" Isabelle mutters, relinquishing the book and promising herself that she'll get rid of the evidence of her transgressions as soon as she's able.

Eva just grins shallowly, the high overhead light casting shadows over her unattractive features. Never beautiful at any given moment, Eva's face always became downright ugly when distorted with cruelty. "Why would I do that, Sister Isabelle," she coos, "when I can just use it against you anytime later—at perhaps a far more advantageous moment to me?"

Eva then turns on her heel, leaving the library in a flurry of delighted, gleeful steps, as upbeat as Isabelle is down.

28

MARGARET

No matter how long I sat on that window sill, I could not seem to come up with a magical, perfect answer that would tie this all up with a neat bow. I never had an epiphany that solidified my decision. I just sat there thinking about Trevor and my faith and my vow to the church until my brain was throbbing and my heart was heavy.

Only when I realized that breakfast was starting soon, and I shouldn't be late and call more attention to myself, did I force myself to my feet and slowly begin to make my way through the winding halls towards the dining room.

I had no appetite whatsoever, but Mother Antonia would notice if I wasn't there, and I didn't want to give Eva any more reasons to tell the mother superior what she'd seen. Catherine had been trying to comfort me by saying Eva had no proof, but Mother Antonia wouldn't need any evidence of my sin to punish me: she was an "act first, think later" type of disciplinarian. I shudder and inspect my palms, which are now mostly healed but still have faint red lines across them from when she'd struck them.

"Sister Margaret," a kind voice draws me out of my reverie.

I tip my head up to see Sister Ruth walking through the hall towards me. She smiles gently, placing a hand on my shoulder when I force a smile and greet her back.

"You look pale as a sheet," she says softly. "Go lay down and take a rest. I'll tell the reverend mother that you're ill."

"Are you sure?" I say in surprise, but the elderly woman nods and winks.

"I'll even bring you some soup later. Go rest, child."

Grateful to escape everyone for a while, I turn and walk the opposite way down the hall. When I pass by the stairs leading to the room I share with Cat, I catch sight of someone else running late for breakfast.

Sister Grace kneels in front of a large stained glass window, adorned in the rainbow of light pouring through the pane. It seems to turn her habit gold. I look up the stairs, considering going to my room, but then approach her instead.

As I kneel down next to her, her soulful, dark eyes flutter open and she turns to look at me.

"Good morning, Sister Margaret," she says with a smile.

The pious woman's cheeks are pink and flushed, the same shade as her supple lips. For a moment, I'm captivated by her delicate beauty. When I concentrate my thoughts on last night, I can still taste Trevor's rough, hot mouth on mine. Now I wonder what it would feel like to kiss gentle Grace.

"Morning ..." I murmur distractedly, clasping my hands in front of me and turning my face towards the stained glass.

I'd prayed endlessly over the situation with Trevor, and then Eva, and whether or not I was making the right choice in choosing my vows to the Catholic Church. Now something about Grace's calm vibration had drawn me to her. I couldn't tell her anything that was going on, but being near her was comforting.

Her eyes drift shut again, hands clasped in front of her chest. "I saw you earlier and it looked like you have a lot on your mind. Like you would need prayer. The kind of prayer that Sister Catherine can't help you with," Grace adds, cracking open one eye to glance at me from the corner of her vision.

So true. Catherine is great at many things, but she isn't the best prayer partner. She will put up with it for a while, but then she gets bored and fidgety and starts pestering me to move on to different topics, namely gossip.

"You're right," I sigh, clasping my hands tighter. But when I close my eyes to pray, my mind wanders away from holy words and thoughts, drifting towards the sight of his body under the rain, and the way it felt to be clutched against him so tightly.

Grace continues to look at me and I hesitantly turn towards her. I try to organize the whirlwind of my emotions and thoughts into something that makes sense, but I'm having a hard time focusing.

"Why did you become a sister, Grace? What brought you to the convent?" I whisper urgently.

Grace sighs. She opens her eyes and pensively stares up at the beautiful stained glass, as if searching for an answer that she'll find in the window; after a while, she looks back at me and her pretty face breaks into an easy smile. She looks so very content, her peaceful state of mind really emphasizes just how lost I am.

"I became a sister here at the Blessed Virgin convent because I felt a call, Sister Margaret."

I lean a little closer. "A call?"

Before, I'd thought I'd felt that, too. But the call I feel to escape back into Trevor's arms is even greater than anything that came before. Is it momentary, fleeting lust? Or is it more?

Grace gives an eager nod. "It was this deep, rooting feeling in my soul that I was meant to come here to be among my sisters and to spread the Holy Spirit around the world."

She settles down from where she was perched upright on her knees, easing into a seated position. "Have you been reconsidering your oath, Sister Margaret?" she presses carefully, unwilling to make an assumption before I say anything.

I don't answer, my jaw gritting and suddenly terrified of her scorn, though Grace is always sweet-tempered—except when she's been deprived of food for a week.

Mulling the unsaid question, Sister Grace gently begins to speak. "The call is yours to follow, whether it's within the Church or not. If you stay here when you're not meant to, then your relationship with your faith will get strained, don't you think? Maybe you need more freedom than you believe. Pray on it, Sister Margaret, and I'm sure the answer will come to you in time. I'll pray for you, too, that you find clarity."

"Thank you," I whisper, sudden gratitude rolling through me like a tide.

I'd forgotten how nice it is to talk to Grace. Though quiet and shy and beautiful, she has a way of thinking that makes me feel more secure. While Cat is quick to judge and quick to make a decision, Grace takes her time.

"Mags!" Catherine calls from behind me, lurching forward. She falls to her knees next to us, chest heaving. "I've been looking for you. You need to come with me right now. I need to tell you something I found out ..." Cat trails off, frowning at Grace, who closes her eyes and returns to her prayer.

Thanking Grace one more time for her kind words, I push myself to my feet and allow Catherine to take my hand and pull me towards the stairs. Cat is slightly prone to dramatics and you can never be too sure when she actually has something important to share, or when she just wants to gossip.

"I went down to the kitchen to talk to Erik, when I heard Trevor in there," Catherine whispers quickly, pausing to suck in another breath.

The gardener's name is like an arrow to my heart. I immediately flinch, closing my eyes and waiting for my racing heart to slow down. But it won't oblige and continues to throb wildly, as I long for him more and more.

"I don't want to talk about Trevor, not right now. I have a lot on my mind and thinking of him is only going to make me more confused," I interrupt firmly. "For a little while I'm just going to focus on me and my prayers until I sort out how I'm feeling. I don't know if it's normal to be as conflicted as I am, but I need more time to decide."

Cat stops mid-step, her hand tightening on my arm. Her eyes are serious when she looks up at me.

"You don't have time, Maggie," Catherine exclaims urgently. "Trevor is leaving the convent. You have to make a choice and you have to make it now."

29

TREVOR

I slink back into the shadows, eyes shifting from corner to corner of the locked room high up in the convent.

If I'd thought it was creepy on just the lower floor of the nunnery, up here it was like being in a haunted house. The entire fortress-like convent creaks and groans and every stair and floorboard seems to squeak in protest. Of what, I wouldn't know. Maybe the plight of women who've been stuck in here for decades.

The passageway from the kitchens had led up to a winding staircase and a small door that I'd been able to unlock. When I peeked out, I found a room covered in dust with windows draped in grimy, gray cloth. But with the sun shining, at least, the room isn't as bleak as it might be. I also found a trail of footprints leading back and forth many times over from a door at the front of the room to one of the windows.

Erik hadn't exactly been forthcoming on any details regarding Cat's use of the passage. He'd simply said that she was the type of woman who occasionally needed privacy, and she'd convinced him to share the key to the top room:

he had the keys to the passage and all the doors in it. I'd asked what the other doors led to, but he'd been tightlipped about that as well.

After a few minutes, I hear the sound of footsteps approaching and flatten myself back against the wall, just as two women in robes open the door.

"Cat, I don't understand why we're up here. We're not allowed ..." Maggie trails off, when suddenly Catherine points at me through the darkness and pushes Maggie through the doorway.

Without a word, Maggie rushes forward, throwing her arms around my neck and crashing against me. She clings to me like she's holding onto a life raft for dear life.

"You two have a lot to talk about, but you don't have a lot of time. This is basically the only place in this prison where you can have a private chat, but you need to make it quick. Got it?" Catherine blurts out, excitedly.

"Yes, Cat, thank you!" Maggie gushes.

I give my thanks as well and Catherine closes the door quietly behind her. Beyond the doorway, I can hear Catherine take a seat on the stairs outside to make sure we aren't interrupted.

Maggie and I hold each other for a moment, basking in delight at being able to be in one another's arms yet again, if only for a few minutes. Even though she'd claimed when I last saw her that I wouldn't again, her eyes are shimmering with joy as she gazes at me, her pupils dilated. I press a tender kiss against her forehead and she clings to me, her body shapely even with the thick robes separating us. I instantly feel aroused.

No matter how hard I try to focus on the woman in front of me, just feeling the heat of her breath on my neck as she embraces me makes my vision hazy, electric desire curling through my core. She's so close and so beautiful, I'm longing to taste her lips again.

"You're leaving the convent?" Maggie gasps, clinging to me. "Why didn't you tell me?"

I brush her veil back off her forehead so I can sweep my hands through her curls. She doesn't object and my finger traces down the curve of her pale cheek.

"I wanted to but the time wasn't right earlier. You sounded like you made up your mind about wanting to remain at the convent," I answer.

Her plump, delicious lower lip is sucked beneath her upper teeth as her brow furrows in concentration. "At the time I was sure ... but the thought of you leaving and me never seeing you again ... I don't know if I could stand that. It's all so confusing. I don't know what the right choice is."

"All I want is for you to be happy, Maggie," I answer, my voice pained. "That's all. Whatever choice you make, it'll be your own, I won't pressure you. But if you asked me, I would take you away from here in a heartbeat. You'd never feel trapped or isolated every again." My nose brushes hers as I speak, my arms tightening around her body.

Her fingers slide through my hair, knotting against my scalp. I feel her pillowy breasts pushing against my chest.

"If I choose to let you go, I may never feel your touch again. I want to feel it now," she murmurs tenderly. "I want to memorize your body so that when I remember you, I can see it and touch it and taste it again .... I want you to touch me, too. Know me. Feel me. So you can remember me." She gazes up at me imploringly, and it's impossible to deny her.

I swallow hard and brush my fingers over Maggie's body, taking my time. I swirl my hands over her breasts, tracing my fingers over her nipples; they harden as I tweak and tease them lightly. She moans and puts a leg up around my ass—I can tell she wants me inside her. I slip an arm under the leg that's around me and pull her other leg up so that now I'm carrying her, her body straddling mine. With her arms holding tight around my neck, Maggie's lips passionately press my own. This time, she welcomes my tongue into her mouth, responding with her own while we kiss deeper and deeper. Our bodies begin to grind together. She gasps, feeling the bulge of my cock pushing insistently against the thin fabric of her panties.

Even though it's inside my pants, when she tentatively strokes my swollen erection, it's almost too much to bear. I've been fantasizing about this moment for so many days that it makes stars burst in front of my eyes. My breath hitches and, still holding her, I kneel down on the floor, then sit on my haunches. Maggie's straddling my lap as I shove aside her habit so it's draped over her thighs behind her.

I moan as we continue our deep kissing and she knots her hands in my hair. I clutch her against me, our hips grinding over our clothes. We collapse back and I pin her down on the dusty floor.

"How do I know which call is the one I should follow?" Maggie asks suddenly, gazing up at me with eyes glazed with lust as well as uncertainty.

I wish I could tell her to come with me. I wish I could make that choice for her. But at the end of the day, she has to make that choice herself because it's she who must live with the consequences. To follow me and give up the veil, or to keep the veil and lose me?

"Would you even want me?" she asks suddenly, our bodies going still.

We're still completely dressed, but her hand is between my legs, rubbing my swollen cock over my jeans. Her pupils are dilated with desire.

"I want you more than I've ever wanted anything in my life," I answer, grabbing her face and pressing my forehead against her own.

Her eyes burst into tears and she clings to me, hiding her face in my shoulder.

"Now, now," I say soothingly, and nudge her head up so she's facing me again. She looks so sweet, I just have to kiss her. Our mouths explore each other ravenously again as she grabs her habit and drags it up around her waist.

I momentarily take in the vision of Maggie, her smooth, flat belly, those long, white legs, and in between, heaven itself: that white lace-covered triangle. I swirl my fingertips lazily over the lace mound, making her emit little shrieks of pleasure. Stroking harder over her panties, I locate her clitoris under the fabric and rub it vigorously up and down. She begins to gasp, her breath coming in small pants. When it's clear she can't take another second of this, I push her soaked panties to one side, my hand plunging between her thighs and cupping her pussy. Maggie moans, quivering under me, as my fingers slip between her inner lips. I glide one finger up and down over her hot, drenched slit, biting back a feral groan of my own. My cock is so swollen that the pressure of it on my jeans makes it throb with desire. As she grinds against my hand, eyes rolling back, I slowly push one finger inside of her and start pumping it in and out. This is as much as she can stand, and she throws her head back, her spine arching as my thumb swirls around her clit.

As her lips form a perfect, plump "O," I bend down to crush her mouth with my own, muffling her screams of ecstasy as her entire body tenses all at once, then her pussy clamps down on my finger, repeatedly. We collapse together on the floor and I hold her in my arms, tight against me.

Though I feel like closing my eyes, I refuse to shut them and lose even a second of this special moment.

My cock throbs in my pants, impatient for his turn. But that isn't to be. Because all too soon, Catherine knocks on the door and tells us we have to hurry, our time is running out. If we stay up here much longer, someone is going to come looking for us. It's already a miracle that I've been able to sneak away from my work as long as I have. Henry is probably hunting me down right now.

"I want to give you as much time as you need, Maggie," I say softly, kissing her again. "But the fact is, my time is limited, I'm leaving early tomorrow morning. Tonight ... we'll either meet for the last time or we'll run away together."

Maggie's eyes brim with tears but she nods. "Tonight. I'll have my answer by then."

Catherine gazes at us, her gaze determined.

"Seven-fifteen," she says quietly. "You two can meet in the church. No one uses it on Saturdays because the priest is away and I'll make sure you're alone. After that, Trevor, you've got to leave right away. If Maggie decides to stay, you being here even a few more hours is only going to make it worse for her. Maggie, if you go, you'll leave with him tonight."

Again Maggie nods, biting her lip.

I turn back to Maggie, brushing my fingers over her soft cheeks. A single tear escapes, snaking down her cheek, and I brush it delicately away.

"It's not goodbye yet," I whisper. "I'll see you tonight."

She doesn't respond and I kiss her one last time, savoring it for as long as possible. If I'm leaving tonight, I need to get some things in order, as does Maggie. It will be the hardest thing in the world to say goodbye even for just a few hours, but she needs space to make her choice either way.

I pause beside Catherine, patting her shoulder gratefully before exiting the small door and descending down the passageway once more. I step out cautiously into the kitchen, where Erik's eyes lock on my own. He nods his head, looking after me as I race out onto the lawn, only to have someone grab my collar and drag me backward.

Copper eyes flashing, Henry stares furiously down at me.

"Do you have any idea what you've done, boy?" he growls.

I rip forcefully away from him, putting as much distance as possible between him and me. I turn and dash across the grass towards the staff apartment building as Henry shouts after me, "Don't say I didn't warn you. You'll have to face the consequences now!"

30

While Mother Antonia loves Fridays and Sundays, she despises Saturdays.

It never fails for things to be hectic on Saturday, between the arrival of the laundry truck in the evening, as well as the farmers coming in all day to drop off local produce and goods at the kitchen. It is rather nice that she was able to pawn off so many duties onto Sister Ruth lately, especially the end-of-the-week mail which always needed to get out before the post offices closed on Sunday. Since Ruth now handles the transfer of all goods coming and going from the convent, this eases Mother Antonia's clerical burdens immensely.

So, the reverend mother supposed, she should take a moment to cherish this Saturday where she wasn't running all over the convent like she normally would be. With any luck, Ruth wouldn't be at the nunnery much longer. While that meant those responsibilities would fall back on Mother Antonia, at least until a suitable replacement could be found, Mother Antonia is fairly certain she would rather have more tasks to delegate, than pesky Sister Ruth sticking her nose where it didn't belong.

If only it didn't take such plotting and planning to be rid of the elderly nun. If Ruth would just die, it'd all be so much easier. Mother Antonia crosses herself hastily, promising the Lord she wouldn't wish an untimely death on any person, but tactfully adding that he should take Ruth whenever he had the time.

She settles back, intent on at least trying to enjoy herself today.

Breakfast had been tasty and quiet. A few of the girls had been missing, but Ruth had whispered in Mother Antonia's ear that there was a bug going around and not to mind the absences.

The meal, as usual, had been delicious. She'd had scones and blueberry compote, but her extra plate of French toast had been waiting at her desk when she returned. It was delightful, though she was missing her fruit bowl. She'd have to have a word with that aggravating chef.

Erik was another on her list of people she wanted fired once Ruth was gone. His tongue was crass and his face far too handsome. He did make a fine meal though, even she had to admit. At least he was earning his employment at the convent.

While she was eating her sweet breakfast, she'd received word that the gardener Trevor was going to be relocated Sunday morning. This thrilled her. She could tell that Sister Margaret pined for him and that enraged Mother Antonia. The faster Trevor was gone, the faster the mother superior could crush Margaret back into submission. Because forgiveness was essential, Mother Antonia believed, she would forgive Margaret for straying off the beaten path. Eventually. And only after a harsh penalty.

Yes, all the pawns on Mother Antonia's board were falling into perfect place.

The reverend mother was so giddy that she decided she should have a little treat. But Mother Antonia had only just unlocked her secret drawer, when there was a sharp, almost frantic, knock at the door.

"What is it?" she barks, not at all interested in entertaining any of the young nuns' tears or complaints at the moment. What she wanted was a solid five minutes without interruption. Could she not have a single cookie without it seeming to summon someone to her door?

She's glad she stuffed her cookies back in the box, however, because without another second's hesitation, the door crashes open.

In charges Sister Eva, her eyes wide and happy, a state Mother Antonia was not expecting. She frowns at the young nun, irritation prickling inside of her: it was even more infuriating to be interrupted because a girl was happy, then it was to be interrupted because she was sad.

"What is it?" Mother Antonia snaps once again, irate. So help her if she has to repeat herself yet a third time.

Without a word, Eva slaps a worn and crumpled notebook on the mother superior's desk. With extreme distaste on her face, Mother Antonia pushes it away with a pale fingernail, unwilling to actually touch it. The disheveled notebook looks like it was forgotten outside overnight, like a misbehaving dog.

"Your Reverence, you'll want to see this," announces Sister Eva, her eyes glimmering. She can barely contain her delight, which makes one of Mother Antonia's brows twitch upward. "I've been listening to my sisters just like you told me to. You were right about Maggie—I mean, Sister

Margaret—you were right to watch her carefully. She's been cavorting with the men outside our walls."

Now Mother Antonia pays attention. She straightens sharply up, her eyes widening. "Are you certain of this?"

Eva eagerly nods. "I saw it myself. She was kissing the new gardener. Trevor, I think his name is."

At the last moment, Eva decides against telling Mother Antonia about what she saw Catherine doing upstairs. It was best to take out the girls one at a time so she could rise in power here; she didn't need to get greedy and take out two at once. Besides, she doubted the mother superior would even bother with Catherine once she heard this news about Maggie.

The sound of soft footsteps comes from outside and Mother Antonia frowns, noticing that the door was still half open from when Eva had dashed inside.

"Close the door!" Mother Antonia barks to Eva. Meanwhile, she bends over the notebook with interest.

Eva rushes over to the door, eyes locking with the sparkling blue ones of Sister Ruth in the hall. Ruth says nothing and simply gazes at the younger nun, with a faint shake of her head. Eva swallows, pushing the door shut and leaning back against it. As she watches Mother Antonia wetting her lips and cackling over the notebook, a strange doubt begins to bubble inside of Eva.

What was that feeling, the girl wonders. It wasn't something she was used to. Uncertainty? She'd had to give the mother superior the notebook, hadn't she? She was only following the rules.

"Who was it?" Mother Antonia asks, distracted by the notebook before her. She'd seen it before. The gardener frequently had it in his grubby hands.

"Sister Grace," Eva replies, before her mind could catch up with her tongue.

She doesn't know why she lied, but it's too late to correct it now. The disappointed way Sister Ruth had been looking at Eva remained in her head, making that slight doubt churn in her core. She does her best to push it aside. She has to look out for herself, no one else will, and anyway, Margaret is the one who misbehaved, not her.

Mother Antonia shrugs at the mention of the mousy, dark haired nun, then gives a gasp when she comes to the drawing of Margaret with her curls billowing and the curve of her naked breast drawn on the page.

Then, Mother Antonia cackles with glee, her head thrown back in delight. Eva had never heard the reverend mother laugh before and it made her skin crawl. Her hand clenches down on the doorknob behind her, but she can't yet convince herself to move.

Mother Antonia picks up her phone and dials a number before pressing it to her cheek. The call goes through and Bishop Frederick's assistant answers.

The mother superior can't stop gazing down at the portrait: this is exactly what she needed. Now, she can bring down the final hammer and get Sister Ruth out of here for good. She hadn't expected to reach checkmate in her game so quickly, but she was grateful for what the Lord had provided her. He'd listened to her prayers.

"Hello, Your Excellency," Mother Antonia purrs. "Yes, I'm afraid I need to speak with you urgently about a serious matter. At your honorable behest, I ordered dear Sister Ruth to take over more duties including lessons with our young nuns, but under her guidance things have gone terribly wrong. If you can come by later, I'll show you the proof."

As she continues the call, Mother Antonia strokes

Margaret's face on the page, following the curve of her chin. With a muted giggle that Bishop Frederick wouldn't be able to hear, she crushes the girl's plump lips with her thumb until the pencil mark is smeared over the paper. She beams down at the marred picture of the lovely woman.

The pretty ones are *meant* to be destroyed. It's the only way to save them.

31

MARGARET

How is it so hard to watch Trevor leave?

Catherine stayed with me for a while, her arm around my shoulders as the gardener reluctantly left us. She hasn't asked any questions about what happened in that room, but I can't stop thinking of Trevor's hands all over me as I numbly walk down the stairs, gripping the rail because my knees are trembling so hard. I can still feel the touch of his hands on me and in me, holding me so firmly while my body shook with pleasure. It'd been exhilarating when I'd touched myself, but when he did it, it was mind-blowing. I'm still riding the aftershocks of pleasure, my knees shaky and legs weak.

I'd been so close to begging him to ravish me there on the dusty floor of that abandoned room. Had we any more time, I just might have.

Who knew that rough hands could be so very capable of tenderness? His mouth had been so warm and sweet on my own. And to tell me that he loved me, what more could a girl ever desire? Is my oath to the church worth giving *that* up?

If only there was a way to know for sure. What if I make the wrong decision and regret it all later?

"Sister Ruth!" cries Catherine suddenly as we make it to the bottom of the stairs.

I glance up at Cat, surprised by the relief in her eyes.

The elderly sister turns around, her typically warm face pensive and drawn. She swallows hard at the sight of us and then attempts to smile, not that it convinces either of the two of us.

Catherine parts her lips to speak, concern for the older nun mounting in her eyes, but then she changes her mind. She glances up and down the hall and then digs down into the top of her habit, withdrawing what looks like a crumpled piece of paper towel with hasty writing on it.

"A letter," Catherine states simply. "Will you deliver it for me?"

Ruth takes it and presses it carefully into her pocket, after glancing at the name written on the folded paper. "Of course, child. It would be my pleasure. Since Mother Antonia gave me all these increased duties around the convent, I'm glad I can be of use in any way possible to my sisters."

I feel like the two of them are talking in some strange code that I can't quite decipher, but I'm too exhausted and drained from my emotional day to question anything right now.

All I know is, Trevor is leaving. If I don't go with him, I'll never see him again. So which is pulling me stronger, my commitment to the veil or to him?

Cat smiles again and then turns towards me with a wink. "Ruth, will you keep an eye on Mags here for a few minutes? She's been feeling under the weather. I'll be right back."

"Certainly. Come, Sister Margaret. Let's sit a spell," Ruth says softly, before guiding me to a nearby room.

She closes the door and then heaves a sigh, taking her veil off and laying it aside. Her hair is surprisingly beautiful, falling in silver ringlets around her cheeks. She invites me to sit at a small table and I do so. I've never been in this room, but it's small and cozy and has a simple cross on the wall and a cot. I realize abruptly it must be Ruth's room.

Settling down beside me at the rickety table, she gazes at me solemnly. Her face is wrinkled but lovely, her eyes gentle even though her countenance is grave.

"I do believe you have a dilemma on your hands, child," she sighs. "I don't want to frighten you, but I believe Mother Antonia is aware of certain ... rules being broken."

Ruth chooses her roundabout words carefully, but the meaning is clear to me. Ice moves up my spine, making me sit rigidly in the chair. I can feel my face grow even more pale than it was a few minutes before.

Sister Eva has turned me in.

Ruth leans back in her chair and gazes up at the ceiling in deep thought, her brow knitting. "Sister Margaret, you aren't the first to wish to be free of this place. And though escape is difficult, it is not impossible. Some of the other girls confide in me and I do my best to guide them, but it seems to me that you've already made up your mind."

"Have I?" I whisper back, biting my lip.

She laughs and just looks at me, head cocking expectantly to the side. Tears again well in my eyes and I fall forward, burying my face in my hands.

"I love him," I croak, the words raspy. "I truly do. I want him with every fiber of my being, more than I ever wanted to be a nun. I followed this profession because I thought it would make my family proud and I thought I would love it, but meeting him has changed me to the core. He changed my heart."

"Yes, child," Ruth sighs, patting my hand again and patiently listening.

I can tell by her tone that she'd heard this before, a few times over, and she doubts it'll be the last time, either.

"Am I doing the right thing?" I whisper, desperate to know for sure.

If anyone could give me clarity, it was wise Sister Ruth.

Ruth frowns. "You know that no one can answer that difficult question but you. What I *will* say is when you leap into the unknown, it's one thing to be afraid of the fall, but it's quite another to be afraid of even jumping in the first place."

"What do I do now?" I murmur. "If Mother Antonia has already found out about Trevor and myself, then it may be too late."

"You have to leave," Ruth answers quietly, just as there's another knock at the door. Ruth glances over, going silent, and when the person knocks again Ruth inhales a nervous breath.

Before she can move, the door cracks open and Eva appears there. Eva's face is a maelstrom of emotions, so many that I can't even begin to place which one predominates.

"You will make the right choice, Sister Margaret, because the only wrong one is to doubt yourself," Ruth assures me, ignoring Eva for a moment, who lingers in the doorway looking furious at her own indecision. "I hope you will as well, Sister Eva," Ruth adds with a glance at the young woman.

Eva pales, gritting her teeth. She takes a step back and

bumps into Catherine, who'd reappeared as well. Eva pushes Cat away and rushes down the hall before pausing and whirling back around for just a second. In a strangely strained voice, Eva hisses, "I warned you, Maggie. I told you I was going to tell. Mother Antonia knows it all."

32

TREVOR

When I approach the staff apartment, Cliff darts abruptly out the door and grabs me by the elbow, before hauling me around to the side of the building. He glances around the corner of the dorm and then turns back to me, a stark frown on his face.

"I heard what happened," he whispers. "What were you thinking getting involved with a nun here?"

"It just happened," I shrug before pulling away from the tall guy. "Neither of us meant it to. How did you find out?"

Cliff grimaces and drags a hand through his dark hair, gaze shifting back again towards the convent before returning to me. "The thing about living and working at this convent is, rumors spread like wildfire. All it takes is one eavesdropping ear and suddenly everyone knows everything."

Sucking in a shallow breath, I whirl around towards the convent, eyes skimming over the spires that pierce the blue sky.

"If you know, then Mother Antonia has to know everything, too. Maggie could be in huge trouble!" I groan.

I have to protect Maggie. It's a nearly feral instinct, a compulsion. If anything were to happen to her, I would lose my mind. Even if we can't be together, she needs to be protected. Cliff grabs me by the arm again, clutching me so hard his fingers dig into my flesh and leave a bruise. He leans closer and shakes his head.

"If you go storming in there and making a huge ruckus, you're only going to make it worse for Sister Margaret. Mother Antonia isn't the type to go easy on her girls. You need to calm down and take a breath. What's your plan?" he asks, releasing me from his hold.

I fall back against the side of the building, my body suddenly heavy and tired. My head lolls against the old brick wall that's warm from the sun. My eyes press shut while I try to calm the whirlwind of my churning mind. "I'm leaving tonight. I don't have a plan yet. It all depends on Maggie."

"She's going with you?" Cliff asks, surprised.

I don't open my eyes but I shrug my shoulders. "Honestly, I'm not sure. She's thinking it over now and making her choice. I'm going to see her one last time before I go."

It hurts to think of leaving Maggie behind, but I know that Catherine is right. I can't stay here now that everyone knows about us, it's only going to fuel Mother Antonia's fury more. I won't be the reason Maggie is harmed. But it's going to take everything I've got not to drag her out of the convent with me—the last thing I want is to leave her alone out here.

"And how are you getting out?" he presses. His arms fold over his muscled chest, his head tilting to the side with interest.

This time, I can't help but laugh. I crack open an eye and grin at the man in front of me. "I have no idea. Maybe I'll just take off running in the direction of the town."

"It's a forty-five minute drive," he answers doubtfully. "Your legs will fall off before you get there."

I shrug a second time. "No legs would be better than staying here."

Would Maggie agree? Again, I look back at the convent with its formidable stone walls. Is she safe? When we first ran into each other, I saw what had happened to her palms. So what would Mother Antonia do to her for being with me? If Maggie did decide to stay at the convent, would she be punished for the rest of her days?

At the sound of approaching feet, Cliff and I both stiffen and listen intently. The footsteps are heavy and unsteady on the grass and Cliff peers around the side of the building before stepping out.

"Sister Ruth!" he exclaims curiously. "What are you doing all the way out here?"

The old woman beams, accepting the kind doctor's arm when he holds it out to steady her on the grass.

"Don't you worry about me, Doctor. I'm out here because of our reverend mother," she says cheerily.

Ruth has a bag over her shoulder that she digs through for a moment. Inside, I can see a stack of stamped envelopes each labeled in black ink. From among them, she pulls out a crumpled paper towel that I recognize vaguely. Where had I seen that?

When she holds it out to the doctor, he frowns at it in apparent disgust.

Catherine, I remember. She'd scrawled a hasty note on the paper towel in the kitchen. What was it doing here now?

"It's for you, Doctor!" Ruth chuckles. "Special delivery. Mother Antonia has me handling all the mail."

"And she wrote me a note on a paper towel?" Cliff answers suspiciously.

Ruth laughs again. "I don't read the letters I deliver. That would be wrong, Doctor."

When Cliff doesn't move, I take the crude letter for him and unfold it. As I begin to read it, Ruth turns away to go back to the convent. Changing her mind, she pauses and turns to me, her eyes locking on mine. Though her face is typically kind, the sun now illuminates stern lines on her face.

"Not only am I handling the mail, Trevor, but the laundry service as well. Just so you know, everything must be on the truck at nine p.m. sharp. Again, that's nine p.m.— I'm a stickler for punctuality."

Then, her face bursting into a radiant smile, she turns and hobbles away while humming a hymn I'd often over-heard the sisters singing.

Cliff peers over my shoulder, curiously inspecting the note that Catherine had written.

"It's time for everyone's annual flu shots, isn't it? Tonight at 7 p.m., Main Hall."

"What in the *world?*" he mutters irritably. "I never do them at night! Who even wrote this?"

I swallow hard and hand him the paper towel, watching him reread it a few times, in the hopes it would make more sense.

"Tonight, you really should do what this asks," I respond quietly, gritting my teeth. I don't know how this all ties together, but I know Catherine wouldn't have requested the doctor to distract everyone if she didn't have a plan. "It would mean a lot to me if you did."

Cliff stares at me, his gray eyes just barely widening with understanding.

"I see," he murmurs, arching an eyebrow.

He asks no further questions, probably because, like

Ruth, he wants to know as little as possible: it's safer that way. Mother Antonia can grill anyone she wants for answers, but she won't get anywhere if no one has more than one piece of the puzzle. He inspects the note one last time and then rips the paper towel into tiny shreds, tossing them into the garbage can. The breeze interferes, and a handful of flecks of paper drift over the grass like snowflakes, floating back towards the convent where Maggie is waiting for me.

Only a little longer now.

33

The purple dusk is deepening as Sister Ruth hobbles down the gravel road to the convent mailbox. She hums as she flips through her bag of letters, glancing over the various addresses. Though she truly does not snoop through the letters that Mother Antonia asks her to mail, there can be a lot of information gleaned from the addresses.

She prepares to thrust the entire stack into the mailbox at once, when a single letter addressed to a judge in Boston a few hours away, slips free. Mother Antonia had never written a letter to such a judge before, Ruth knew, and she also knew that Trevor had come from Boston. Considering he was working here through a program that kept him out of prison, the mother superior was probably contacting the judge regarding Trevor's recent transgression.

The envelope flutters towards the ground and—before Ruth can convince her oh-so-tired and oh-so-old limbs to properly react—falls into a large puddle left over from the heavy rains.

She clicks her tongue, shaking her head as she watches

the ink of the letter slowly dissolve as it slips further and further into the water. She could have reached down and grabbed it, but Mother Antonia was very clear that Ruth was not to handle any of the letters, beyond taking them out of her bag and putting them into the mailbox.

This was, of course, entirely accidental. She'll just have to tell Mother Antonia to rewrite that particular note. That is, if her feeble old mind could remember such a thing later: she did have so many other tasks to handle these days, thanks to the mother superior.

With a shrug, Ruth shuts the mailbox and trundles back to the convent.

Following the sound of Ruth's humming, Mother Antonia abruptly whips around the corner, eyes smoldering.

"I was looking for you, Sister Ruth," she snarls, her lips cruelly furling upward into a jack-o'-lantern-like grin. "You should be ashamed of yourself."

"For what, exactly?" Ruth responds sweetly.

"Our young sisters are being led astray by temptation!" Mother Antonia bellows, "It's all your fault! They follow your lessons and your example and they are behaving no better than harlots!

She shakes her head dramatically. "I thought by increasing your duties that you would be less inclined to cause trouble, but clearly that is not the case."

"Is it?" Ruth replies. It's a personal game of hers to respond to everything Mother Antonia says with a question.

Mother Antonia bristles, irritated with the constant questioning. "I've been communicating with Bishop Frederick about this matter for some time now. He's on his way here and he's going to have a strong word with you tonight."

Ruth doesn't even blink. "Is he now?"

The mother superior glowers, her pleased grin fading slightly with annoyance. Ideally, she'd expected tears or at the very least a good bit of blanching from the elderly sister, but Sister Ruth seemed as nonplussed as ever. Mother Antonia frowns now, the fun of her game derailed.

Oh, well, surely when the bishop tells Ruth she's going to be expelled from the convent, then Mother Antonia will get some sort of reaction out of her. Until then, the reverend mother would try to be patient.

"Have you seen Sister Margaret?" Mother Antonia then asks, her eyes wandering up and down the halls. "Or the gardener?"

"Recently?" Ruth asks, pondering what exactly "recently" may truly mean. It could be defined as some point within the last week, or within the last ten seconds.

"Yes, *recently!*" spits the mother superior before giving an irate growl and shaking her head. "Sister Eva mentioned she saw Sister Margaret with you before your mailing rounds—you know what, never mind. I can tell you're going to be of no use to me."

"Mother Antonia!" the kind voice of Doctor Cliff calls, interrupting the two women.

The reverend mother spins around, fury distorting her face. "What are you doing inside?" she snarls ferociously.

Cliff just beams. "Strictly medical business, Reverend Mother. I understand your need for the cloister, but I believe health concerns rise above all. Correct?"

"Not above all," Mother Antonia mutters, eyes lifting towards the Heavenly Father above before glowering at Cliff, who doesn't seem perturbed.

Typically, as much as she hates men in general, Mother Antonia likes the doctor, but today she has no time for him. She needs to get everything in order for the arrival of the bishop. Everything must be in place before he reaches the convent.

Cliff lifts a clipboard, tapping it with his finger. "We missed our flu shots last winter, and now with the flu epidemic these days, flu shots are definitely due. Care to be the first, Mother Antonia?"

"What? What flu epidemic? No, I—" she mumbles, utterly discombobulated, as Cliff takes her gently by the arm and begins to coerce her in the opposite direction down the hall.

"Now, now, there's no reason to be afraid … it'll only take a minute, just a little sting … We'll just assemble all the nuns and staff …" he says, his voice drifting off while Mother Antonia continues to argue.

Sister Ruth simply gives a slight bow of her head and then continues her ambling pace towards her room. It's time she lay down for a nap. She wouldn't want to be too tired when the bishop arrived, and she still needs to get the laundry out.

She pushes her door open, noting that it's now empty. She'd left Catherine and Maggie inside while she took care of the mail, and now the room is so quiet that it almost makes the older sister sad.

She's going to miss sweet Sister Margaret. She knows it's only a matter of time before she misses Sister Catherine as well, and perhaps even a few more of her young charges.

These nuns are beautiful, but they're not meant to be caged.

34

MARGARET

atherine is not a woman who's used to feeling wild emotions, but I can feel her panicked energy as she races through the hall of the convent while dragging me along. She moves erratically, her feet noisy on the stone floor.

"Where is everyone?" I ask, looking around.

"The doctor is distracting them so I can sneak you in here," she answers quietly.

"That was nice of him," I answer, surprised that Cliff would help Cat do anything insubordinate.

Catherine just shrugs. She works in mysterious ways, that one. Our hurried feet slow to a stop as the quiet church doors loom into view. She turns towards me, taking my hands in hers.

"I'm so relieved that you've decided to leave," she says softly. Her eyes are shining. "I never doubted you would. I've known since you two met that he would steal you away." She speaks affectionately, though her eyes are sad. "Somehow, I woke up today knowing it would be the last time I saw you."

"Come with me, Cat," I plead earnestly. "Come with us. You don't want to be here either."

Catherine bites her lip and then hugs me again. This time the hug lingers and Catherine presses her cheek against my own.

"I can't," she whispers, truly sad for perhaps the first time. "At least not yet ... I haven't paid for my sins yet. I want you to be happy more than anything. He loves you, Mags. I can see it in his eyes. And you love him." Catherine was used to faking emotions, but right now there was nothing fake about the sincerity in her eyes.

"Your sins?" I whisper in confusion. "What sins?"

Cat's eyes are sad but she shakes her head and refuses to speak further on the topic.

"Are you ready?" she adds.

I nod and give her hands a squeeze. I am ready to leave my habit and my oath behind. I'm ready to toss aside every vow I've made to the Church and step into a new world with vows to Trevor alone.

Catherine walks with me to the doors, helping me ease them open as quietly as possible; there isn't a single light inside. Dusk is fading into darkness now, making the interior of the church swirl with shadows.

Trevor stands up from a pew, his hands extending towards me. I leap into his arms, eager to feel him against me.

"Stay here until at least midnight," Cat whispers. "Then you can sneak away." I nod and Catherine vanishes back out into the hall, shutting the doors.

Our mouths find one another as he clutches me against him. There is intense yearning in the way he embraces me, fingers spreading out over my hips and spine so that he can feel as much of me as possible through my habit.

"Maggie ..." he whispers against my lips, "I thought I could leave without you, but I don't know if I can anymore."

Kissing me lightly all over my face, he opens his eyes to stare at me. My hands spread over his chest.

"Then don't go without me," I answer breathlessly.

A flash of shock jolts his handsome features. His jaw drops and he presses his forehead to my own. "Are you sure you want to leave?"

"Completely," I answer, "Even wearing this habit right now feels unbearable, like it's trying to suffocate me. Take it off of me, *please.*"

This time, he doesn't ask if I'm sure. Because even I can hear the conviction in my words. Have I finally become brave?

He takes my veil and pushes it back off of my head. My mane of dark, curly hair tumbles down my back. Then he bends down and takes hold of my habit, slowly pulling it up and over my head, then tossing it aside.

Slowly, his eyes rake over me. I stand in front of him in a thin, white slip. I reach up my hands, taking the straps of the slip and easing them gradually off my shoulders and my arms, 'til the fabric glides off my body and forms a silken pool at my feet.

He breathes in the sight of me, staggering slightly back-ward and grabbing hold of one of the pews to steady himself. This gesture is so exaggerated, I almost giggle, but I'm too lost in the heat of his gaze as it takes in every exposed inch of my body. Though I want to cover myself, I boldly resist the urge, because I'm not doing this for just any man, I'm doing this for Trevor. I push my white lace panties down. They join the pile and I step out of them.

"Maggie, what are you doing?" he asks.

"I want you," I whisper, my voice quavering. "I want to

be one with you, completely. I need ..." I pause, cheeks burning pink no matter how hard I try not to blush, "I need you inside of me."

Trevor rushes forward, pulling my naked body into his strong arms. The heat between us is so intense, the air so electric, I feel the sparks flying between him and me as I rip off his clothes and he's stripped as well. Then I step back, allowing myself to take in the beauty of the man's figure. I've seen a naked man before—but only in paintings and sculptures—and so I revel in the way the fading light outlines his broad shoulders, his strong chest and chiseled abs. But it's what I find between his legs that truly takes my breath away.

His erection is swollen thick, curving up towards me as if it were beckoning me towards him.

Though I'd managed not to bashfully cover myself, Trevor's face is red and his arms fold uncomfortably over his chest. I ease forward, pressing my palms against his chest so that he sits down on the pew behind us. He does so, tilting his head to look at me. His fingertips sweep slowly up and down my sides, his eyes again wandering over every curve of my body.

"You're so beautiful," he whispers. "I'm afraid to break you."

"You're not going to break me," I murmur, "you're going to put me together." I straddle his lap and press my mouth eagerly to his. We kiss deeply, passionately. He grips my hips, pulling me towards him so that our naked chests crash together. My full breasts crush against him; his body feels so warm and strong, it makes it hard to breathe. I feel his swollen cock—Catherine had taught me that crude word—rigid against me, poking my lower abdomen. I can't resist looking down and touching it, it's fascinating and new to me. I marvel how big and thick it is, and how it responds to my strokes, becoming as hard as steel —it seems to have a mind of its own. And it seems, too, that I'm the one on its mind! As I encircle it with my fingers and try rubbing it up and down, it only gets bigger, and Trevor moans and starts panting in short, shallow breaths.

"Enough, Baby," he growls, scooping me up and laying me down on the pew. As he crawls on top of me, his bicep muscles strain as he keeps his weight from pressing down on me. I wrap my legs around him and bring him down towards me, eager to feel his body against mine again.

His lips capture mine, his tongue stroking my lower lip. I wrap my arms around his neck, fingers in his hair. We open our mouths wider and deepen our kiss, our tongues pulsing together in an intoxicating, passionate dance.

Trevor's guides his cock between my legs and caresses the throbbing lips of my slick pussy with it, the same way his finger had, making my eyes roll back in my head. Every pore of my body is steaming with feral heat—I want him so bad I could scream.

"Fuck me," I plead into his ear, cheeks blushing. I'd never even thought that word, let alone said it out loud.

He gives a faint growl and slowly eases his cock deep inside of me. He doesn't stop when I clutch him tighter or begin to whimper; I don't stop squeezing his hips with my thighs.

As my virgin pussy stretches to fit his cock inside of me, it hurts a bit, but at the same time, I feel incredible pleasure. By the time he's buried inside of me to the hilt, the room is spinning and my hips buck against his own.

"Fuck me," I beg, more urgently this time.

"Maggie, you feel so damn good," Trevor growls in my ear, pinning me down on the pew as he slowly pulls out of my pussy and then thrusts back in again. Each carnal stroke makes my body spasm with ecstasy. As he pumps, I dig my fingers into his muscular ass, pulling him towards me again and again, reveling in this feeling of being one with him. Full. Complete.

Then I rest my arms behind my head and Trevor's hands interlace with mine. We rock against the pew, inhaling one another's moans and gasps of pleasure. I don't know how much longer I can go before I explode, when all of a sudden he groans against my mouth.

"I'm going to come, Maggie," he cries. "You feel too good!"

I can only respond with a savage shriek of ecstasy, as my entire body suddenly begins to violently twitch with pleasure, all the muscles inside of me tightening at once—the rubber band is snapping, over and over.

As Trevor moans and buries himself one last time inside of me, he collapses on top of me, his shoulders damp with sweat. As the first stars become visible through the high windows, we cling to one another, one unified organism quivering with euphoric bliss.

I can't believe I'd been ready to deny myself this forever. Now I want Trevor *inside* of me forever.

He lifts his head and kisses me tenderly, his shaking fingers stroking my face.

"Maggie, I'm so grateful I found you," he murmurs, his eyes shining though his voice is thick with sleep.

"I feel exactly the same way about you, Trevor," I answer softly.

This, I believe, is what faith should feel like. It shouldn't be captivating or enthralling, it should be liberating. Exhilarating. Orgasmic!

We curl up in this pew where we're hidden from anyone

peering in through the windows, holding each other. When I shiver, he grabs his shirt and slides it over my shoulders.

"What will we do until midnight?" I ask, stroking Trevor's face as his eyelids slowly fall shut.

"Don't worry," he whispers before yawning. "I have a plan. I just need a few minutes to rest. It's been such a crazy day ..."

"Of course," I answer, kissing his forehead.

Trevor drifts asleep, one arm around me, and I stare up at the ceiling and then at the windows, as night envelops the convent.

Then, suddenly, I hear a faint scuffling at the door. I try to sink lower against the pew, but I recognize the face of the person peering in.

It's Sister Eva.

My heart drops when her eyes lock on mine, but she doesn't shout for Mother Antonia or take off running. Instead, she gestures me towards her.

Carefully, I untangle myself from Trevor and pad forward towards the woman, tugging his shirt lower over my thighs.

"How did you know we were here?" I ask grimly.

Eva waves this away, her lips pursing before she speaks. "I heard you're leaving. I just wanted you to know that there's a notebook that Trevor had in his possession ... it had a drawing of you in it."

"What?" I murmur.

Eva stares at her feet. "I only saw a glimpse of it, but it looked like it was something he treasured. If you two are leaving, he may want it back. Mother Antonia has a drawer where she hides things. She's with the doctor right now so we can slip in."

"Why would you do that for me?" I ask suspiciously, not moving from the doorway of the church.

Eva looks at me as though she's surprised I would question her. "All I really want is for you to be gone, Margaret. You and Catherine both. If you two leave, I can be the one who everyone listens to. I want to be the one with the power. Monica and the twins and Grace are easy to control, Mother Antonia taught me that, but you and Catherine aren't. Do you want the notebook or not? You don't have long."

"Fine," I mutter, glancing back one last time at Trevor's sleeping figure.

We walk together in silence to Mother Antonia's office. We slip inside and Eva produces a key from her pocket, gesturing at a small drawer at the bottom of the mother superior's desk. I unlock it quickly, finding a weathered notebook inside resting upon what looks like a tin cookie box.

I open the notebook, gasping when I see the beautiful image inside. Trevor had drawn this, and of me?

When I look up, Eva's face is slightly pained.

Before I can ask what's wrong, the head gardener lumbers into the room. He stands behind Eva, grinning as I shoot to my feet, clutching the notebook.

Before I can even manage a scream of surprise, Henry grabs me. He spins me around and pins me against his chest with ease, his rough hand covering my mouth and nose as he shoves aside the grotesque crucifix statue to reveal a passageway in the wall I'd never seen before. I struggle against him, kicking and biting, but he just laughs at my attempts.

The last thing I see are Eva's wide eyes as the passage door slams shut.

35

TREVOR

I jerk awake to the first rays of moonlight shining in through the nearby window. Two pairs of curious eyes stare down at me. I gulp and leap up, recognizing Sisters Monica and Grace peering down at me.

Suddenly remembering my nakedness, I cover myself with my hands before fumbling around for my jeans, then pulling them on. While Monica's eyes curiously graze over me, Grace flushes scarlet and covers her eyes with her hands.

What are you doing in here?" Monica asks lightly, while a much more critically-toned Grace adds, "Men aren't allowed inside the convent!"

"Maggie ..." I murmur, rubbing my eyes and looking around. "Where is she?"

Monica shrugs. "With the doctor, I assume. He's giving flu shots. Sister Grace and I already got ours, poor Gracie almost fainted."

Grace peers through her fingers to pout at her friend. "It wasn't because of the shot, it was because he kept holding my arm. He had to pull up my sleeve and I felt so naked ..."

her eyes drift back to me, who was recently actually naked, and she gives a faint yelp and covers her eyes again.

While Monica barrages me with questions about why in the world I would be naked in a church, I look wildly around, noting the discarded habit still laying on the floor where Maggie left it.

Something is wrong. My gut is twisting and turning like snakes have replaced my intestines. I rush towards the doors of the church that lead into the convent, but Sister Monica grabs my arm and stops me.

"Where are you going?" Monica asks. "If Mother Antonia sees you, she's going to have a fit."

"You don't understand, Maggie was supposed to be here with me!" I cry out in a panic.

Sister Grace's eyes flicker over towards the discarded habit, her cheeks going pink. She hugs herself, arms wrapping tight just under the curve of her ample breast. Monica frowns, as well, her head tilting curiously to the side.

"Why?" Monica asks innocently.

I start to tell them the details, but then I cut myself off. I shouldn't get these girls involved. Not with how dangerous Mother Antonia is. The less they know, the better.

"I've got to go." I push away from them and run out the other doors that lead outside, looking urgently around the empty convent courtyard.

Where could Maggie have gone?

I whip towards the kitchen, charging over towards it and throwing open the doors. The kitchen is empty, aside from the head chef.

Erik points a spatula at me, shaking his head. "How many times do I have to tell you?" he glowers. "You have to order in advance!"

"No, I'm not here about any damn food, Erik!" I shout furiously. "I need Catherine. Have you seen her?"

Erik lowers his spatula, considering my panicked face and deciding to keep his smart comments to himself.

"Yes," he says simply, narrowing his eyes on mine. "Catherine is with a girl. The serious looking one."

"Where did she go?" I press.

Erik says nothing, but points his spatula at the closed double doors that lead into the dining room.

'Hang on, Maggie,' I mutter inaudibly. 'Just give me a little longer.'

36

Sisters Eva and Catherine stand at a distance in the dining hall, the room empty and quiet: Saturday's traditional early dinner hour had already come and gone.

Eva swallows hard, her fists clenched tightly. Catherine sinks languidly down into one of the dining hall chairs, dragging her black cloak up over her knees and letting her feet rest on the table. Eva's eyes rake over the fishnet stockings, her throat suddenly dry. She forces her gaze back onto Catherine's own, refusing to give her the reaction she knows Catherine wants.

Catherine smirks faintly, her head tilting from side to side as she analyzes Eva's face. With Maggie and Trevor safely hidden away, she could resume taunting those around the convent she didn't like. If she didn't, Mother Antonia would almost certainly get suspicious. Catherine was quite surprised she wasn't already being hounded for details on Maggie's disappearance, but she supposed Dr. Cliff was just doing an exceptional job keeping Mother Antonia occupied.

Catherine enjoyed watching Cliff from her private room upstairs. She could just see into the clinic, and at times he would change into his running clothes after his shift was over. He had the muscled body of a Greek statue, and Catherine appreciated the view.

"What were you doing alone with the chef?" Eva asks dryly, stalling for time.

She hasn't made up her mind about what she wants to do, or whether she's going to tell Catherine what happened.

Catherine's eyes drift over to the dining room doors, thinking of the chef and the way Erik pushes up his sleeves, showing off muscles and rippling tattoos which Catherine enjoys with interest. She'd always wanted to run her fingers up and down the man's arms, and maybe some day, she would. Erik, gruff and coarse though he is, has a tender heart. Catherine is many things, but tender isn't one. At least not towards anyone other than Maggie.

At its core, she and Erik have a business deal.

The chef is Catherine's connection to the outside world, and the way she gets all of her illicit paraphernalia smuggled into the convent, such as chocolates and steamy novels and fishnet stockings. It'd taken some convincing to get Erik to do her bidding, but everyone can be convinced if one makes the right offer. Catherine has always been cunning— she knows how to get what she wants, especially from men. Even if they're not interested in her "that way."

"He's a friend," Catherine muses. "Not that you would know what that means."

Eva glowers, her heart torn in two directions.

All she can think about is Maggie's tormented face and what that man may be doing to her. When Mother Antonia told Sister Eva to bait the young woman out of the church hall alone, Eva hadn't known that Henry would seize Maggie. They'd been gone for a while and Eva had been hoping to catch the man returning, but there was no trace of him yet.

What if he hurt Maggie? Would that be on her?

She wanted power, but she didn't want anyone physically injured. No, that would be just too much. Besides, emotional torment was way more fun.

Before Eva can say anything at all, the doors behind her and Catherine fly open. Eva whirls around, while Catherine just nonchalantly turns her head. At the sight of the panicked and grim-faced young gardener, though, even Catherine shoots up to her feet, nearly knocking over the chair behind her.

"What are you doing out here, Trevor?" Catherine cries irritably. "You need to be with Maggie! If someone sees you, it'll be over."

"She's gone," Trevor answers, his chest heaving. "Maggie is gone. I can't find her, Catherine."

Catherine turns towards Eva, her eyes wide. "You knew, didn't you? Is that why you brought me back here. Are you trying to distract me so I can't help find her?"

Eva's already pale face drains of color. Her dark eyes shift between Catherine and Trevor, her lips moving but no words coming out. Trevor charges forward and grabs Eva by the shoulders, giving her a rough shake. Eva trembles in his arms, trying to writhe free of him.

"Where is Maggie?" Trevor demands, looming over the slender nun. "You tell me right now or so help me—"

"The man, Henry. He took her," Eva whispers faintly. She knows she can't undo the choice she made to help Mother Antonia, but she can help get Maggie out of this situation. "He dragged her away behind the crucifix statue. I don't know where they went."

Catherine grabs Trevor's wrist, dragging him back towards the kitchen.

"I do," she growls.

37

MARGARET

In the dusty upstairs room, I peer through the darkness at the shadowy, looming figures of Mother Antonia and Henry.

The mother superior stands directly in front of me, illuminated only by a sliver of moonlight through the grimy drapes covering the windows. Behind her, Henry leers, his eyes wandering over my body. The way he openly gapes at me makes my skin crawl, but I refuse to be intimidated. In the struggle in the reverend mother's office, some buttons on the shirt I'd borrowed from Trevor had ripped off, so it was now hanging open in the front, exposing me. My hair is mussed, curls falling freely over my shoulders. I'm sure my lips are still bruised from the intense kisses Trevor and I shared, and I know I have love bites dotting my neck and breasts. I wear those with pride.

"Henry, the door," Mother Antonia hisses, pointing a gnarled finger at the passageway door that Henry had dragged me through earlier.

When I'd started screaming as soon as he released me, he'd laughed maniacally and told me that no one would hear me. I could scream until my throat burned and someone would just think a kitten was mewling in the distance. Judging by how raw my throat felt right now, he was right.

Under Mother Antonia's command, he grabs a hammer and some nails from his back pocket and begins to seal up the door. My pulse quickens but I remain calm, glaring at Mother Antonia with my chin lifted.

I'd been afraid of her for so long that now it feels odd to no longer be under her control. Odd and liberating.

"Why are you dressed in that man's shirt, Sister Margaret?" the woman asks frostily, her gaze piercing.

I don't think she's blinked since she brought me up here. When I don't answer immediately, she steps closer and thrusts a finger against my chest.

"Did you let him touch you, girl?" she snarls. "Did you let him have his way with you?"

"How did you know we were in the church?" I ask firmly, unwilling to give her an answer without first receiving some information of my own.

Mother Antonia narrows her eyes. "You did have sexual intercourse with him, didn't you?" she growls, rage igniting the woman's cold, gray eyes.

"I *did*," I whisper back, grinning lasciviously. Though each nail Henry pounds into the passageway door is meant to keep me locked in here for God knows how long, I will not be silenced.

There'd been so many times I wanted to speak my mind to the mother superior, but I'd always been afraid. She'd left me trembling in my shoes, too cowed to ever raise my voice. But I was no longer the weak little girl that Mother Antonia could push around: I'd bloomed, finally, into the strong, beautiful rose I was meant to be—and just watch out for my thorns. Meeting Trevor had helped me find my roots and blossom, though I'd had my doubts and questions long before.

That was why I was so drawn to Cat, who is so unapologetically fierce. Knowing her and Trevor have brought me at last to myself.

"You vile wench!" Mother Antonia shrieks, shuddering at the thought of a man's hands on my body.

"And I *loved* it, Antonia," I smirk as I disrespect her with her first name, my fingers curling into fists. I lift my chin even higher, still grinning rebelliously despite her intention to cage me away. "I loved the way it felt when he pinned me down on that church pew, the wood rough on my back and his mouth crushing mine. I loved it when his cock thrust so deep inside of me that it made my head spin—"

Mother Antonia's palm suddenly collides with my cheek in a loud smack, knocking me backward from the doorway where Henry has been standing guard.

I stagger back, clutching my cheek, but the more furious Mother Antonia gets, the bigger my grin becomes. Her chest heaves as she frantically clutches the rosary at her breast.

"You wretched girl!" shrieks the mother superior, "You had carnal knowledge of a man in our sacred church? You defiled our holiest of sanctuaries?"

"That's not *all* I did in there," I taunt her, remembering the self-pleasuring appetizer I enjoyed there, before Trevor introduced me to the far more delicious—and meaty—main course.

Mother Antonia drags in a heaving breath, stepping sideways so she can press a hand against the wall to steady herself. I've literally thrown her off balance. She'd thought surely the first girl to pull something like this would be

Catherine, but instead it was me. Something about that thought inflates me even more, and my grin just widens.

I have faith that the mother superior will not get away with locking me up. Trevor wouldn't stand for it. But more importantly, *I* won't stand for it. I've spent my entire life sitting pretty like a doll on a shelf, doing as I'm told and only caring what authority figures think. But now, I'm weak and frozen no more, and so help me God, I will *not* be *tyrannized!*

"How could you do this to yourself?" Mother Antonia cries out, her tone bitter with condemnation. "Your virginity was your only value, and now you're worthless both to me and in the eyes of your Heavenly Father!"

"I am not worthless," I whisper back. Though my voice is quiet and I cup my aching cheek, my eyes blaze fiercely. "If there is a God, he will love me as I am, whether I've slept with Trevor or not! You can't keep me cooped up here. I'm getting out of this hellhole, one way or another!"

"If there *is* a God?" Mother Antonia shrieks. "How dare you, you blasphemous whore!" she screams, finally losing her last measure of control. She lunges at me and grabs me roughly by the shoulders, shaking me. I don't hit her back or shove her—leering into her face is so much more effective. "You ungrateful, spoiled bitch! I gave you a home here, a bed. I fed you. I cared for you. And this is how you repay me?"

I don't flinch when Mother Antonia's hands move down, fingers digging into my upper arms. My lip curls in disdain as I deliver my own shock and awe. "Your title may be that of 'Mother Superior,' Antonia, but don't kid yourself, there's nothing maternal about you. You're not capable of nurturing and comforting, only damage and destruction. And as for the "superior" part, superior to whom—a serial killer?"

She slaps me again, harder, but I refuse to stagger this time.

"We'll just see how you feel after a week of being locked up here alone without food and water, Sister Margaret!" Mother Antonia snarls. "You'll change your tune—they always do."

My knees tremble slightly but I straighten up even more. My own outrage has given me all the strength I need. "You can't keep me locked here forever. I'm going to leave and when I do, I'm going to go back to Trevor. I want his hands on me, Mother Antonia, all over me." And knowing it will infuriate her even more, I say, licking my lips dramatically, "I want him to fuck me day and night—that's a heaven you'll never know."

Mother Antonia shrieks and covers her ears, but I keep talking. She will no longer be able to silence me. I've found my voice and my passion, and I'm going to pursue them forever.

"I *will* get out of here. I *will* live my life. You can't control me!" I shout, even as Henry starts trying to hush me.

I don't care if I have to claw my way out of here, I'm getting back to Trevor and getting out of this place for good!

38

TREVOR

Catherine wrings her hands, talking so rapidly that she trips over her words. Her face is pale, her glassy eyes wide and distraught. As much as I adore Maggie, I can tell that Catherine cherishes her just as much, and is equally worried about her safety.

I have to get Maggie away from Henry and Mother Antonia. I've met a lot of bad people in my life, but Mother Antonia really tops them all.

There'd been a part of me that'd wanted to furiously shake Sister Eva even more than I did, but I know what I have to focus on right now is finding Maggie and getting her the hell out of here. Besides, all my energy needs to be devoted to saving her, not to retaliating against one of her sisters. Anyway, Eva is just another victim of Mother Antonia's, if a more willing one.

"Is my kitchen a damn train station?" Erik grumbles with a roll of his eyes, watching Catherine and I discuss our plan of attack.

Catherine shoots him a withering look. After awkwardly

clearing his throat, he quiets, and turns back to preparing the special croissants he makes for Sunday breakfast.

"Do you remember the room way upstairs I sent you to before? The one where you and Maggie met earlier. That's where she's being held, I'm sure of it," Catherine explains hastily, dragging in a shallow breath. "We've got to go get her, Trevor. We can't wait any longer."

I grasp her shoulders and shake my head. She stares at me, her face agitated with frustration. "Trevor, we don't have time to just talk anymore!"

"Catherine, no," I interrupt. "*We* don't have to go get her. *I do.* You can't be any more involved in this than you already are. It's clear to me now how dangerous your mother superior is, and I'm not going to let you or any of the other people at this convent get in trouble for the choices that Maggie and I made. Once she and I are gone, I want to make sure there will be no one else for Mother Antonia to blame."

"But, Trevor ..." Catherine whispers, biting her lip. "Maggie is my best friend. I can't just sit by and do nothing."

Eva emerges from the back of the room, trembling. Erik watches us with interest, sitting on a stool like he was settling down to watch a television show. She swallows hard, making a point of not looking at me—I think she's afraid of me.

"... I know something you can do, Sister Catherine," she announces quietly.

"Why should we believe you, Eva?" snarls Catherine, stalking towards her like a lion hunting its prey. Eva's chin dips towards her chest. "You were the one that got Maggie into this position in the first place! You took her to Henry and let him take her!"

Annoyance crosses Eva's face and for a second, I think she's contemplating just turning and leaving. Instead, she begins to speak. "I got in over my head, Catherine. I didn't realize how bad this was going to get. I made a mistake. I have no interest in being your friend or in ever helping you again, but this one time I can make an exception."

"Go with Eva, Catherine," I tell the blue-eyed nun. "Like you said, we have to move now and I believe her. I don't know why, but I do. Don't worry, I'm going to get Maggie. She's going to be okay."

Catherine stares at me with pleading eyes, giving me one last chance to change my mind and allow her to come with me into the passage. When I say nothing, she flings herself against me and holds on tight.

"You take her as far from here as you can, okay? And I swear if I hear you've so much as made her cry one drop of sadness, I'll make you regret it," she says, sniffling and stepping back from me.

I open the passage door and take one step in, smiling back at Catherine. "Don't worry. From this point onward, every single one of her days will be happier than the last. I promise you that."

Catherine's chin dips in a shallow nod. She stares after me as I rush down the passage, until Eva grabs her hand, dragging her out of the kitchen.

Up ahead, I hear angry voices. Though they would be muffled in the main building, in this passage they seem amplified. There's Mother Antonia's voice, shrill and demanding; Henry's quiet and forceful way of speaking; and then Maggie's rising above both of theirs.

My heart races, feet pounding against the stone floor. She's so close.

When I reach the small door, the open lock dangles from the latch. Assuming the door is open I push it, but it doesn't budge. With a roar, I charge at it with all of my might

—dust and nails and shards of wood fly through the air. Mother Antonia whirls, shocked to see me.

"Stop him!" shrieks the mother superior. "He's going to try and take the girl!"

Henry staggers forward, one of his fists pulled back, but I let my own fist fly first.

I grew up in tough homes and tough situations, and if there's one thing I know, it's how to defend myself. This catches Henry by surprise and my clenched fist collides with his soft nose, crushing it with ease. He groans in pain, holding his face, and falls over backward while I turn to Maggie.

Mother Antonia stares at me, her jaw dropped and gaping like a fish, but I ignore her and sweep Maggie up into my arms. She beams at me proudly, her entire body shaking but with a radiant smile on her face.

"It's you," she whispers before I lift her up in my arms to press my mouth eagerly to hers. If possible, this kiss is even sweeter than our last. Our sweetest *ever,* in fact.

"We have to go!" Maggie cries urgently against my lips.

I turn back towards the passageway but Mother Antonia lumbers into my way, desperately scratching and clawing at me. "Put the girl down, you brute!" she screams, "She belongs to *me!*"

Before I can react, Maggie kicks out one of her legs, squarely planting her foot on the mother superior's chest. "I don't belong to *anyone,* Antonia! Least of all, *you!*" she shouts as she forcefully shoves Mother Antonia with her foot. The reverend mother staggers backwards and crashes in a heap on the floor.

Dodging Mother Antonia—who's sobbing and struggling to get her stout body up off the floor—and the passageway door leading back to the kitchen, I run past

Henry's still-crumpled body to kick open the room's regular door and descend down the stairs to the second floor of the nunnery.

A few of the older sisters, drawn out to the hallway by the noise, watch us in shock as we hustle by. I have to get us out of here fast. I know Henry and Mother Antonia are going to be right behind us. I can already hear them moving, Henry's clumsy feet storming down the stairs, while Mother Antonia frantically shrieks behind him, "Stop them!"

Catherine's voice suddenly ripples down the hallway, and my head twists in that direction. She's walking towards us with a tall, white-haired man.

"And if you come this way, Your Excellency," Catherine says airily, "our ever dutiful Mother Superior is having a private meeting with one of our sisters—oh my!" Catherine gasps when she sees us, playing the part of stunned, saintly nun more flawlessly than any Hollywood actress could.

Bishop Frederick gapes at me carrying Maggie dressed in just my ripped shirt, just as Henry bursts into view behind me, holding his nose as blood spews between his fingers. Then Mother Antonia comes barreling to a stop behind him, red-faced and furious.

I don't hesitate even a second and, my adrenaline pumping, look wildly around for an escape route.

Then, my eyes lock on the nearby open laundry chute where Sister Monica stands, caught between staring at us, open mouthed, and stuffing a last-minute load of clothes down for tonight's weekly pickup. That's it, the chute—it's our only chance.

Bishop Frederick delicately wraps an arm around the trembling and sweet-faced Sister Catherine, turning her towards him so that he can cover her eyes to prevent the innocent nun from having to witness such crude behavior as has just been displayed.

Catherine gives a choked sob and collapses against him, tearfully wailing with just the right amount of tears.

"What is going on?" Sister Catherine cries. "This is ... this is truly indecent!"

"I agree, my child!" growls the bishop, scowling intently at the mother superior and the man nearby. Never before had he seen such behavior in a sacred convent.

He steps in the way as the reverend mother attempts to give chase to the two receding figures, who dash around a corner of the hallway. "Mother Superior Antonia!" he admonishes her loudly, his face pale as a sheet. "What on earth is going on here? Someone gets this man a doctor!" One of the equally shocked older sisters hastens away to find Dr. Cliff.

"It's ... it's all because of Sister Ruth!" cries Mother Antonia, flustered and stammering. She is not used to being caught off guard and unprepared. This was not at all the scene that she wanted the bishop to see when he arrived. How had everything gone so terribly wrong? "This is all that dreadful woman's fault!" she sputters. "As I explained to you before, it's Sister Ruth's teachings that have gotten the girls to behave so sinfully."

Bishop Frederick blinks unconvinced eyes. He looks down at the quivering lips of the sweet young woman in his arms. Catherine gives a small shake of her head, clutching to his robes. "Sister Ruth is a beacon of light in this blasphemous world, sir. She keeps us strong and guides us steadfastly towards our blessed futures of service to our Lord and Savior."

The bishop nods and releases the charming nun. "Of course, Sister. Please, go. Be free of this situation."

"Thank you, Your Excellency. I'll go to my prayers," Catherine says with a gracious nod of her head.

Heading down the hall, she takes a few steps behind the bishop, then turns around, shooting Mother Antonia a triumphant smirk that makes the reverend mother's blood boil.

Dr. Cliff comes running down the hallway. He takes in the sight of Henry and his bloody nose, almost wishing it were he who had the honor of inflicting such damage. He then shakes his head and pushes that thought aside. After all, his duty is to heal, not wish harm, even on men as weird as Henry. Cliff unwraps a gauze bandage from its package and gives it to Henry, instructing him to press it on his nose to stop the bleeding.

Bishop Frederick turns to Mother Antonia. "Do you still say this commotion is the fault of Sister Ruth?" he asks dryly, glowering at the mother superior.

She bites her lip and gives a faint nod. "I know how this must look, Your Excellency, but really, you need to expel Sister Ruth from the convent. She's only going to continue to make it impossible for me to keep the young sisters on the path of righteousness."

Bishop Frederick tips his head back and mutters a quick prayer to the Heavenly Father, requesting patience. He'd come here hoping to have a nice chat with the sisters and staff, and announce some exciting changes to the convent, and instead he had to deal with childish issues among catty women. This is why he rarely visits the convents, there's always something going on. The monks' monasteries were far less irritating.

"Really, Mother Antonia? You're going to stick to that claim? Because when I arrived, Sister Ruth was greeting the laundrymen and going about the tasks that you had set out for her. Yet judging by the long list of duties you've unfairly assigned that poor woman, I doubt she has time to even say her evening prayers. Are you really going to say she had a hand in any of this?"

The mother superior pales, grasping at every rebuttal she could think of, yet unable to come up with something that would convince him. Her eyes drift down the hall, wondering just how far Sister Margaret and that beast of a young gardener had gotten.

Having lost her bid to condemn Ruth, she seizes on a strategy to salvage her reputation, which is all she can fight for, at this point. "I was trying to protect my nun's purity," Mother Antonia states gravely. With exaggerated drama she drags in a shuddering breath and clasps her hands in front of her breast. "Sister Margaret is young and has no one but me to look out for her. Was that so wrong, Your Excellency?"

Bishop Frederick gives a slight sigh, his irate face softening. "Of course not, Mother Antonia. I understand where you're coming from. I don't doubt your dedication to the protection of the women in your convent. Come. We need to discuss this further, away from the nuns' ears."

He walks over to Mother Antonia and gently puts an arm around her shoulder, as easily swayed by her fake appeal as he was by Catherine's. The mother superior dabs at her eyes and nods, gesturing towards Henry.

"He heard the commotion and came to assist me. He got into a fight with the young man who took Sister Margaret from the convent. How is he, Doctor?" she asks.

Dr. Cliff clears his throat and nods his head. "He'll be just fine. There's no need to worry," he says with a polite grin. Cliff had considered straightening the bone back into place, but he didn't want to touch Henry, and Henry didn't seem to want Cliff to touch him, either. So, instead, Cliff just stood at his side and helped him stanch the bleeding.

"Let's head to your office, Mother Antonia, so we can chat," Bishop Frederick says, guiding the woman towards the stairs. "I'll bring in Sister Ruth, as well, to get more of the details of what happened here."

Ruth, hearing her name from upstairs, tips her head curiously towards the stairs before checking her watch. She frowns slightly, biting the corner of her mouth just as Erik rounds the corner and approaches her.

Though Erik frequently rubbed the nuns and staff members of the convent the wrong way with his prickly demeanor, when it came to Sister Ruth, he was as sweet as any grandson might be, despite their lack of blood relations.

"The laundry guy is getting a little impatient, I think," he says, hands on his hips as he looks at the oversized cart of dirty clothing. "He says he's getting behind schedule."

Suddenly, above both of their heads, there's a thunderous sound inside the laundry chute. Erik lurches to the side, staring at the chute with alarm.

"Did you hear that?" he gasps, noticing with amazement the way Sister Ruth doesn't even flinch.

She giggles and beams at him, shrugging her shoulders. "Oh, dear. You know my hearing isn't what it used to be. I didn't hear a thing."

Funny, Erik thought, he'd never noticed Ruth having an issue hearing anyone before. In fact, Sister Ruth seemed almost perfectly healthy in every way, despite the occasional stiffness in her knees.

Just as she finished speaking, behind her two bodies tumbled out of the chute and deep into the laundry cart, landing softly among the clothes to be washed. Erik stared behind her, his jaw dropped, but Ruth just blinked innocently and gestured towards the cart.

"Could you be a dear and push this out to the laundry van for me?" Ruth asks, pointing at the doors. Erik gives a blank nod, grabbing the cart and beginning to push it away.

"You really should hurry, Erik!" she calls after him. "Those deliverymen can get rather irritable when it comes to punctuality!"

40

———

MARGARET

Even though the clothes smell sour and I'm pretty sure I'm lying right on top of my rain and mud-soaked habit from the other day, I've never been so thrilled in my life to have anything to do with dirty clothes.

The cart rumbles as it begins to move across the cobbled stone floor, the muffled voices of Sister Ruth and the head chef drifting in through the layers of clothing.

I dig through the layers of clothes, searching for Trevor. Though we'd been holding on to one another when we jumped into the laundry chute, the rough ride down had separated us. I'd felt his weight when he crashed into the laundry cart with me, but the clothes had piled up so fast that I hadn't been able to grab hold of him.

His face appears through the clothes, a huge grin on his face. He reaches out towards me, squirming between the clothes as if he were swimming, and grabs hold of my hand. Our fingers lace, our eyes locked on one another.

The cart rumbles forward and I careen into Trevor as it tilts upward: we are being pushed up the truck's ramp. "We made it," he whispers when the cart is righted and safely inside the delivery truck that will take us to town. His eyes glitter, even though he's knocked his head on the side of the chute and he's got a bump growing there. "We really made it, Maggie."

His mouth captures mine and we share a kiss of pure, delirious joy. Even though Mother Antonia had done her best to bring us down, we'd overcome her and we were free, gloriously free. Nothing mattered anymore as long as Trevor and I are together—I'd go anywhere in the world with this man. In fact, I hope we will go all over the world. There are so many things that I want to see. I want to meet new people and taste new foods and experience all the life I almost deprived myself of.

I also want to spend thousands of hours exploring Trevor's body, delighting in the way he reacts when my tongue traces every inch of him. After all, God wouldn't have made Trevor so tantalizing and delicious if He didn't want me to savor him.

"Why are you looking at me like that, Maggie?" Trevor teases, pulling me against him. I giggle and stroke my hands down his face and then down his still-naked chest.

Then, softly, I press my forehead against his.

"Thank you," I whisper, earning a slightly confused look from the young man. I press a soft kiss to his lips, still allowing my fingers to sweep over the curves and crevices of his toned body. "For saving me, Trevor."

"Oh," he answers, a sweet blush forming on his cheeks. He averts his eyes for a moment and then brushes the tip of his nose against my own. "I don't think I can really take credit for that, Maggie. I heard the way you were standing up to Mother Antonia and Henry. You were going to get out of that room, whether or not I busted down that door."

I giggle and shake my head. "No, silly. I'm not talking

about that. You saved me by showing me what love and passion and ferocity felt like, by showing me that I could feel that, too. Had I never met you, I would've carried on thinking that love was the lackluster devotion I had to my faith."

For too long, I'd believed love was about repression, but now I know it is about freedom.

And looking back on it all, I'd been so blessed! What would have happened if Mother Antonia hadn't chosen me to punish that morning for Sister Monica stealing her chocolates? What if she had picked Sister Grace or Sister Isabelle or even Cat to whip with that wooden cross? Would it be one of those girls in Trevor's arms now?

Seeming to sense my thoughts, Trevor hugs me tighter. "If I saved you, then you saved me, too, Maggie. I had no drive. I was lost and had no sense of purpose in life. But being with you makes me feel so strong—you make me want to be a better man."

We share another tender kiss. Once again, I feel that heat begin to pulse through my veins. My hands wander over him, wondering how he could have not felt strong before meeting me, when his body is so massive and muscled.

His hands wander over me as well, pushing up the shirt I'm wearing so that he can grip my naked hips. I bite back a moan, a shudder rippling through me. It feels so good, so right, to have his rough fingertips on my naked body. I find the fly of his pants and unzip it so that I can slide one of my hands inside. His breath hitches, eyes closing, as my eager fingertips find his cock, now swelling under my exploratory touch. I stroke my hand against it, feeling the smooth heat of it against my palm, and then wrap my fingers around it.

I hold Trevor's cock in my grasp, slowly stroking up and

down the great, stiffening length of it as he twitches and moans. Fascinated, I scrutinize its tantalizing thickness and the way the swollen veins strain against my fingers, the way the bulbous tip has beads of cum already forming at the tip of it.

"I want you," he murmurs, his eyes opening to stare at me piercingly.

My heart thumps, butterflies fluttering in my stomach. I gulp and nod faintly, not even able to speak. Will I ever get used to having someone so incredibly attractive, attracted to *me?*

He grabs me roughly and flips me over, but when he's just about to push inside me from behind, the faint noise of a commotion ripples outside. There are men's voices and another female one. Trevor pulls me back against him so that my back is pressed to his chest. He wraps one arm around me, the other poised to defend us. Outside, the female voice shrieks, "Wait!"

Somebody clambers up the ramp. Then, just as suddenly, clothes are ripped away from our faces. Catherine stares down at Trevor and me, her face bright and shining.

"I made it," she whispers, tears brimming in her eyes. "I wanted to say goodbye, Mags."

"Goodbye, Cat," I start to say, but Catherine throws half of her body into the laundry cart and grabs my face, her lips pressing directly on mine.

The taste of jasmine and honey bursts against my lips and she pulls back, eyes glittering. I stare back at her, red as a lobster. Cat giggles, looking pleased as ever to have taken me by surprise.

"Go, be happy, Mags. I love you," she whispers with a wink, hurling herself out of the cart and then running down the truck's ramp.

I stare into the space where she just vanished, one hand pressed to my lips. Trevor continues to hold me, his breath hot on my neck as he presses a gentle kiss on my tingling flesh.

"Get out of here, boys!" I hear Catherine shouting from outside as the ramp goes up and the back of the truck is secured.

As we're plunged into darkness and the truck lurches forward, I close my eyes, praying that one day Catherine is able to get away from Mother Antonia, just like I have. One day, her time will come, and Cat will know the freedom and happiness I feel.

41

___

TREVOR

Maggie's fingers intertwine tightly with mine, her head heavy on my shoulder as we walk up the stairs to the room I'd rented for us in a tiny, local hotel a forty-five minute drive from the Convent of the Blessed Virgin.

When we walk into the room, I go over to the window. You can just barely make out the tiny speck that is the convent, its lights glowing in the remote distance up in the hills. I shut the blinds before turning back to Maggie, offering a gentle smile and sitting down on the bed.

She smiles back at me before walking forward, slipping down onto my lap and wrapping her arms around my neck. She presses her forehead to mine, gazing into my eyes.

When the laundry truck had pulled to a stop, the driver had been amazed to find Maggie and me waiting patiently in the back. I'd patted his shoulder, passed him a twenty dollar bill, and then scooped Maggie up into my arms to walk over to the hotel across the street. It was only two stories and the room was cramped and smelled faintly of cigarettes, but it was all ours. To us, it may as well have been the White House.

"What are you thinking about?" Maggie asks sleepily, fingers lazily brushing through my hair. I kiss her right cheek, hands stroking up and down her back as she gives a faint shiver.

"I'm just imagining us on the beach in a few days, Maggie. We'll be living right next to it.We'll be able to take a walk by the ocean every day when I'm done with work. And play in it. And surf, maybe." I grin at her, squeezing her gently, and she gives a faint giggle.

"I've never seen the beach," she murmurs dreamily. "I've seen pictures. Is the water really the same shade of blue as sapphires?"

"It is, plus baby blue, and aquamarine, and turquoise, and all kinds of blues," I murmur, brushing her curls from her eyes.

She places her hand on my own, lacing her fingers into mine. Gently, she pushes me back on the bed so she can crawl on top of me, her fingers unzipping my pants and tugging them down. I arch my back up so she can free them from my hips.

Her lips find mine, the tip of her velvet tongue gliding lightly between my lips. I respond, sucking gently on her plump lips, top and bottom, then thrusting my hungry tongue in her mouth. We share a deep, passionate kiss that makes us ache for more. A moan of desire rumbles up in my throat, my cock already swelling just at the thought of having Maggie again.

I reach up, pushing back my shirt from her shoulders so that her lovely, pale body is fully exposed. She gazes down at me, her brunette curls cascading over her breasts as her hips straddle me. I reach up and run my fingers up and down her body, mapping the swell of her full, ripe breasts before I lean up, eyes still locked on hers, and capture her pink nipple between my lips. She gives a faint whimper of pleasure, her fingers knotting against my scalp as her head falls back and her hair tumbles down her spine.

My teeth just barely graze the sensitive rosebud trapped in my lips as I grab her hips, maneuvering her pussy over my engorged cock. She tries to ease down on top of it but I make her wait, sucking on one nipple, then the other, nipping and covering them in little bites that make them stand at attention. She moans and writhes, ready for me to pound her hard.

But I'm not done with teasing her. With one hand I guide my thick cock up and down her slick pussy, while my other hand strokes and swirls around her inner thighs, up into the sensitive creases of her groin and on top of her mound. My fingers thread lightly through the black curls that cover it. The sight and the touch of it—so womanly, so sexual—just makes me harder, if that were possible. Continuing my exploration, I lightly trace her outer lips, now swollen with desire. All this light stroking has totally lit her up, and she moans and sways her hips rhythmically. She wants me bad.

"Please, Trevor, get inside me," Maggie pleads, breathlessly. But I just shake my head, grinning.

As I keep moving my cock up and down the outside of her pussy, the swirling fingers of my other hand travel inside those sweet lips to her clit. I flick it lightly with my finger until it starts to become engorged; her breath has now quickened into shallow pants. But then I vibrate her clit with my finger, first lightly, then increasing the intensity. Now Maggie shrieks with pleasure, her gasps begging me to bring her home ... *now*.

Only then do I pull her hips down to sit on my swollen cock, filling her with one powerful thrust. She cries out in pleasure and brings her face down to kiss me passionately. Then, effortlessly getting the gist of this position, she sits back and bounces up and down on me while I pump my ass up and down, impaling her on my cock. As the headboard bangs against the wall, the bedsprings squeak rhythmically along with us, accompanying our moans. Maggie shrieks wildly, and my grunts are no less savage.

"Oh, my sweet baby!" Maggie cries. "I'm going to co—" Maggie begins as her words dissolve into a feral scream. I come with her and with my loud groan added to the noise, we collapse on the bed, two wild animals, finally at peace. Undoubtedly, the entire hotel came with us, too, judging from the noise we made.

Sweaty and elated, she holds me in her arms and presses her mouth to my ear.

"I love you, Trevor," Maggie murmurs, her voice quivering with ecstasy.

I gaze at her, cupping her face, overwhelmed by the way she makes my heart soar—she's enthralled me, heart and soul. She's all I'll ever need, all I'll ever want. Maggie is mine. Forever.

"I love you, Maggie," I whisper, overcome with emotion.

In a few days we're going to be in a brand new place, starting a brand new life. I've never been more excited for a tomorrow, and for the first time ever, I've got a purpose: I'm going to make Maggie happy.

42

As they sit in her office, Bishop Frederick frowns at Mother Antonia. Meanwhile, the mother superior, who is doing her best impression of Sister Ruth, smiles pleasantly back.

Inside, however, Mother Antonia is furious. Her blood boils, giving her a cheeks a ruddy flush that the bishop will mistake for humiliation when really it is pure, concentrated rage. Her foot taps the floor not with anxiety, but because she's doing her best not to charge out of here and start shrieking at each of her young nuns. She desperately needs to figure out exactly what went wrong.

She can't believe how things have turned out for her. Everything was going so well until it all fell apart at the end. She's been going over the events of the last few days again and again, trying to find the one cog of the wheel that came loose, but she hasn't been able to figure it out.

It certainly wasn't her own fault. Mother Antonia is guided by the light of the Lord Himself, and He would never allow her to make a mistake. It wasn't anything Sister Eva had done either. Mother Antonia was certain she had that groveling girl squarely under thumb, just where she wanted her.

On the other hand, Sister Catherine almost definitely did have something to do with her plan falling apart, as that was just Catherine's usual way to interfere ... but for everything to have gone so disastrously, was it merely a tragic coincidence?

Mother Antonia believes in coincidences as much as she believes in unicorns.

Her eyes dart towards Sister Ruth, who sits at Mother Antonia's side looking tranquil as a freshwater spring. She nods faintly as Bishop Frederick speaks, her attention rapt. When she senses Mother Antonia's scornful glare, the elderly sister smiles at her, which only furthers the woman's internal rage.

The mother superior had to accept now that there was probably little she would ever be able to do to rid herself of Sister Ruth. Now that Bishop Frederick had come and seen what he had, Mother Antonia would never have the power to get Ruth transferred to another convent, or have her expelled from the sisterhood altogether, unless Ruth suggested it to the bishop, herself.

That was, perhaps, something Mother Antonia could strategize. She would have to play her cards differently next time, but she wouldn't lose twice. Not with the Lord on her side.

"Is there anything else you want to add, Mother Antonia?" Bishop Frederick asks, reaching across the desk to take Mother Antonia's hand in his and hold it delicately.

She stares at their hands, somehow restraining herself from jerking away, and keeps that polished and professional mask on her face.

Men are all the same, she muses, whether they're of the

cloth or not. She almost feels sorry for Margaret, that she will be at the whim of that gardener's desires, but the mother superior is too furious with the dark-haired former nun to feel pity for her.

"It was all just a misunderstanding, Your Excellency," Mother Antonia says calmly.

Now that she'd had a few minutes to collect herself, she was feeling more confident in her explanation. All she had to do was apologize, and bat her eyelashes, and feign contrition and he would be on his way, while she could return to her duties. After all, her young nuns needed her now more than ever: with the loss of their sister, they might well continue to rebel. Things of this nature, Mother Antonia found, are contagious. An anarchic fire could spread from girl to girl, one that only she can properly snuff out.

Mother Antonia forces herself to give the old man's hand a squeeze, which he seems to appreciate. "I do apologize greatly for this ... er ... situation. It's only because I have such passion for our Lord and Savior that I have acted in this way. All I wanted was to protect young Sister Margaret before she was defiled. I only wish I could have prevented the terrible sins that took place ..." the mother superior, choking up, dabs at her dry eyes.

Bishop Frederick shifts his gaze from Mother Antonia to Sister Ruth, who is polishing her glasses on her sleeve.

"Do you know what happened to the young lady and the young man?" he asks.

Ruth heaves a sigh and nibbles her lower lip. "I'm afraid not. Mother Antonia keeps me rather busy, and I was just trying to get on with my tasks. But I don't have any reason to believe Margaret is in danger with that boy. You know how young love can be. If Margaret wants to return, we would adore to have her back. Our doors will remain permanently open for her. I'm sure in time she'll reach out to one of her friends here, and then we'll have word of how she's doing."

"Of course, Sister Ruth. And regarding your responsibilities, though you are assistant mother superior, it pains me that you have too many obligations; I'm sure they're too taxing for you. Mother Antonia, you will take back the greater bulk of your duties," Bishop Frederick declares, pulling his hand away from the mother superior's.

"Of course, Your Excellency," Mother Antonia mutters, bowing her head and internally seething.

"And the girls are to continue their duties around the convent helping the staff, as well as in the nearby town," Bishop Frederick continues. "One of the hallmarks of our order is our helpfulness and commitment to our community, and I won't have you isolate the sisters."

"Of course," Mother Antonia repeats, fingernails digging into her palms.

"Now then, on to other matters," the bishop says, leaning forward eagerly in his chair. Mother Antonia frowns at him, wondering what she'd been left out of the loop on. "The reason I came out here was not only to see you about recent events at the convent, but also to inform you that we are beginning long-overdue renovations in a few weeks. You can expect carpenters and construction workers to arrive, too many to reside in the male dorm, so a few will have to be accommodated here in the convent. I'm sure you can find them rooms an appropriate distance from the sisters."

Mother Antonia nods, gritting her teeth. Men? Sleeping in *her convent?* This was an abomination. She wants to lash out at the bishop, but he's left no room for argument: this has already been decided without the mother superior's counsel.

Bishop Frederick then stands, shaking hands with both

Mother Antonia and Sister Ruth before heading to the office door. He pauses in the doorway, glancing back.

"Oh, and Mother Antonia. Do keep the dramatics here to a minimum or you'll risk your seat at the Catholic conference in Boston. Understand?"

"Yes, Your Excellency," the reverend mother utters, gritting her teeth and mumbling to herself as Sister Ruth climbs to her feet. Without saying goodbye, Ruth heads out into the hall.

Mother Antonia sinks into her chair, furious. She may have lost one nun, but she sure isn't going to lose any more.

43

MARGARET

I ease back against Trevor's chest, my head reclining on his powerful shoulder. Over our heads, the sun is a great golden ball in the sky that makes my skin melt with heat. I swear, it feels like we're lightyears closer to the sun here, everything is so warm.

"How in the world did you even get this number?" I ask, shifting the cellphone in my hand from one ear to the other, before stretching my legs out in front of me.

Since abandoning my habit a few months ago, I'd been working on a tan. My legs are long and freckled, extending out from a pair of cutoff jean shorts I'd been delighted to buy. I'm not a materialistic girl, but having a closet even half full of clothes that aren't long black and white cloaks is exhilarating.

Trevor leans back, palms sinking in the soft sand. The sun shimmers over the peaking crests of breaking waves as they assault the bay in front of us.

The beach had been even more beautiful than I could have imagined. The first time Trevor and I went for a walk on the sand, I'd been unable to stop crying at the majesty of it. I'd thought the closest I'd ever come to such beauty were images in books Cat snuck into the convent, or the artistry of the nunnery's stained glass windows, but this was more lovely than my heart could bear.

Since arriving here, Trevor and I come frequently to the ocean. Recently, we'd even started coming at night when the beach was deserted and the ocean was still. Only the moon illuminates our naked bodies as we make love among the still sun-warmed dunes.

"You should know by now that I always find a way to get what I want. But I can barely hear you with all this construction work going on at the convent," Cat giggles into my ear. "Oh, Mags. You sound so happy."

"You sound pretty pleased yourself," I retort. "Have you gotten your fill of construction workers yet?"

Cat pretends to gasp. "Me? Margaret, I am a devoted sister of the cloth. I would never do such a thing as to seduce a hunky rock of man who knows how to work a jackhammer—if you know what I mean."

We laugh together until Cat gives a faint groan. "I've got to go, Eva is coming this way and I don't want her to know Erik snuck me a cellphone. Monica and the twins and Grace all say hello. We miss you like crazy, Mags."

"I miss you too, Cat," I say, closing my eyes and savoring the sun. Trevor's fingers gently brush my sandy arms. "Remember to tell me every exciting detail about life at the convent."

"Exciting?" drawls the nun. I can already see her rolling her eyes. "Please. The last exciting thing that will ever happen here is you, half-naked, jumping down a laundry chute with a half-naked man."

I crack open an eye, smiling at the ocean waves. "With you there, Cat, somehow I doubt that."

ALSO BY LILY MILES

THE SAGA CONTINUES WITH

NASTY HABITS,

BOOK TWO

FORGIVE US OUR TRESPASSES

ENJOY THE FOLLOWING EXCERPT!

Monica

As I approach the door, I peer in through the small peephole and curiously find what appears to be an empty room. The exam table with its crisp, white sheet sits undisturbed, the window open as a warm breeze floats in and rustles the pretty white blinds. I peek up and down the small hall, but the other rooms are empty as well, and this is the one with the little note on the door saying a patient is inside.

Perhaps whoever the patient was had gotten scared and jumped out the window to run away. It wouldn't be the first time. Usually it was the children who were terrified of Dr. Cliff and his needles, but occasionally an adult would be just as bad. I'd always have to leave the room to contain my laughter when that happened. Cliff told me I should be sympathetic, but it's hard when a fifty-year-old man is sobbing over one little injection.

I crack open the door and peek uncertainly inside, startled to find a big man standing in the corner of the room, flipping through some of the textbooks that Dr. Cliff kept.

With his back to me, he stands tall and tan, his muscled arms the same bronze color as a shiny penny, and his dirt-stained white tee shirt wet from sweat between his broad shoulders. His beat-up jeans ride low on his narrow hips, just tight enough to highlight his sculpted butt cheeks. My throat goes suddenly dry, the tray in my hands tipping until it clatters to the ground, metal tools scattering over the tiled floor.

Immediately, the patient whirls around, his dark, chocolate eyes locking on me from the corner of the room.

His body hunches slightly, lean muscles taut like an animal getting ready to spring in escape. I can only just stare at him, taking in his body with the same admiration others might look at fine artwork. In all the fairytale books I'd read when I was young, he was exactly the type of man I always imagined Prince Charming would be. I stop myself from gasping—he's just gorgeous.

"Are you lost, lady?" he says, his deep voice quiet and gruff and not nearly as kind as I expected my Prince Charming's might have been. A few strands of dark brown hair have fallen onto his forehead—he casually rakes them back with his big, beautiful hand. I'm dazzled.

I manage to collect myself. "Lady?" I echo, bristling. "I'm a sister. Sister Monica, to be precise. If the mother superior hears you calling any of us 'lady,' you'll never hear the end of it."

His head tilts, that dark hair falling once again into his eyes. "Sorry. You surprised me. I'm Brett." He flashes a devastating smile, his teeth a slash of bright white against his pink lips and stubbled cheeks.

My heart is thumping so hard it's going to vault out of my chest. Nevertheless, I succeed in saying "It's nice to meet you, Brett. Can you sit down for me?" in my most professional voice. This is my first time doing any sort of procedure without the doctor at my side, not to mention, doing a procedure on Prince Charming himself—to say I'm nervous is the understatement of the century.

He walks over to the exam table and hops up onto the edge of it— it's only then that I see the gash on his arm. It's a round, slightly jagged puncture mark, like he'd been stabbed with something. I grimace, watching thin trails of blood slither across his tan skin.

He follows my stare and then half turns his arm so it's not facing towards me.

"Is the doctor coming in soon?" he asks. "I really need to get back to work."

"I am the doctor," I answer before giving a faint yelp, "I mean, I'm not the doctor, but I'm going to be the one giving you stitches today."

He nods his chin at the fallen tools, including the once-sanitized thread and needle I would have been using. "Not with those, I hope."

I break into a grin and shake my head, grabbing the tray and setting it down on the corner of a counter before digging through some of the cabinets. I find a medically sealed baggie containing more needle and thread.

"We've got spares. So, what happened?" I continue, going to his side and inspecting the injury. The sight of the blood streaking across his arm makes my head swim.

"I'm one of the carpenters. There was a … mishap," he adds vaguely, not adding in any further detail than that.

It sounds like he wants that conversation to end, and so I don't press for more information, but apparently he doesn't want silence either, because a moment later he starts talking.

"Do you do this a lot?" he continues idly, watching as I pull on a pair of latex gloves and carefully thread the needle.

When I approach, he swallows hard and tips his chin up so he's looking away. As I swab his arm with alcohol, my eyes follow his throat and the motion of his Adam's apple. He smells like sun and wood and I lean closer to breathe in the smell. There's also some strangely heady fragrance that I assume is cologne, before I realize it's just his sweat. I'd never been this close to a man before. Not even our priest, who always keeps a very respectful distance even when we kneel together on the church floor to pray.

All of a sudden I'm aware of some strange, new, magnetic energy pulsing inside of me. It's low in my stomach, slithering through my core and twisting itself deep within. It's odd and unfamiliar, and actually thrilling, despite the fact that it makes the room feel like it's spinning slightly.

I blink hard and shake my head, forcing myself to focus, even though the thought of touching this man's bare arm has sent goosebumps up my arms.

"Nope," I answer honestly, inhaling deeply before taking hold of his arm and turning it back towards me. I stare down at the jagged flesh, say a silent prayer, and then glide my needle into the fragile, tan skin.

ABOUT THE AUTHOR

I'm Lily Miles, and it's my pleasure to welcome you to my world of romance. I've been a writer for many years in various genres under different names, and now it's my great pleasure to contribute my voice to the romance scene as well—considering romance flows through my veins, it may as well flow from my pen! I live in New York City, a place of glamour and excitement that has been the one constant lover in my life. I'm passionate about travel and exploration of any kind—I *live* for adventure. And whether I'm pursuing romance on my laptop or between the sheets, I always have a good read on my night table.

I hope my books will be the good reads on yours.

Yours in romance,

Lily

facebook.com/LilyMilesRomanceAuthor

twitter.com/LilyRomance

instagram.com/lilymilesromance

www.ingramcontent.com/pod-product-compliance
Lightning Source LLC
Chambersburg PA
CBHW072002180726
48291CB00002BA/514